Green Witch

Green Witch

Kelly McKain

LODESTONE
BOOKS

Winchester, UK
Washington, USA

JOHN HUNT PUBLISHING

First published by Lodestone Books, 2023
Lodestone Books is an imprint of John Hunt Publishing Ltd., No. 3 East Street,
Alresford, Hampshire SO24 9EE, UK
office@jhpbooks.net
www.johnhuntpublishing.com

For distributor details and how to order please visit the 'Ordering' section on our website.

Text copyright: Kelly McKain 2022

ISBN: 978 1 78904 741 7
978 1 78904 742 4 (ebook)
Library of Congress Control Number: 2021949490

A CIP catalogue record for this book is available from the British Library.

Design: Stuart Davies

UK: Printed and bound by CPI Group (UK) Ltd, Croydon, CR0 4YY
US: Printed and bound by Thomson-Shore, 7300 West Joy Road, Dexter, MI 48130

We operate a distinctive and ethical publishing philosophy in
all areas of our business, from our global network of authors to
production and worldwide distribution.

For Green Witches everywhere.
For here, now, everything, always.
And for my beautiful Mr T. K.

Chapter 1

The skittering, pounding dance track was thumping right through Delilah. It was stressing her out, but she hadn't dared ask the cabbie to turn it down. He was clearly already pissed off about loading all her bags into the boot at the train station and now, as they turned down a bumpy, single-track lane, he started swearing about what it was doing to the suspension of his decade-old Merc.

He pulled in alongside some rusty iron gates and Delilah peered through the tangle of ivy and bindweed growing up them. The grey stone manor house beyond looked desolate in its ragged, overgrown gardens, as if it had stood alone for a hundred years. The gable at one end was crumbling, threatening to fall down completely. For a moment, she imagined finding Sleeping Beauty inside. Instead, she would find Great Aunt Edie, who'd developed dementia in the last couple of years. She knew she'd be staying for the summer to help look after her, before sixth-form college began. Beyond that, she had no idea what to expect.

"What the heck have you got in here?"

Delilah hurried out of the cab to find the driver wrestling her bags out of the boot, a cigarette hanging from his mouth, threatening to drop hot ash over the beautiful leather. She wanted to take over and do it herself, but she didn't dare say anything. She was trying not to step in the mud; suede high heels probably hadn't been the best choice, in retrospect. But then, she'd imagined the manor house as more like a country spa hotel than this crumbling old pile surrounded by tangled weeds and oily puddles.

"Careful with that one," she ventured as the cabbie wrenched at her pink Louis Vuitton tote. "It's got fragile-" She winced as the bag came free, swung in an arc in the air and landed hard on

1

the jagged edge of the tarmac. If her mother's exquisite vintage perfume bottle – which still held the faintest trace of her scent – was broken, then she'd… *What? What* will *you do?* jibed a voice in her head. *Nothing,* another answered. *Why start standing up for yourself now?* She was still getting used to the spacious feeling of not having to be on alert all the time for Shayla and her friends. They made sugar-coated comments with a sharp centre and dropped their voices to a whisper when she entered a room at school. Being a boarding school, there had been no getting away from it, but they never overstepped the line enough for it to actually be stopped.

"Twenty-two fifty," said the driver gruffly.

Delilah rummaged in her purse, pulled out a twenty and five and handed them to him. "Thanks," she said, automatically. He didn't say it back. Instead, he shut the boot and strode to the driver's door—to get her change, she assumed.

As she reached down for her pink bag, the cab's back wheel began moving. As the Merc bumped off down the lane, she stuck her middle finger up at it, then quickly put it down, thinking that the driver might see in the rear-view mirror and come back to start something.

She shouldered her pink bag, inched one of the gates open and wrestled her way through. Putting the bag down carefully on the path, she managed to heave the gate open a little wider, then went back for her cases. She moved her stuff further and further down the path, clicking back and forth in her heels, trying not to let them sink into the mossy gaps between the paving slabs. A jangling, nervy feeling started up in her stomach—what was *that* about?

It's only an old house, she told herself. *Nothing spooky. And Edie's inside. And I've been here before.*

She had stayed with Great Aunt Edie when she was six. A whole decade ago now.

Right after…

"*Don't,*" she told herself firmly. She shook her head hard, sending her hair whipping around her face, as if that would shake the thoughts away. Even though it had been ten years ago, she still couldn't bear to think about the accident. Whenever a fleeting thought about it crept into her mind, she tried to push it out before it turned into images of screeching tyres, an echoing smash, cars on fire and bleeding, twisted people sprayed with shattered glass.

Her mother among them.

Sometimes she managed to catch the thought before the images came – quickly putting the rec room TV on loud or dashing out into the grounds for a run. She did that a lot to get away from Shayla too.

Delilah and all her bags had almost reached the front porch. She was surprised to spot a compact red car at the side of the house, parked on a slim gravel driveway. So there *was* a more sensible way in to the place, then. As she went back up the path a little way for the last bag, she almost slipped on some weird-looking mess on the paving. She couldn't stop herself from leaning down for a closer look. She stared at it for a few seconds, waiting for her brain to make sense of it. Then she recoiled. It was a dead baby bird. A scrawny scrap of goo with a few sad feathers and a bulging, foetal eye. She clamped her hand over her mouth and walked far around it, over the mulchy grass, *sod the suede shoes.* She looked up at the manor house again. So this was her new life, for a while anyway. The bird didn't seem like a good omen.

As there wasn't a bell, she rapped hard with the iron knocker, but no one came. She waited way past the polite amount of time then knocked again. Nothing. She turned the latch and pushed at the heavy, weathered door, which—to her surprise—swung open.

She stepped tentatively inside. "Edie?"

When there was no reply, she made her way up the hallway,

her heels echoing on the flagstone floor. It smelt like the boot room at school. She passed aged photographs on a side table and paused, noticing one of herself as a child, with her mum. Quickly, automatically, she put up a block in her mind against images of the accident. It didn't always work but this time it held. The edge of the photo was ragged in its gilt frame—someone had been torn out. She noticed a couple of other pictures of her with Miranda, and one of Great Aunt Edie with them both. They'd all had the tearing-out treatment too. It served him right.

Just then, the sound of two singing voices carried down from upstairs. Delilah followed them, up the grand staircase, taking care not to trip on the frayed edges of the carpet. *Row, row, row your boat, gently down the stream. Merrily, merrily, merrily, merrily, life is but a dream.* The voices were coming from a room off the upstairs landing. As Delilah put her head round the doorframe she found it was a bathroom. Containing a bath. With her great aunt in it.

Fortunately, there were a lot of bubbles. Edie looked a lot older than Delilah remembered, and, obviously, far more naked. A large, cheerful woman in a carer's uniform sat beside the bath, a towel on her lap. Neither of the women had noticed Delilah yet, so, before she spoke, she tried to wipe the surprise off her face and look like it was no big deal for her to walk in on a—what, eighty-year-old?—in the bath.

"I did ring the bell, but—"

The carer glanced round and smiled warmly. "Delilah! Lovely to meet you, honey. I'm Jane. I've heard all about you, haven't I, Edie? Edie told me that when you were a little girl you came to stay. Didn't she, Edie? And now she's back, all grown up!"

As Jane spoke, Great Aunt Edie continued to poke a sponge around in the water, not registering Delilah at all. Then suddenly she looked up and smiled. "Hello, my dear!" she said. "Gosh, how rude of me, I must—" She made a sudden move to stand up, dislodging her bubbles.

"No, no, you stay there!" cried Delilah, alarmed.

Luckily Jane was quick to steady Edie back down again. "You'd think you were twenty, leaping around like that! Now, if you're ready to get out, we'll get you out sensibly." She got to her feet, holding up the towel.

"Oh, no, please, don't rush for me. It's fine, I'm fine. I'll wait downstairs. I'll get the kettle on..."

"If you're sure—" Jane began.

"Sure, I'm sure," Delilah insisted, backing out of the room. As she made her way back down the hall, she couldn't help but hear their conversation.

"Who was that?" asked Edie.

Jane laughed gently. "She's your great niece, remember? Miranda's daughter. God rest her soul. Delilah's going to stay for a while. Keep you company."

"Oh, that does sound nice," said Edie. "But who's Miranda?"

Delilah's heart skipped a beat, and she stopped dead at the top of the stairs. Edie didn't remember her mother? How could that *be*? She understood about dementia, of course, well, she'd read a little bit about it, but still, how? How could anyone forget beautiful, laughing, chaotic, creative Miranda?

* * *

About half an hour later, Jane appeared in the kitchen, to find Delilah fiddling with her phone, a glass of water within reach. There didn't seem to be any 4G coverage here, or even 3G, so she was offline and just scrolling through photos – but at least there was a bit of signal. "Didn't you find the tea things?" Jane asked.

"Oh, I'm okay with water, thanks." In fact, she'd been gasping for a cup of tea, but one look at the grimy, battered tins and ancient pot with its cracked spout, and she'd decided against it. Jane put a saucepan on the stove, turned on the gas and lit it with a match. "Edie's tucked up in bed. I'll take her cocoa up and then I'll get going—"

"You're leaving?" cried Delilah, panic rising in her chest. "But what about Edie? She didn't even know me. I don't think I should be in charge of her. I mean, I'm not qualified or anything—"

"You'll be fine," Jane told her. "She's not always so confused."

"I won't have to do her bath, will I?" She instantly felt unkind, and railed at herself, but Jane chuckled. "Not unless she puts yogurt on her head again, no."

Delilah didn't know how to take that. Was it meant to be a joke?

"Look, honestly, don't worry. I come in the mornings and evenings, well, me or one of the other ladies, and you can call me if you need anything. You can book extra time via the agency if you're going to be out."

Like babysitting, Delilah thought.

"To start with, just do what you're comfortable with and let's see how we go," Jane continued. "If you want someone else here more of the time, we'll arrange that and add it to the account. You're here mainly for company, and you shouldn't feel that you have to be on hand twenty-four seven. We're all aware that the situation isn't ideal, with Edie still living here, but her condition has deteriorated very suddenly in the last couple of months, and we're still catching up. Arrangements are being made for her longer-term care in a specialist residential home, and that should all be sorted out by the end of the summer." She gave Delilah a smile and turned to the stove, stirring the cocoa.

Delilah felt like she should say something mature, informed and insightful, but only one stupid thought would come into her mind, over and over. "Jane," she began. "I know this is silly, but..."

Jane turned, wooden spoon in hand, eyes twinkling with

amusement. "She can go to the toilet on her own."

Delilah studied the table. "Right. Good."

"Are you okay for money?" Jane asked then. "For shopping and things?"

"Oh yes, got Daddy's credit card," she mumbled, embarrassed. "I'm one of *those*."

"You're a good girl," said Jane firmly. "Good on you for coming. I don't like seeing my oldies with no family around them."

Delilah smiled at this. *Now this is something I* can *do*, she thought wryly. *Just be related to Edie.* She couldn't fuck that up, at least. Jane picked up the steaming cocoa, which was in a delicate, flower-patterned cup and saucer. She must have noticed Delilah looking at the chipped rim, because she said, "I know, but she won't have any other cup. This one's her favourite."

"Another thing I didn't know," said Delilah flatly.

"You'll soon get the hang of the place. Right, well, the keys are in this drawer. My number's on the fridge."

"Thanks. Oh, but- Where do I find the code for the Wi-Fi?"

This seemed to amuse Jane. "Honey, your great aunt only had a land line put in a year ago, and that was because social services insisted."

Delilah tried to hide her shock, not wanting to look like a total Gen-Z cliché.

"Maybe you can talk some sense into her," Jane said.

"Maybe... If she ever remembers who I am."

Jane gave her a sympathetic smile. "She's a bit better in the mornings. Really, you'll be fine. It's great that you're here. This is going to work out really well for both of you, I'm sure."

Delilah was far from sure, but she didn't really know what else she could say. She couldn't exactly turn around and leave. It looked like she and Edie were stuck with each other – and at this point it was clear who had the worse deal. Yes, she was stuck looking after a person who didn't appear to know who she was, but Edie was stuck being looked after by someone with no clue about dementia. *Or life in general.*

Delilah was suddenly flooded with panicky thoughts — what if Edie wandered out of bed at night and fell down the stairs? What if she ate the wrong thing and choked? What if she walked up onto the main road and got hit by a car? Suddenly it seemed like there were a hundred ways that Edie could get hurt, or *die*, on her watch.

She'd never seen a dead body.

Well, apart from her mother's. *Don't think about it.* But she hadn't *understood* that Miranda was dead, in the car. *Don't think about it.* And it had been a closed coffin, of course. Her father had told her this a few years later, because she had no memory of Miranda's funeral. None at all. When the fact that she didn't remember it came up, during one of their infrequent, brief and strangely formal lunches, he'd said she must have blanked it all out.

Delilah glanced up to see Jane blowing on the cocoa and testing the temperature with her little finger, as if for a child. Jane seemed to have no inkling of the huge personal freak-out she'd just been through in her head. "Just right," Jane said, of the cocoa. "I'll take this up and then I'll be off."

Delilah wanted to throw herself across the room, hang onto Jane's ankles and beg her to stay. Or at least to sit down with her and have a sensible discussion regarding her misgivings about being left in charge. But instead all she could manage was a small, "Okay then."

Pathetic, she told herself scornfully. Then she pulled on a smile for Jane, which faded the second the carer had bustled out of the room.

* * *

When Jane had gone home, Delilah ate a lonely supper of

random cold food from the fridge, while trying to watch the flickering black and white TV on the counter. By nine o'clock, she'd washed up her few dishes and made herself a cup of tea in the least chipped and stained mug she could find. She drank it while staring out of the window at the gathering dusk.

The kitchen looked onto the side of the house, where Jane's little red car had been parked. She thought for the hundredth time how much easier things would have been if the taxi had pulled into the drive, if she'd known about it.

Then she wished she didn't have the kind of mind that obsessed over silly little things when it was too late to change them. It would be so lovely to be one of those robust, jolly people who just got up in the morning and cracked on with *living*. Sometimes her whirring mind felt like a prison she couldn't escape from.

She tried to think positive—that was what you were supposed to do, right? At least the perfume bottle hadn't been broken in the end. When she'd checked it, after finding Edie in the bath, she'd actually sobbed with relief. *Things are not the people they remind us of,* she told herself sternly. But there were so few things of Miranda's. Fewer stories. Hardly any memories at all.

When the tea was finished, there wasn't really much else to do. She didn't fancy staying in the cavernous kitchen as it grew dark, especially as the blind was stuck open – now, that really *would* send her mind into overdrive. Woodland flanked the house to the back and sides, and as the trees became black silhouettes and the sky turned an inky indigo, she made her way upstairs.

Looking at the stack of bags by the front door, she realised that they contained everything she owned in the world. Her father hadn't kept any of her things—he liked steel and glass and strange spiky sculptures. It hadn't been until a brief visit to his apartment in the school holidays that Delilah had thought to ask about Miranda's belongings. But she'd been too late. They'd gone. She didn't know where. And he'd been angry — there was a new pink mountain bike in the hall with a bow on it, wasn't that enough? She hadn't asked again. Ever. She assumed most of it had gone to the charity shop.

As she passed Great Aunt Edie's door, she had a sudden panic that perhaps she'd been supposed to look in on her every half an hour or something (is that what carers did? She had no idea.). She peered around the doorframe, braced for something awful. But Edie was sitting up in bed, *not* lying in a cold bone-broken heap on the floor. And she was laughing at a TV show, *not* lolling lifelessly, having somehow been electrocuted by the remote control. Delilah smiled a little, but then, *Don't relax just yet,* she told herself sternly. *If she survives the night then, okay, you can congratulate yourself.*

Only then did she realise that she didn't know which room she was staying in. "Hi, Edie, where do you want me to sleep?" she asked brightly from the doorway, in the same cheerful tone Jane had used with her great aunt. But Edie didn't take her eyes from the TV – she was completely absorbed, open-faced, like a child.

Delilah thought for a moment about going right in, standing in front of her and asking again, but she held back. What if Edie still didn't remember who she was, or had forgotten she was even there at all, and completely freaked out? Instead, she crept past the doorway – she'd have to work things out for herself.

Further down the hall, one of the doors was half open and she stepped through tentatively. She found herself in a pretty but faded and dust-ridden bedroom, with little antique tables on either side of a double bed. The room also held a chest of drawers and a large wardrobe, and there were faded pressed flower pictures on the walls, their colour almost completely gone. It was stuffy in there, so she crossed over to the little casement window and opened it wide.

The room was at the back of the manor house and looked

out onto the overgrown gardens and the woods beyond. Delilah heard an owl hoot in the distance and the trees rustled faintly as a light wind blew through the wood. Apart from that, there was no sound at all. She couldn't even hear the cars speeding up the main road into town from this side of the manor.

She began to draw the curtains but that disturbed so much dust that she decided to leave them alone, at least until she could take them down and give them a good shake outside. Then, just as she was about to turn away from the window, something caught her eye. She gasped as a stunning white owl swooped low right outside it. Admiring its beauty, she craned her neck to watch it for as long as she could, until it disappeared into the wood.

She flicked the switch of the bedside lamp nearest the window, expecting it to be broken, but the bulb leapt into life. She put the other lamp on too and took off her shoes. Feeling the grittiness of the floor under her bare feet, she instantly put them back on again.

Bracing herself for a mouse corpse or something, she pulled back the bedcover and sheets. They smelt stale and, pressing a hand on them, she felt a slight dampness. She pulled them back up, deciding that she'd rather lay on top with her dressing gown on. And that she'd have a spring clean in the morning.

She had briefly wondered about looking for another room further down the hallway, but it seemed unlikely that there would be a freshly polished one with crisp lavender-scented sheets magically waiting for her. Jane was obviously a lovely lady, but she was a carer not a housekeeper. After a quick wash in the bathroom, and a change into PJs and the dressing gown, Delilah crawled onto the bed, abandoning her shoes at the very last moment. She lay there looking up at the cracked ceiling, trying not to think about spiders. Or moths, gnats, mice, rats. *Rats? Oh, God, stop,* she told herself firmly.

The canned laughter from Edie's TV show drifted in from

the hallway and the moonlight flooded through the window, sending a stripe of silver right across her body in its fluffy, fabric-conditioner-scented dressing gown. It was the last thing she'd put into the laundry before leaving school. That familiar smell would fade and wear off altogether soon – and be replaced with something else.

Just as school, which had been her home, was now replaced with this. This manor house, and its overgrown garden and an end wall that looked like it might fall down, and the moonlight filling the dusty room, and Great Aunt Edie, and...

She fell asleep thinking of all these things, still steeped in the comforting smell of her dressing gown.

* * *

In the dead of night, the silence of the manor was shattered by screams. Delilah woke and shot upright all at once, her heart pounding, every sense on alert. Her first thought as she leapt off the bed was *Edie*. But as her initial shock subsided, she understood that the sound was coming from outside the window.

It was a sickening noise, like shrieking, terrified women. She was about to lunge for her phone when she realised—vixens. They screamed when they fought. Thank God for that.

Her heart steadied itself as she walked over to the window, tiptoeing to get as little of the floor-grit on her feet as possible. She looked out. The insistent screams came again, shearing the air. But this time she didn't react. It was just nature, red in tooth and claw. Foxes, free and wild, roaming the woods, under a glistening moon. There was nothing to be afraid of out there. Nothing at all.

Chapter 2

Delilah spent most of the following morning doing a complicated puzzle with Edie, who still didn't seem entirely sure who she actually *was*. She had been too anxious to mention her mother and risk having to hear Edie's confusion over Miranda again, so she'd settled on saying she was a friend of Jane's. She pulled the lid of the puzzle box upright to work from the image—a complex fifties seaside scene—when she noticed that there was something written on the inside of it. It was some kind of poem, written in pencil—in Edie's writing from before she got ill. The inside of a puzzle box lid was a strange place to write a poem. It wasn't just scribbled there, but neatly scribed, perfectly horizontal despite the lack of guiding lines. It was titled "One", and as she turned the box towards Edie, she registered that it had five short stanzas.

"Edie, what's this?" Delilah asked, flexing her wrist awkwardly around the side of the box to point to the writing.

Edie peered at it. "It looks like a poem, dear," she said. "Did you want some paper from the bureau? You shouldn't have to go writing in puzzle boxes."

This made Delilah smile, and feel sad at the same time. Bless Edie. "*I* didn't write it," she said gently. She didn't insist to Edie that it was her own handwriting. She didn't want to risk confusing or distressing her. She knew for sure it was, though, because her great aunt used to send her birthday cards to school without fail every year. She felt a rush of affection for Edie and found herself putting her hand on hers and squeezing it gently. "It's lovely to be here," she said. "Getting to know you at last."

"Yes," said Edie warmly. "It is. It's lovely." But clearly, she didn't really understand who she was getting to know.

* * *

As it neared lunchtime, Delilah was making her way into town, struggling along the busy, pavement-less main road in skinny jeans and another pair of high heels from her collection of unsuitable footwear. She was also on the phone to her father. His name was Gerrard, but he was known to everyone but Delilah by his surname, Hardcastle.

"Daddy, it's literally the middle of nowhere," she told him. "Like, the *actual* middle. And Edie's much worse that you said."

She squealed and staggered backwards as a truck blazed by her, blaring its horn. Her father had said something she didn't quite hear, but she knew it wasn't, "Oh dear, why don't you come and stay with me instead?"

When she spoke to him on the phone, she always imagined him standing in his shiny, minimal London office, probably with a sexy PA handing him papers to sign. She wondered where he imagined she was at that moment, if he thought about it at all – probably *not* stumbling down a muddy roadside in wildly unsuitable shoes almost getting hit by passing trucks, anyway.

"Don't you care?" she asked, knowing the answer.

"Of course I care, darling," her father insisted. *Yeah, right.*

"Jane the carer is liaising with the council about a specialist nursing home for Edie," she began, as she picked her way past some thorny bushes. "She—"

"Huh! Not bloody likely!" blustered her father. "Do you know how much those places cost? And it's only her mind that's had it. She could go on for years… We'd have to sell the manor to cover the costs, and that's your inheritance."

"What?! *I* don't want it!" she cried, alarmed. It was the first she'd heard of *that*. "It's a crumbling, spooky old pile!"

"It's twelve luxury flats waiting to happen," Hardcastle said, sounding pleased with himself. "The start of your career, following in the family footsteps."

Huh. So that was his plan. She hadn't been sent here on a mercy mission to help her great aunt, after all. When her father had told her about Edie's dementia and suggested (well, more like commanded) that she go and stay, she'd wondered whether he was finally softening.

Perhaps, she'd thought, because Miranda and Edie had been so close.

She should have known there was something else behind it. Something that involved property and money, wheeling and dealing. She'd often felt like just another one of his investments herself, tucked away in her lovely little school, growing steadily and quietly.

Now it was time for him to cash her in.

Of course, Great Aunt Edie would rather leave the whole place to a cat rescue charity than give him any part of it, but Delilah could see that *she* was a different matter. She had a part of Miranda in her. She was a blood relation. It made sense that Edie would have included her in her will. But until this moment, at the vile roadside, shrieking as she got splattered with muddy puddle water by a white van, she'd never even thought about the subject.

"Delilah?" came her father's voice, and she realised that, as far as he'd heard, she'd been silent for a long time, then shrieked loudly. For all he knew she could be being abducted and murdered. Or fallen down and hurt herself, at least. She wished he sounded more concerned than impatient, but she knew better than to hope for that by now.

"You've got it all planned out, haven't you?" she said bitterly.

His reaction to that was explosive and furious—something about *ungrateful, spoilt little...* She didn't hear it all as she cringed away from the phone. She stumbled backwards onto the grass verge and ended up with dog poo smeared over one of her shoes.

She rubbed the side of the shoe against the grass, gagging at the smell. "I'm just saying... I've been boarding every holiday since I was six, and I thought maybe, for my first summer..."

More anger, defence and justification came down the phone.

The shoe still wouldn't get clean. Delilah resigned herself to the fact that they were ruined and walked on. "I know you have to work."

Hardcastle sighed, through gritted teeth. Then he made a determined swerve to an upbeat tone. "Look, I've got to go, darling. Client lunch. Ciao."

The familiar fob-off exasperated her. "Daddy, I'm way out of my depth here!"

"Regards to Edith!" he called, ignoring this. She knew he was already walking out of the office door – she could hear his expensive Italian shoes on the marble floor, the swish of his suit jacket as he swung it over his shoulder.

"She's torn you out of all the pictures, you know!" she shouted, a last-ditch attempt to keep him talking.

It didn't work. He'd hung up.

"*Ciao* to you too," she said with venom.

She pressed the red button on her screen and slid the phone back into her bag. Something ominously soft beneath her right foot made her leap backwards, as a gagging stink filled her nostrils. She clamped her hand over her mouth and looked down to see a maggoty road-kill fox blocking her way. "Excellent," she said, through her fingers. "Just excellent. Happy summer, Delilah."

* * *

About twenty minutes later, Delilah found herself on what appeared to be the main street of the local town, Bernhurst. The taxi she'd taken from the mainline station hadn't come this way. Calling it *run down* would have been a compliment. It was shabby and desolate, with closed-down shops, graffiti and dropped rubbish everywhere.

We're not in Kansas anymore, Toto.

Delilah wandered up the empty street, looking for signs of life. She spotted a shoe shop further along that looked open and made a beeline for it.

But once she was outside it, she hesitated. Cheap, out of fashion shoes sat jumbled in wire baskets by the door. In the window were freaky disembodied mannequin feet wearing more horrible shoes, and doomed flies buzzing against the inside of the glass.

She looked up and down the street again, hoping for an alternative. But she hadn't somehow accidentally walked past a pristine branch of Dune.

She sighed. Her current shoes may be Valentino, but they were also mud-soaked, and covered in dog poo and traces of decomposing fox.

There was no choice, it was this shop or nothing.

She went inside to find the place empty apart from the teenage assistant, who was staring blankly at the shelf of shoes she was dusting. Yes, dusting the actual shoes. *My God, how long have they been there?*

She said hello and smiled. The assistant didn't even look up, let alone do the whole "may I help you?" thing.

Scanning the shelves, she spotted a pair of trainers, which could only be described as utterly vile. However, they were slightly less utterly vile that the other options on display. When she picked them up to check, she found that they were her size. She felt the cheap fabric and tried not to make a face. Not that the assistant was looking at her anyway.

She walked up to her, pulling on a smile. "Excuse me," she began, "do you have anything like this, but more…"

The assistant turned and gazed blankly at her. "More what?"

"Well, I mean, less…" She was trying to work out a way to say *more stylish and less gross* without being rude. But there was no non-rude way to say that, so she petered off into silence.

"We just have what's there," said the assistant, looking at

Delilah as if she were from another planet.

"Fine, I'll take them," said Delilah. "I'll wear them now."

A few minutes later, having wrapped up her beautiful, ruined shoes in the trainer box and handed them to the (very nonplussed) assistant for disposal, Delilah emerged from the shop in the vile trainers.

She was about to cross the road in search of something to eat when a motorbike came tearing down the empty street. She stepped back, anticipating the roar of the engine as it passed her. She'd always had a strong reaction to loud noises. They seemed to jolt her more than they did other people – to rattle her right down to the bones. But as it reached her the bike slowed.

The guy riding it looked her up and down as he went past, blatantly checking her out. She knew she should be outraged and stomp off, on behalf of all womankind, but instead she found herself dropping her bag hurriedly so that it covered the vile trainers. His strong, muscular torso in the leather jacket looked, well… It made her stomach flip over.

The only part of his face she could see was his eyes—his helmet covered the rest—and they were dark and intense. He was looking right at her.

For a moment they held one another's gaze—and then he turned his attention to the road, revved the bike and roared away. "Arrogant twat," Delilah pronounced, as she crossed the road. Which he had been. But that wasn't quite the whole story. "*Intriguing* arrogant twat, then," she corrected, with a small smile to herself.

On the other side of the road, a little further down, was a place called The Chinese Chippy. Its peeling, wonky sign and graffiti-covered front wall didn't make it look exactly *appealing*, but when she glanced inside, she saw that it was clean, at least. There were a few Formica tables along the wall opposite the counter, so she could sit down too.

She went in and joined the queue, behind a group of dusty,

rowdy workmen. She kept her distance and pretended to be very interested in the contents of the counter—saveloys, pies, golden-battered fish—hoping they wouldn't notice her. She didn't want them to start making lairy comments, or equally bad, say, "Cheer up, love, it might never happen." During Saturday free time at school, she and her friends had sometimes gone round town, and she'd had that shouted at her a few times. She knew she worried too much, and it probably did show.

Fortunately, the men didn't pay her any attention, but just got their orders in and left in a contented rabble, clutching open containers of pie and chips, and guzzling from cans of fizzy drinks.

Delilah shuffled forward and found herself standing opposite a part-Chinese girl about the same age as her, with liner-slicked sloping eyes, long dark hair, and a tight T-shirt which said simply, *Fuck Off.*

"Succinct," said Delilah, impressed.

The girl flashed her a smile for that, then quipped, "We don't do salad. Sorry."

"Oh, well, I…"

"Joke," said the girl. "So, what do you want?"

Delilah felt herself relax a bit and smiled back. "What's good here?" she asked.

The girl looked pleased—that seemed to have been the right thing to say. "Watch."

She put the gas on under a wok and slopped some oil in. Then she bobbed down, took a bowl from the fridge under the counter and peeled off the cling film. She grabbed up a big handful of what looked like a rice, prawn and vegetable mix and threw it into the now-sizzling wok. It spat and steamed so much when it hit the hot fat that it made Delilah jump.

The girl shook the wok hard, dousing its contents with various sauces from squeezy bottles. Her hair slipped back over her shoulder, revealing bright orange and electric blue flashes.

Holy Mother of Cool.

"It smells delicious," she told the girl a moment later, as a savoury, chilli-piqued fug filled the air.

The girl grinned at her and gave the wok another violent shake. "You wait. It'll taste even better."

* * *

"You're right, that was really good." Mae was now wiping down the table next to hers. She'd been offered a plastic fork but she'd asked for chopsticks instead, which had earned her finding out the girl's name.

Mae smiled, looking suddenly sweet and all at odds with her antsy T-shirt. "My grandpa's recipe," she told her.

Delilah finished up the prawn fried rice from its cardboard takeaway carton, chasing the final bits around with her chopsticks. "Is there Wi-Fi in here?" she ventured. "Looks like my 4G doesn't work round here—it must be my network."

"No customer Wi-Fi in here, and the 4G coverage is awful in this area, for some reason." Mae said. "You have to go to the library. Old school."

Delilah tried to hide her surprise that there was such a lovely thing as a library in this godforsaken hellhole. Now she'd just have to find it. She stood up, uncertain. "Oh, right, well, thanks. And which way is that...?"

Mae strode back to the counter and binned her cloth. Then she grabbed a sports bag, which she slung over her shoulder. Delilah thought she wasn't going to bother answering her, but as she made for the door, she said, "Come on, I'll show you. I'm heading that way." Then she shouted, "Dad! I'm going to the studio. I'll be back to open up later."

A careworn Chinese man came through the beaded curtain at the back of the restaurant. He was clutching a pile of paperwork. "Straight there and back," he said sternly. "You know I don't—"

At that moment he noticed Delilah standing there and obviously decided to hold back on their private family business. "Just remember what we talked about," he said, fixing Mae with a meaningful look.

What with the T-shirt and the feisty attitude, Delilah thought Mae might give him some lip, but she just nodded, looking deeply respectful. "Yes, Dad."

"Good girl," said her father. He nodded to Delilah and she gave him a shy smile, which he didn't return. Then he slipped back through the curtain and Mae bustled her outside, turning the "open" sign to "closed" as they went.

* * *

"So, how long have you lived here?" Delilah asked Mae as they walked up the main street.

"All my life," she replied, suddenly defensive. "I'm proud of my Chinese heritage but I'm as much of a local as everyone else."

"I meant, because I only got here yesterday," Delilah said hurriedly. "I'm staying for the summer, to help my great aunt, Edie. She's pretty old, but that's not really the problem. The thing is that she has dementia, so she's confused. She didn't even know who I was when I got here, and I'm not sure she does even now. And my dad thinks she's fine in that big old house on her own with just me, and a proper carer coming twice a day, or if I go out for ages. But Jane, that's her main carer, is arranging a specialist nursing home and I can understand why she–" Delilah noticed that Mae was looking at her with an expression that could only be described as *Woah*. "Sorry, T.M.I," she said quickly, then made herself shut up.

"I'm sorry about your aunt," Mae said.

"Thanks."

Mae stopped suddenly on the pavement and Delilah realised

that they'd arrived at the dance studio. It was actually some kind of community hall. Like the rest of the place, it was covered in graffiti, and one of the windows was boarded up. She flicked her hair back over her shoulders and Delilah almost said, "I like your flashes," but she stopped herself, thinking it would sound incredibly lame. And she told herself that asking Mae whether she'd like to hang out sometime would be even lamer.

"The library's that way," Mae was saying, gesturing vaguely down the street. "Ask for Milly. She's my friend. She'll help you with anything." As she spoke, a teenage boy in a leather biker jacket, not the guy who'd checked her out earlier, slid round the corner. He saw Delilah see him and pressed a finger to his lips. Then he slunk up behind Mae and grabbed her round the waist.

"Cal!" Mae half-screamed. She glanced up and down the empty street, then turned in his arms. "I hate you," she said, shaking her head.

"I hate you too, baby," said the boy called Cal.

Delilah was feeling awkward enough, but then Mae and Cal started in on a long, passionate kiss, his hands on her backside, pulling her close to him with a sort of *grinding* motion that made Delilah blush a deep red.

"Well, thanks, then. I'll..." Delilah said vaguely to herself and began to walk away.

Mae must have heard, because she pulled away from the boy and called, "Wait! This is Cal, my... Well... Look, just don't tell my dad, okay?"

Delilah nodded, then shook her head, not sure how to convey, *Yes,* I will *not* tell him.

"This is Delilah," Mae informed Cal.

"Nice to meet you," said Delilah, automatically holding out her hand to shake his (her school produced lovely *well-mannered* young ladies). Instead of taking it, he held his in the air and said "Hey". She quickly said "Hey" herself and copied his gesture, while cringing inside. *Shaking hands? "Nice to meet you"? Oh my*

God, there really is no hope for me, she thought. *I'm a disgrace to the name of teenager.*

"You going to the party tomorrow night?" Cal asked her.

Delilah was taken aback. "Well, I—"

"You should come," said Mae. "It's in the woods by the old manor house. It should be—"

"What, *my* woods?" Delilah cut in. Seeing them staring at her in surprise she hurriedly added, "Well, I don't mean they're mine but they're next to where I'm staying."

"Your great aunt lives in that massive manor house?" asked Mae, eyes wide.

Delilah nodded.

"Oh my God, is she loaded?" That was Cal.

"No, she's really not," Delilah insisted. "It's falling down—"

"Is it haunted?" asked Mae, looking thrilled at the idea. "I bet it is!"

Cal pulled her tight to him. "You don't really believe in that kind of stuff, do you?"

Mae wrapped her arms round his neck. "So, you'd stay the night there, would you?" she asked him, in a flirty, teasing way. "In a creaky, crumbling old house? It's, like, *hundreds* of years old. Think how many people must have died in that place."

"It's actually okay," Delilah said quietly. It looked like the kissing was about to recommence, so she was just thinking of an excuse for a quick exit, when a motorbike came roaring down the road.

It was that guy again. *Intriguing arrogant twat.*

He slowed the bike as he neared them, and this time she composed herself. If he looked her up and down again she'd give him the full outraged feminist face she hadn't quite managed earlier. He did check her out again, and she did start giving him the face, when, mortifyingly, he came to a complete stop. He walked the bike along a couple of paces so that he was right beside them, and Delilah tried not to notice the way his thigh muscles moved under his jeans, or how noticing that made heat rise up her throat and flood her cheeks.

It got worse when he took off his helmet and his eyes locked onto hers. Neither of them could look away.

There was something about him, apart from his strong shoulders and angular good looks, and almost-black, dark-lashed eyes. Something *more*. Something almost feral. Primal, even.

He looked at her hungrily, and she couldn't help but look back, deep into those dark eyes, with a lust so animal that the second she became aware of exactly what she was feeling, she blushed deep red again.

She tore her gaze away and saw that Mae had been watching them. The playfulness she'd had with Cal a moment before was gone. Now she looked uneasy. She was winding her hair tight round her finger, creating a black, orange and blue twist.

Cal broke the silence. "Gotta go," he said to Mae.

They kissed again, quickly this time.

Mae turned to Delilah. "Come to the party, yeah?" she said.

Delilah realised she was staring at the guy on the motorbike again, as he adjusted his leather gloves. Flushing even redder, she forced herself to refocus on Cal and Mae, and tried to sound vaguely normal. "Maybe. If I can. Thanks."

Cal started walking away, heading for the alley down the side of the building. "Bring booze," he called, over his shoulder.

"Well, I'm not sure..." she said weakly, then trailed off as he vanished out of sight.

The Intriguing Arrogant guy (scrap the *Twat* part, Delilah was now thinking, and go heavy on the *Intriguing*) nodded at her and Mae.

"Ladies." It was all he said. All he'd said *full stop*. But something in his voice caught at Delilah, making her breathe in sharply, as her stomach flipped over.

Then Intriguing Guy (as she'd decided he was now—

24

confidence wasn't the same as arrogance, right?) put his helmet back on and revved his bike.

Cal came roaring out of the alleyway on a motorbike then, making Delilah jump backwards. He had a helmet on, and he and Intriguing *Sexy* Guy (might as well state the obvious) tore off up the road.

Delilah stood with Mae, watching them, listening to the gear changes as they gathered speed. "Is *he* going to the party?" she asked.

"Yeah," said Mae. Delilah glanced at her as she watched the bikes round the corner. There it was again, that look. Uneasiness.

When Mae finally focussed back on her, Delilah looked at her questioningly, but she didn't say anything about the guy. She just gave her a tight smile, said "Laters" in a cool way that Delilah knew she personally could never pull off, and headed up the steps of the dance studio.

* * *

Delilah found the library with only one wrong turn and she now sat at an ancient-looking computer terminal in what was (a bit optimistically, she thought) called the "Tech Room". Milly, Mae's friend, was leaning over her, tapping at the keyboard.

Delilah had been surprised when she'd asked for Milly at the counter and a sweet, hippy girl in a vintage flowery dress had said, "Yes, that's me, how may I help you?" She'd just assumed that any friend of Mae's would be as full of attitude as she was and wearing some kind of similarly sweary-sloganed T-shirt — perhaps, *If you don't like libraries, go screw yourself.*

When Delilah had explained about needing Wi-Fi, Milly had showed her to the computers. Now she was leaning across her, setting up a user account. As Delilah watched her slim, delicate fingers flying over the keyboard, she caught a waft of her perfume. It was rose maybe, something natural anyway.

Something *aromatherapeutic*, if that was even a word. She almost asked her where she'd got it from—started a conversation. But she didn't, *typically*.

"So, that's you all set," Milly told her, straightening up. "Just create a password and you're good to go."

"Thanks," said Delilah. Then, as some sort of stab at friendly conversation, she added, "I hate being out of touch with my friends. Last time I got online was on the train down here, yesterday lunchtime."

Milly looked at her with genuine horror. "Twenty-four hours with no Wi-Fi? Wow. Well, I'll leave you to it. Did Mae tell you about the party?"

Delilah nodded.

"Great. Maybe see you there then."

"Maybe, yeah. Thanks."

Milly gave Delilah a smile and swished away in her long dress.

Delilah sorted out her password and got onto Facebook. But the initial excitement she'd felt about being back in the loop soon faded. Her tanned, relaxed-looking friends all seemed to be having the time of their lives on the beach, at sumptuous champagne-fuelled parties and, in Yolanda's case, on some fit guy's yacht. They were more like nice people she knew than friends, as such. She'd never really got close to any of them – to anyone, actually. But, unlike Shayla and her tight, bitchy circle, they were open and breezy and didn't seem to mind her hanging out with them. The cursor blinked at her from the status box, and she went to type something, but as her fingers hovered over the keys she hesitated.

Really, what could she say?

She typed: *Had an awesome morning doing a puzzle with my eighty-year-old great aunt, who has only the vaguest idea of who I am, and who, by some miracle, has not yet suffered any serious injury under my woefully underqualified and clueless supervision.*

Then she deleted it, as she'd known she would. She didn't want them feeling sorry for her (or worse, laughing at her) and she didn't want Shayla reading it. They were friends online, of course. Not being wasn't an option. With a sigh, she exited the page and logged off. Then she headed out, thanking Milly again as she passed the help desk.

As she walked back through the desolate town, she tried very, very hard not to think about dark, captivating eyes, or strong shoulders, or taut thigh muscles, or steady leather-gloved hands revving engines.

And failed spectacularly.

Chapter 3

Delilah had stripped the covers off her bed, changed them, and washed the old ones in a hot wash. Now, the following morning, as she put the dried and folded sheets away in the linen cupboard in the hall, she heard Jane and Edie's voices drifting out of her great aunt's bedroom.

"Now, come on, Edie. You can't leave your hair like that. Let me pin it up for you."

"Alright then," said her great aunt, with a sigh. Delilah was only half listening. She wasn't going to fit her sheets on top of the pile of linen, which was wedged in against the shelf above. She pulled at the pile, thinking she'd take out the big blanket from the middle of it and put it somewhere else.

"They don't like me to have it loose anyway," Edie remarked.

"Who doesn't?"

"The teachers, silly!" her great aunt exclaimed. "Loose hair spreads lice! Everyone knows that."

Delilah registered this and grimaced. She noticed that the *lice* bit had grossed her out but the fact that Edie seemed to think she was still at school hadn't really registered. She was obviously starting to get used to things round here.

She and Edie had survived another night together and, although she desperately wanted to ask Jane to book a carer to stay over every night, she'd been too embarrassed about looking completely incapable to say anything. She had asked for that evening, though, in case she decided to go to the party. Not that she would. She definitely wouldn't, in fact. But it was a good excuse to get someone to stay over, and it would give her a break from waking up worrying about Edie every couple of hours.

She put the new sheets on top of the pile, then supported the whole lot with her knee as she wiggled the blanket free and dropped it to the floor. To her surprise, a photograph fluttered out too, and she crouched to pick it up.

It made her smile suddenly, unexpectedly.

It was of Edie, at about the same age as Delilah herself was now, with very similar long brown, reddish-tinged hair flowing down her back, in a beautiful green velvet dress. Edie smiled out enigmatically at whoever was taking the picture.

Delilah thought that such a beautiful photo shouldn't be shoved to the back of the linen cupboard. She took it into the room, bringing the blanket too, which she draped across the end of her bed to make it look cosier. She put the photo on the top of her chest of drawers, leaning it against Miranda's perfume bottle until she could find a frame for it.

Jane left just after ten and the day went quickly. Delilah watched some TV with Edie in the sitting room, then, when the sun came out, she helped settle her with the radio on the back porch. She made some lunch for them from the fresh ingredients that Jane had bought, a Bolognese. Delilah couldn't help but watch Edie closely as they ate, hoping Jane was *really* sure that spaghetti wasn't dangerous, and on alert for the first signs of choking.

Edie ate her yogurt without putting any of it on her head, to Delilah's relief (and she wondered now if Jane had been joking about that), and Jane came back at five to find them in the sitting room, listening to Edie's record collection.

Delilah had managed to keep her great aunt alive all by herself for a whole day, and she was starting to think she was getting the hang of things. In fact, when Jane had called down the hall to ask her to bring a towel into the bathroom for Edie, she'd found herself walking in and handing it over without even thinking *eeek, there's my naked eighty-year-old great aunt in the bath*.

That was definitely progress.

Jane left again just after eight o'clock, and by nine, Delilah was reading her book in the kitchen. The clock seemed to be ticking extra loudly in the silence, making it difficult to concentrate. She put the book face down in her lap and tapped her nails on the kitchen table.

She thought about the party in the woods.

She'd just sort of assumed that she wouldn't actually *go*. And she wouldn't. Probably not. Almost definitely not. Even though Edie would be fine, as she was already asleep and Ewelina the carer had arrived for the night an hour before and was now watching TV in the sitting room.

After all, she'd only spoken to Mae and Cal for a few minutes. And Milly for even less. She wasn't shy exactly, but a big party in the woods where everyone was drinking and she only (barely) knew three people? It didn't seem like her kind of thing.

She went back to her book, but she couldn't get into it. The text blurred and she found herself staring out of the window at the gathering dusk. It was June, so although it was past nine, there was still plenty of light in the sky. Plenty to find her way through the woods by.

And she'd know a fourth person, of course.

The guy on the motorbike.

Just thinking about him made her stomach flip over again. Mae had said he was going too.

Delilah put her book on the table, stood up and stretched. She looked down at her jeans and comfy jumper. Yes, it was cashmere, but... It wouldn't do for a party.

Feeling a swirl of nerves and excitement in her stomach, she headed for her room.

* * *

Half an hour later, and now dressed in a sparkly clubbing dress, with silver and black eye make-up to match, Delilah came back down the hall. The vile trainers were disgusting, yes, but necessary — she wasn't ruining another pair of heels (or even her running shoes or Uggs) in damp, loamy woodland earth.

She said goodbye to Ewelina, then headed out, locking the heavy front door behind her and putting the comically huge key under a flowerpot full of weeds – it would be safer than possibly losing it in the woods. Ewelina had a sensible-sized key for the side door, so she wasn't locking them in or anything. She didn't need a bag – her phone had just died and was charging in the kitchen. She'd remembered what Cal had said — *bring booze* — and was clutching two bottles she'd found in Edie's drinks cabinet.

As she walked along the lane by the field that led up to the woods, she saw a line of badly parked cars, some battered and some souped-up. A path led up from the layby through the field to the woods. At least she knew roughly where to go now. Mae hadn't given her any directions, or a phone number or anything, and she hadn't really thought she'd come, so she hadn't asked. Besides, how sad would that have looked? She might as well have asked for a formal invitation printed in gold on embossed card.

By the gate where the path to the woods was, a cluster of motorbikes leaned on their stands. Seeing them made her heart beat faster. She couldn't pick his out, Intriguing Sexy Guy's. She hadn't been looking that closely at it — she'd been kind of busy being utterly transfixed by the person *on* it. But the presence of bikes suggested he was here, and that set her stomach flipping with nervous tension and excitement. She took a deep breath and pulled at the bottom of her dress anxiously, wondering what the others would be wearing, hoping she looked okay.

As soon as she'd followed the path under the cover of the trees, she heard music, voices, laughter. She followed the sound, which grew louder and louder as she made her way deeper into the wood. There was a bonfire smell too, like Mr Rowe the caretaker burning dry leaves at the edge of the sports field at school.

She turned a corner to find a clearing up ahead, and roughly twenty people gathered there. The path leading to it was much narrower, so she had to push branches away from her face as she walked, and the vile trainers slipped on the tree roots and mud-rutted ground.

It made her sad to see graffiti on some of the trees, and when she reached the clearing, she noticed that the beautiful oaks surrounding it had been sprayed with swear words and tags. And there was rubbish all over the place.

There's a party going on and that's what I notice? she thought. *What a geek.*

She focused on the people as she neared the clearing. A fire crackled in the centre, lighting them up in silhouette in the dusk light. Slivers of still-bright moonlight sliced down between the trees, giving the scene a background glow.

Delilah reached the edge of the clearing but stayed under the trees, watching, gathering courage. Some of the figures were dancing, some were lolling around on big logs, chatting. Some were kissing. Most had a can or bottle in their hands.

Suddenly someone sloshed petrol on the fire, and Delilah leapt backwards as the flames went up with a *whoosh,* to whoops and cheers. Sure, now, that this really wasn't her kind of thing (*Petrol? Jesus*), she decided to slip away.

But just then a voice rang out over the chatter. "Hey, you made it!"

She squinted across the clearing. It was Milly, sitting next to Mae and Cal, waving at her. Too late. She'd have to go over now. She couldn't not, not after all her years of nice young lady politeness training.

Pulling on a smile, she made her way over.

"Great, you came!" said Milly.

Delilah's smile was real now. "Good to see you again," she said. It really *did* feel good. There was a gentleness about Milly that put her at ease, and she felt like maybe they would have stuff in common. She turned to Mae and Cal, and said simply, "Hey."

No handshake this time. Go me.

"Hi," said Mae, detangling herself from Cal.

Cal raised his hand in a casual greeting and took the bottles from her. "Interesting choice," he said, peering at the labels. "What's advo-cat?"

"Asks the barman," said Milly, amused.

"*Advocaat*, you idiot," said Mae, with a teasing grin.

Cal pulled a face at her. "Seventeen percent, however you pronounce it," he said good-naturedly. "Not bad."

Milly shuffled up along the log and patted the space beside her, saying, "Come and sit here."

Delilah sat, guessing that Milly must have been feeling like a complete spare part next to the entwined Mae and Cal. *She* certainly would have been.

Cal inspected the other bottle, which was Stone's Ginger Wine. "Awesome old lady bevvies," he said, adding her offerings to the collection of bottles and cans at their feet.

"Oh, well, I—" Delilah began, feeling flustered.

"She's gone vintage, it's cool," said Milly.

Delilah gave her a grateful smile. She could usually manage to act reasonably confident in unfamiliar places, even when she felt the complete opposite inside, but this situation was so far out of her comfort zone that she seemed to have turned into The World's Most Awkward Girl™. Her lovely school for young ladies had not provided any opportunities for unsupervised drinking parties in the woods. There had been a black-tie Leavers' Ball just before the summer, with boys from their partner school, but the ball gown and swing band and fruit punch—even with the compulsory bit of vodka slipped into it from the hip flasks the boys had snuck in—was about as far removed from *this* party as it got.

And she was dressed all wrong.

She wished now that she'd left her jeans and jumper on, or at least put some leggings under the dress. She heard her name and emerged from her thoughts to find Mae teasing Cal again. "You should say, 'Hello, Delilah, how are you?' not just be like, 'What booze did you bring?'"

"Oh, no, it's fine, I—" Delilah blustered, her cheeks reddening.

Cal gave Mae a cheeky smile. He seemed to like her teasing him. He turned to Delilah and grinned widely, and as she smiled back, he gave her an elaborate bow and said, "Hello, Delilah, how are you?"

"Yes, how *are* you?" came a voice from behind her. A voice that made her skin prickle.

She turned to find the motorbike guy standing there, looking no less intriguing and if possible, even more sexy, in black jeans and his leather jacket.

The jokey atmosphere changed in an instant. Once again, she couldn't tear her eyes from his.

The connection between the two of them was so animal, so *raw*, that she felt embarrassed, like she was standing there naked and everyone knew how she was feeling.

What she was thinking…

And him… He looked like he was feeling the same way—she felt his eyes eating her up, drinking in her face, her hair, her body.

Delilah heard whispering nearby and managed to pull her gaze away from his for a moment. A group of girls were giving her the evils. Like it was *her* fault his attention was on her and not them, when all she ever did was try to look as invisible as possible. That hadn't stopped Shayla, though, and she wondered if acting small had ever made any difference.

Cal took his chance to lighten the mood. "Alright, Tol, put your eyes back in your head."

Tol. So that was his name.

Tol didn't seem to hear this. He didn't take his eyes from Delilah. "Nice dress," he said.

"What there is of it," she heard one of the girls close by whisper. This was followed by sniggering from the girl's friends. She blushed even deeper. *Bitches.* Milly must have heard it too, because she gave them a sharp look and shifted closer to Delilah.

Tol smiled at her then, a slow, lazy, wolfish smile, and sauntered away. Delilah watched him go, feeling almost a magnetic pull, as if she'd *have* to get up and follow him. She gripped the log with her fingertips to physically stop herself. She was desperate to talk to him, to get to know him better. Actually, she didn't even want to do that. She just wanted to be near him, to soak up every detail of his face, to feel his body heat beside her, to breathe in his smell. She imagined touching him, kissing him, his arms tight around her, and she could hardly breathe.

"How's Great Aunt Edie?" asked Mae, pulling her back to reality.

Delilah smiled. "Good thanks. Still alive, even though I've been the one looking after her all day. I'll go back soon," she added, "I don't want to leave her for too long." She didn't mention that Ewelina was there. Needing to go back for Edie could be her insurance policy if she wanted to tap out.

"Oh, we usually walk down together," said Mae, "but if you need to go earlier Cal will walk you, won't you, hon?"

"Sure," said Cal.

"Oh, I'll be fine," said Delilah, but then she thought again and said, "Actually that would be great, thank you." It would be pitch dark in half an hour, and while it had been easy to head towards noise to find the party, she wasn't sure she'd remember which paths she'd taken to get back. "I wouldn't want to end up getting lost out here," she added.

A loaded glance passed between Milly and Mae. Delilah looked at them questioningly, but it was Cal who spoke. "Of course I'm very happy to walk you back down," he said. "Because I am a gentleman," he added, looking pointedly at Milly and Mae. "*Not* because I believe any of this Dark Woods shit."

"But it's true!" Milly protested.

"It's where that weird, twisted tree is, further into the woods," said Mae. "The evil-looking one!"

"Trees can't look evil," Milly cried. "All trees are beautiful, like all babies."

Cal spluttered into his drink at this. "You obviously didn't see my little cousin Sammy when he came out." He hummed the music from *The Omen* and Milly giggled despite herself.

Ignoring this, Mae turned to Delilah. "I heard they used to hang witches there. That whole part of the wood is poisoned. My friend Courtney's sister went up there for a dare and stood next to that tree and she said it was like this evil force was dragging her down, sucking the life right out of her—"

Cal cut in. "This *is* Courtney who also says she has a recording contract with some label in Santa Monica, right? The same Courtney who reckons her real dad's that Canadian wrestler. Oh..." He paused, thinking. "What's his name..?"

"Captain Chaos," Milly supplied.

"Captain Chaos, that's it."

Mae wasn't going to be steered off course, though. "Still, she swears down that Tara nearly died up there."

Cal snorted. "Broke a nail more like."

Milly raised an eyebrow at him. "There are more things in heaven and earth, Horatio, than are dreamt of in your philosophies."

Delilah smiled and Mae nudged Cal's arm. "Mil's getting literary on *yo ass*!" She framed *yo ass* with air quotes in a cute, ironic way. "You won't catch *me* up there, anyway!"

"Hamlet," Delilah said to Milly. "My favourite. Well, along with Macbeth."

Milly smiled at her warmly. "Mine too."

"You like a good tragedy, huh?" said Cal. When Mae snorted, he added, "What? I do know *some* stuff."

"So, what do *you* think?" Mae suddenly asked Delilah.

"I think Cal does know *some* stuff," she said, using the joke to buy her time. They all laughed at this, but they didn't stop looking at her, waiting for her take on Courtney's tale. She realised she'd been holding back from giving an opinion. She didn't really like to think about spooky stuff—she was one of those people who only had to catch a glimpse of a scary movie to be up all night, convinced some shadowy force was going to get her. The sooner they changed the subject the better, as far as she was concerned.

She got to her feet. "Well, I don't know about this Courtney," she told them, "but I do know that I need to pee and that you're all going to have to look the other way and hum, because after hearing that story I am only going as far away as that tree." Though she'd never intended to actually pee, only to stop the conversation, she realised she needed to. She had to make sure she was completely hidden by the tree trunk and then do an ungainly crouch on the uneven ground and get it over with as fast as possible.

The awkwardness of trying to have a pee in the woods became funny and she was still smiling to herself as she made her way back towards the fire, enjoying the evening now. But then her gaze strayed over to Tol and her whole mood changed. She felt the animalistic pull of him, and her heart began to beat faster, as the swirly sexy feeling which rose up in her caught her off guard and she gasped. He looked up suddenly and their eyes locked. She felt like the feeling building inside her would rush out and she'd explode and shatter. It was overwhelming and she really thought her body was going to run over there on its own and grab him and...

She looked away and tried to get a grip, forcing herself to

stare at her feet as she made her way unsteadily back to her group.

Once there, she did her best not to keep glancing across the clearing at Tol, who didn't come over to them again. After a while she got into talking to Milly and managed to *not* glance at him for whole minutes at a time. *Go me*, she thought. They chatted to Mae and Cal too, when those two weren't locked onto each other's lips, oozing sex.

Luckily, she hadn't had to resort to actually drinking the "old lady beverages" she'd bought, as Milly had insisted that they share her collection of different organic ciders and cans of vintage lemonade. They drank those down then topped them up with vodka from the communal bottle the three of them had chipped in for.

"Oh, I should have brought some cash with me," she said, when Mae revealed this fact.

"No, no, you're our guest," Milly insisted, as she topped up Delilah's can from the bottle.

"Although, you *are* rich, right?" said Cal, with a cheeky smile. Delilah found herself blushing and Mae nudged him hard, crying "Cal!" But he just flashed her a smile then said to Delilah, "Pitch in next time and we'll get some Stoli instead of this cheap stuff. You could strip paint with this."

Delilah smiled at him. She liked the idea of being included, and of there being a next time. "You're on," she told him.

Cal wasn't like any of the boys she'd met before, either on Saturday afternoons in town or at joint events with the boys' school. In fact, if she'd seen him go by the coffee shop where she used to camp out with Yolanda and Georgia and the hockey girls, she would have thought he was at least twenty, and big, and scruffy and—admit it—*rough*-looking. And if she'd somehow met him down a dark alley in the middle of the night, she would have been terrified. Not that she'd ever *been* down a dark alley in the middle of the night. But, in fact, he was a really sweet guy, and he had a chilled-outness and cheeky humour about him which made her feel more and more relaxed as the evening went by.

It turned out that the vodka had been bought at wholesale price from the pub where he was a barman. "More like a security guard, the kind of customers we get in," he told her. "You might have noticed, it's not exactly Chelsea round here. A fist fight broke out the other day, it was like the Wild bloody West. Last night I had to physically carry this huge, sweaty guy out of the place at closing time *and* he puked on my shoes."

"You should get danger money," said Delilah.

Cal laughed. "I should! At least I've got my room there, though, upstairs, for hardly any rent. Gus, who owns the place, doesn't fancy being there overnight after the last time it was robbed, so I lucked out and got a place to stay."

Delilah was about to ask where his mum and dad lived, but Mae cut in. "Night watchman," she said. "You should get a uniform! Ooooh, yeah," she teased. "Do that, get a uniform. I love a man in uniform! Don't all girls?" She addressed this to Milly and Delilah.

Milly shrugged. "Not my cup of tea," she said.

Mae raised her eyebrows. "The man or the uniform?" she said archly.

Milly smiled good-naturedly. "Neither, as you well know."

"Uniforms still make me think of boys in *school* uniform," said Delilah.

"You had boys at your school?" asked Milly. "Oh! I just assumed..." She trailed off, looking suddenly awkward.

"She assumed you went to some super-posh girls' boarding school," finished Cal helpfully.

Delilah smiled. "I did," she admitted. "They shipped boys in from St Edwards sometimes, just so we knew what they were."

Cal, Mae and Milly all laughed at this and Delilah felt happiness bubble through her. She thought funny things in her head, but she never usually said them out loud, in case people didn't get it and just looked blankly at her, and also because she hated being the centre of attention. But she felt differently now. That was twice she'd made them laugh. *Huh!* she thought. *So, I actually can be outgoing, and relaxed and funny. I just need a large amount of vodka to bring it out in me.* She smiled wryly to herself and Milly picked up on it and gave her a questioning look. Delilah shook her head to mean *doesn't matter*.

She was warming to Milly hugely too, and Mae. They'd talked about how Milly had only come to Bernhurst the year before, because she'd really wanted to work in a library for the summer and there hadn't been any jobs going in her own area.

"When I got the job offer, my parents were freaking out, saying I couldn't go that far away from them, and get my own place and everything—that I wouldn't be able to afford to rent somewhere. When I came here to look round places, everything was way out of my price range, but lucky for me there was this tiny, run-down studio flat—"

"Yeah, 'lucky'," Mae cut in. "That place is a rat-pit, Mil, no offence."

"I'm sorry, *rat-pit*?!" Milly gasped. "How is that *possibly* not offensive?"

Mae grinned. "You know I don't mean it," she said, then turned to Delilah and exaggeratedly mouthed "rat-pit", causing Milly to slap her playfully on the arm. "I just wish you'd come and stay with us instead, be a lodger," Mae continued, to Milly. "My parents would be glad of the money for the spare room." She turned to Delilah. "Things have been tough at the restaurant lately," she explained, more quietly. Delilah assumed she'd lowered her voice to make sure the group of bitchy girls nearby didn't overhear. "It's really stressing them out, especially my dad."

Delilah grimaced. "I'm sorry to hear that."

"I'm sorry too," said Milly, "but there's no way I'm moving

back in with anyone's parents, not just when I've finally got away from my own." To Delilah, she added, "They're kind of... over-involved."

"Oh, I would *love* over-involved," said Delilah, without thinking. Then they were all looking at her and she had to explain, of course. *Stupid alcohol,* she thought, *making me speak up when I should have kept quiet.* She steeled herself and said, "My mum died in a car crash when I was six." She braced against the barrage of gasps, *oh my Gods* and *I'm so sorrys*, which came right on cue. Even now, she could barely stand them. "Thanks," she said quickly, and swerved off the subject. "And my dad, well, he's... he's this big businessman, property developer, into all sorts of God-knows-what. Children weren't his thing, even before Mum—before the accident, so he *really* didn't know what to do with me after that. I had a nanny and then, when I turned seven, I went off to Highoaks as a boarder and... Well, they basically brought me up."

Delilah had mumbled all this into her lap and now she glanced up to see her new friends looking at her with such sadness and pity that she wanted to curl up and disappear. Then, *wow, okay,* she realised *I just thought of them as my friends.* Well, maybe that was a bit premature, but she really hoped they would be, in time.

* * *

The awkward moment when she'd had to tell them about her mum had passed, thank God, and Delilah had asked Mae about dance. Mae had told her all about how she was hoping to get a scholarship to the American Dance Institute in New York and get herself and Cal out of *this hellhole* (Mae's words) for good.

Half an hour later, they were onto a subject that had absolutely nothing to do with Delilah, much to her relief. She wasn't entirely sure what they *were* talking about—the conversation was kind of drifting over her as she focused on trying to stop her head from spinning and on keeping an eye on Tol.

It was properly dark now, had been for an hour or so, and once again she thought that she should go back to Edie. She was sharing Cal's jacket with Milly, and really wished she'd bought some leggings to pull on under the dress. People were getting off with each other now. She didn't want to suddenly be surprised by the sight of Tol with some girl, so she had to keep watching him. He was still with his mates, still drinking, and now they were playing some game that involved stabbing a penknife into a tree trunk, just missing their spread-out hands, so that was okay. He might lose a finger, but he wasn't kissing anyone, at least.

The thought of Tol with someone else sent a sudden jolt of sickness through her, and she had to clamp her hand over her mouth to hold it back. This shocked her, and for a moment she tried to get away with telling herself she'd just drunk too much, and someone would have to hold her hair while she got sick everywhere. But she knew it wasn't that. It was purely the idea of Tol with someone else. And then the shocking rush of thoughts, *I'll kill her. I'll scratch her eyes out. I'll—Woah*, she told herself firmly. *He isn't* with *you. It's up to him what he does. Anyway, there isn't any girl.*

There might be though. Soon. The bitchy girls were dancing seductively by the fire, pretending not to notice Tol's friends casting glances at them. She wished he would come over to her side of the clearing again. Then, for the first time all night, it occurred to Delilah that maybe she should *do* something about all this. That maybe she should go over to *him*.

A few minutes later, his friends were up and messing around with the dancing girls, leaving him alone for the first time all night. As Milly got pulled into a nearby conversation, Delilah took her chance. She lurched across the clearing, almost stumbling into the fire as her brain struggled to balance her, kicking up the embers in a shower of sparks as she veered away from it. Tol was sitting with his back against a broad tree trunk, still drinking from the now almost-empty bottle of vodka. Delilah slid down the tree in an ungainly manner and landed in a heap beside him. "Epic sophistication fail," she muttered, shaking her hair out of her face.

"Ow!" gasped Tol suddenly, wincing.

"What?" cried Delilah, alarmed, scrabbling to her feet and looking for small bitey creatures.

Tol gave her an amused look. "Just cutting myself on your accent."

She sat back down again. "Ha."

"So, what is a nice girl like you doing in a ..." he gazed lazily around him, "in a *wood* like this. Surely you had a better offer?"

Delilah raised an eyebrow at him. "Well, my Great Aunt Edie and I do have a particularly thrilling thousand-piece puzzle on the go, but she goes to bed at nine and I promised not to finish it without her."

Tol snickered at this and took another drink from the bottle. "Cal told me about the great aunt thing," he drawled. "It's a bit weird. Wouldn't you rather be off on Daddy's yacht or something?"

"I'm her only family," Delilah said, feeling protective. "And anyway, Daddy doesn't have a yacht. It's a catamaran."

Tol smiled at this, conceding defeat. *Look at me being funny again*, Delilah thought. *Merci beaucoup, vodka.* She shivered— she'd left Cal's jacket with Milly. Tol noticed, but rather than offering his own, he held out the bottle.

She giggled loudly, as if this was hilarious. He gave her an amused look. "What's so funny?"

"What, just drink it out of the bottle? Just, neat?"

He smiled. "What, do you want a glass? Ice?"

They were flirting, she realised, and it felt great. *Look at me, flirting.* She clamped her lips shut in case her drunk brain decided to announce it out loud.

She gave Tol a slow, sultry smile. "Yeah. And tonic. A slice of lemon."

He looked amused. "Oh, I'm sorry," he said. Getting to his feet, he glanced around. "I really must have a word with the caterer."

Delilah laughed, reaching up her arm and pulling him back down.

It was the first time they'd touched.

And it was electric.

They were instantly serious, their eyes locked, looking so deeply into one another that Delilah felt like she might have to scream, just to let some of the intensity out.

"Come on, let's go for a walk," said Tol, standing suddenly.

Delilah let him pull her up. She glanced around her, waiting for her dizzy brain to stop moving, and saw Milly deep in conversation with Mae, and Cal now swigging the advocaat with his friend Adam, both of them pulling *yuck* faces. She wondered for a moment whether to tell them where she was going. But then Tol interlaced his fingers with hers, and squeezed her hand, and she felt that squeeze bleed heat right through her..

Suddenly it felt like there were only the two of them in the world, and she would have gone with him anywhere.

They lurched along the narrow path, Tol leading the way. Delilah's hand was still entwined with his, and she used his strong arm to steady herself. As they reached the wider path she fell into step beside him and he slung his arm around her shoulders. And then, suddenly, neither of them could wait any longer. At the same moment they moved towards each other, her hands reaching up around his neck, his mouth searching for hers.

The second their lips touched, she felt herself explode with desire for him, with that feral, animal hunger. She revelled in his smell, his taste, his touch. He felt the same about her, she knew—he pushed her back against a broad tree trunk and, as an owl screeched overhead, they kissed, hard and deep.

When they finally pulled away, they stared intensely at each other, sharing in that look that this attraction was something far beyond anything either of them had ever known. Then, as if dragged by a current, they were pulled into another kiss, their hands all over each other, instinctively knowing how to make each other gasp with pleasure.

They broke apart and Delilah leaned her head back, catching her breath for a moment. She gazed up into the trees, revelling in the solidity of Tol's body on hers, her hands sweeping over his shoulders, down his back.

My God, she thought, *so this is how good kissing can be.*

Tol gazed deep into her eyes. It was almost, *almost* too much, and she had to take in a deep breath and stop herself from looking away. "I want to know you," he breathed. "Really know you. Who are you, Delilah?"

She gaped at him. She hadn't been expecting him to say anything like that. "I... I'm..." she began. Her chest was seizing up—it was hard to breathe. No one had ever asked her who she *was*. Not like that. She knew he meant it on a deep level. But when she reached into herself, searching for some well of identity, some source of herself, she just found a gaping hole.

Yes, she was Delilah, but that was just a name. A schoolgirl? Not anymore. She liked running, music and fashion, but those things weren't *her*. She broke eye contact with him, feeling shallow, all surface, all... nothingness. Then she asked herself, in her head, in desperation, "Who am I?" and she found that she didn't know.

Tol was talking. "I'm sorry, that must have sounded—"

"No, no." She waved this away, but she felt angry with him too—for saying that, for making her feel so... empty. But she couldn't share that with him. Instead, she pulled him towards her and kissed him hard. He kissed her back, and then his hands were moving all over her – up and down the sides of her dress, across the top of her thighs, then suddenly cupping her breasts, making her cry out and pull him closer. They pressed their lips hard together again, then held their mouths open for a moment, until it was too much to take, and gasping, they went diving back into deep, strong kisses.

Leaning in to kiss her neck, Tol began pulling her dress up. Horrified, she pushed his hand roughly away. He stepped back, searching her outraged face. "What, did I hurt you?" he asked, looking confused, concerned.

She was as shocked as he was by her sudden anger. "Oh my God, do you think I would go off into the woods with some guy I've only just met and have sex?!" she snapped.

"Alright! Calm down!" he gasped, holding his hands up, looking vaguely amused.

"You *did*!" Delilah shrieked. "Typical." She looked at him with disdain. "I should have known."

"What should you have known?" he asked, looking bewildered, hurt. Before she could reply, he was shouting, with such rage that she stumbled backwards, her heart hammering with fright. "What do you think you know about me? You know *nothing*! You know *nothing* about me!"

Fear turned Delilah's legs to water beneath her as he came right up close. "I—" she began.

He was right in her face. "What gives you the right to judge me, you tight-arsed, stuck-up bitch!" He swung his arm backwards suddenly, fist clenched, and she flinched away, expecting a blow to land, but he whirled round at the last moment and punched the nearest tree, grunting in pain as his knuckles connected with it. Then, nursing his hand, he stormed away from her. Delilah just stared after him, open-mouthed. She jumped again at his parting shout—"Bitch!" Then he stumbled off into the woods, yelling. "You know nothing about me. You know nothing about me. Fuck you, bitch!"

She leaned back against the tree and let the shock give way to hysterical sobs. After a few minutes, the tears ebbed away, and she managed to get her breathing a little more under control. She struggled to wrap her head round exactly how things had gone so wrong between them, and so quickly. Why had she jumped to the idea that he'd wanted sex? Not that she had any experience at all, but she knew there was plenty in between kissing and sex that might lead a guy to pull your skirt up. Hadn't she wanted *any* of it? She didn't even know now. She'd just reacted — just snapped. She'd already been feeling weird, and suddenly angry with him, about what he'd said. *Who are you, Delilah?* That had got her on edge.

But anyway, whatever had made her push his hand away, whatever reason she'd said what she'd said, he'd stopped right away. He'd even been concerned he'd hurt her somehow...

So, why had it gone so wrong after that?

Realisation crept over her... It had been something she'd said. Implied, anyway. *"I should have known."* It had sounded like she was saying all he wanted from her was sex. Of course, now the moment had passed, she knew she shouldn't have said it, but... the way he'd exploded with rage had been terrifying.

He'd shown his true colours then.

He had a temper, like her father. He couldn't control himself. He'd punched a tree, for God's sake. If he hadn't turned at the last moment, it could have been her *face*. Well, at least she'd found out early on, and she vowed to stay well clear of him in future.

It was only when she'd processed through the whole thing, which took longer in her booze-soaked brain, that she looked around her and fully understood that she was alone in the woods with no idea of how to get back to the party. Fighting panic, she tried to shake herself sober, to focus her mind. She registered that she had two options: Try to find her way back in the dark or stay put and wait until dawn.

No contest. Her feet were already moving her back along the path she and Tol had come down. An owl screeching overhead made her jump and her heart started banging hard again as she reached a fork on the trail. She stared at it. She was sure there had only been one single path. But maybe she hadn't noticed the fork, or maybe she'd set off the wrong way in the first place and was now even further from the party than before. Swallowing down her rising panic, she chose the left-hand path and kept walking. She felt safer moving than standing still, even with the ground lurching in strange directions as her reeling brain struggled to keep her balanced.

She moved on, listening out for the party, but all she heard were the screeches of owls and unsettling rustles in the undergrowth which made her heart bang in her chest. She stumbled forwards, hurrying along the now-winding trail as fast as she could go without spinning out, or throwing up. She was sure she'd walked at least five times further than they had when they'd left the party, but she didn't know which direction she was heading in now, or whether she was just going round in circles. Staying where she was wasn't an option, though. She steeled herself and moved on.

A few minutes later she stopped dead. She was sure she heard voices. Not chatting and laughter, but whispering. Her brain struggled to make sense of it. Maybe a couple of people had slipped away from the party for a private chat. Maybe she really had come round in circles and she was closer to the clearing than she'd thought.

Her heart leapt with hope. "Is anyone there?" she cried out, registering how slurred her words were. But all that came back was her lonely echo.

Suddenly, a branch caught at her foot, turning her ankle, and sending her stumbling forwards, crying out in shock. She landed hard on her ribcage, knocking all the air out of herself and getting a mouthful of dirt. She fought to get her breath back and spat on the ground. She looked up, pushing her tangled hair from her eyes.

The whispering was louder now.

And it wasn't from people... it was... it seemed to be coming from the trees that surrounded her. *Wow, I am never, ever drinking again,* she thought. She got carefully to her feet, trying her weight on her ankle. It hurt—like hell—but it held, just about.

Some kind of owl ruffled its feathers in the branches above her, its cold eyes glinting at her in the moonlight.

The whispering was growing louder. She couldn't make out the words, and perhaps it wasn't even in English, but it sounded malevolent, and taunting. She shook her head hard, hoping that would stop it, and almost threw up. Pursing her lips against her threatening stomach, she steadied herself and took a step. A pain shot through her ankle and she tipped sideways and grabbed at the nearest tree for support.

Then the most awful sickening feeling slid through her, as if she'd swallowed black tar and it was slowly crawling down into her stomach. Suddenly all the strength was sucked out of her body and she crumpled onto the ground. The earth itself had a current, dragging her down...

She looked in horror up at the tree, at its spiralling winding bark and wizened twisting branches, and everything flooded into her mind at once.

Mae's story.

The Dark Woods.

The Twisted Tree.

Oh my God. I have to get out of here.

She managed to drag herself up, her arms and legs dead weights. It was like pulling herself out of a swamp. She just had to take a step, then another, and she'd be out of there...

Suddenly the owl was swooping down from the tree, screeching, beak and talons flashing in the moonlight. For a second she just stared at it, open-mouthed. She couldn't take it in. It couldn't be… But it *was*…

It was coming right for her face.

Just as it was about to hit her, instinct kicked in and she threw herself to the ground again. In a flurry of feathers the owl soared away. Heart pounding, mouth dry with shock, Delilah scrambled up and ran, howling at the pain in her ankle. The owl came at her again, talons aimed right at her eyes. She threw up her arms and batted at it, shrieking as it scratched a searing cut into her cheek. Then its talons dug into her arm. She was screaming hysterically now, trying to shake it off, panic-flooded, fear-crazed. It wouldn't let go. The whispering in the trees grew louder, and her vision began to grey over as the owl held still for a moment, looking right at her.

It felt like she was looking into the eyes of pure evil.

Then it lurched for her throat, razor beak wide.

Just before it struck, one thought cut through the primal terror that consumed her.

I'm going to die.

And then the force hit them both. Blowing in like a tornado, it knocked Delilah off her feet, and hurled the owl away, flinging it through the air like a toy. She gasped as she found herself surrounded with… Well, she wanted to say *light*, but it wasn't that the wood was lit up all around her, so it couldn't be. It was strength and energy and power, and the most exquisite kindness, and right in the centre, it was a deep, deep peace, like nothing she'd ever known.

Like liquid love.

And then it was gone.

And she ran.

Chapter 4

Delilah had been stumbling around for nearly half an hour, lost and hysterical. She was terrified that the bloody psycho owl was about to burst through the trees behind her, when she heard a shout. "No luck that way!"

It came from her right, and it sounded fairly close by.

Sobbing with relief, she ran towards the voice. Soon, she saw the fire twinkling through the trees ahead and made for it, wading through holly bushes, not even noticing them scratch and tear at her bare legs, just taking the most direct route. As she stumbled into the clearing, Milly and Mae rushed to her, throwing their arms around her.

"It's okay, she's here!" shouted Mae over the top of Delilah's head, as she sobbed onto her checked shirt.

"Oh my God, what happened?" Milly gasped. "Where have you been?"

Delilah couldn't reply—she was trembling too much. Cal and Adam jogged up, and, seeing the state of her, Cal took off his jacket and slung it around her shoulders.

"I- I- I-" she stuttered, then shook her head and burst into tears.

Mae's glance slid to the group of bitchy girls nearby, who were inching closer, while pretending not to listen. "Come on, we'll take you home," she said protectively, glaring at them. "We can talk on the way, away from *them*."

As they let go of Delilah, they saw the state of her. "Oh my God, your face!" shrieked Milly. "And your arm's shredded!"

Delilah looked down at the rivulets of blood dripping down and running in between her fingers.

Mae cast another look at the bitchy girls. "Let's go," she said, steering her away.

They headed out of the clearing, Milly and Mae half holding

Delilah up. Cal hung back for a moment to do a complicated handshake thing with Adam, then followed the three girls.

About fifteen minutes later, they were almost back at the manor. Delilah stopped, caught her breath and, haltingly told them what had happened with Tol, and the owl.

"What the fuck?" cried Milly. She gestured at Delilah's arm and face. "An *owl* did that?!"

Cal was furious. "Tol shouldn't have left you there by yourself. Or got aggressive. Not with a woman, that's not on. Next time I see him, I'll—"

"Leave it, Cal," Mae cut in, forcing him to look at her. "I mean it. He's not worth you getting in trouble over. *Again.*"

Milly pulled Delilah to her as they walked, in a sideways hug. "I've never heard of an owl doing that. Thank goodness you managed to get away."

Delilah hesitated, not sure how to explain, then she said tentatively, "Well, I had a little help with that."

Her friends looked at her in confusion.

"What, was someone else there?" asked Milly.

"No. No one," Delilah said. "I just mean..."

But... What *did* she mean, exactly?

She suddenly realised how crazy it would sound. Some kind of mysterious force had torn through the woodland and saved her from an evil killer owl?

She shook her head. "Never mind. I probably imagined it. I was..." Her voice cracked and she broke down in tears again. "I was just so scared."

Milly squeezed her shoulder and Mae gripped her hand tightly. "It's okay, you're safe now," Milly said gently. "It's over."

Delilah found herself suddenly anxious. "Tol was so angry with me," she gasped. "And so drunk. And I said about Edie, so maybe he knows where to find me..." She felt panic rising in her chest and fear overrode all her inhibitions. "Will you stay with me tonight?" she asked. "All of you?"

"Of course we will," said Milly gently.

Mae stole a glance at her watch. "Absolutely," she said, after a moment. "I'll have to go at first light, though. I wasn't allowed to go to the party. If my dad catches me out of the flat—" She looked panicked at the thought and Cal took her hand. "He won't, okay?" he told her firmly. "I'll get you back in time."

They had reached the gate to the lane, where the motorbikes were parked up. Cal stroked his lovingly. "You'll have to stay here tonight, Clarabelle," he told it. "I'm wasted."

Delilah managed a tiny smile. "Clarabelle?"

Mae rolled her eyes. "Don't ask," she said.

"Where's Tol's bike?" Cal asked, his brow furrowed. "He's wasted too."

* * *

The manor was still and silent in the moonlight. Delilah lay awake on her bed, her hair still wet from the shower. Luckily Ewelina was sleeping in the room beside Edie's, far down the hall, and they'd managed to creep past without waking her. It helped that both her door and Edie's were shut—Delilah had seen the baby monitor she'd set up when she'd taken her some clean towels before she went out. It made her cringe—poor Edie.

She'd had to brush her teeth twice to get the dirt taste out of her mouth. The nasty scratch on her face was stinging, and the cuts on her arm throbbed under their dressing. Milly had cleaned and bandaged them with calm efficiency, seeming to know exactly what to do. Now she was on the bed beside her, and across the hall, in a dusty bedroom, Cal and Mae were curled up on top of the coverlet, his jacket slung over them both.

Delilah's eyelids flickered and, just as she was thinking that she really should have checked on Edie when she'd got in, she slipped into a vivid dream. She thrashed around feverishly

53

as Milly slept soundly. She was in the woods again, with Tol, terrified by his anger.

You know nothing. *You know* nothing *about me.*

He drew his arm hard back and she instinctively flinched away, sure once more that he was going to hit her. She stumbled and fell, and as she gasped, catching her breath, the ground began to suck her down. Malevolent, inhuman whispers rustled in the branches around her. She glanced sharply up—and found she was alone. Hardly daring to look, but unable to stop herself, she focussed on the tree looming over her. She'd jumped location. It was the Twisted Tree.

Suddenly the owl was coming at her again, screeching like the devil. She threw herself onto the ground, but she wasn't fast enough. This time it buried its beak deep into her throat. She choked out a groan, drowning, eyes wide, as blood arced high from the wound.

She woke at that moment, hands clawing at her neck, eyes wild, feet scrabbling. She registered that she was in the manor, in her bedroom, that Milly was beside her, that she was safe. Slowly, she let herself breathe out, relief flooding through her.

Only a dream.

Then somehow, impossibly, Tol was there.

He towered over the bed. Through her shock, Delilah took in that his face was bruised and battered, his shirt bloody and torn. His right eye was closed, the skin swollen and purple.

Suddenly his lips were a whisper away from her ear. "You know nothing about me," he hissed. He drew his arm back, and instinctively she flinched away. Then, when a blow didn't land, she found her voice, and screamed. Milly woke immediately, shot upright and held her tight.

"Tol..." she whimpered.

"Shh, it's okay, sounds like you had a nightmare," Milly said groggily.

A moment later, Mae and Cal, looking dishevelled, appeared

at the doorway. "What's going on?" asked Cal.

"A nightmare," Milly told them.

"It *was* a nightmare," Delilah said, her voice trembling. "But then I woke up and Tol was here. Right there."

She gestured at the empty space in front of her.

"Oh, hon…" Mae sat on the bed and stroked her arm. "Your mind was playing tricks… After what you went through tonight, it's not surprising."

"Oh my God," muttered Cal, and the girls looked up to find him staring at his phone.

"What's up?" Mae asked.

"It's Tol," he murmured, staring in disbelief at the screen. "He did take off on his bike." He paused and took in a deep, shaky breath. "He crashed it. He was taken to hospital."

"Oh my God…" gasped Milly.

"Is he alright?" asked Mae.

Cal shrugged. "Adam says that's all he knows."

Delilah's shock turned to horror as she felt a terrible knowing uncurl in the pit of her stomach. "Oh my God, Tol's dead," she stuttered. "He must be dead. That's the only thing that explains how he just appeared here, in my room."

* * *

As soon as she'd heard the news about Tol, Delilah had begged Cal to take her to the hospital on Clarabelle. He'd flat out refused, pointing out that he could barely walk in a straight line, let alone handle a bike. Then she'd grabbed her phone, intent on calling a taxi, and been informed by Milly that, round here, cabs finished just after last orders at the pub.

So, she had been forced to wait. Mae had insisted she try to get some sleep, and after a few hours' fitful half-slumber, they'd all crept out of the silent house. They walked into town just after it got light, along the near-empty main road, to wait for the first bus that took the route for the hospital, which was out on the dual carriageway. So she'd had plenty of time to think about the looks on her new friends' faces when she'd blurted that thing out—about Tol being dead. Milly had looked as horrified as Delilah by this, but Mae and Cal had shared a concerned glance, and now she wondered whether they were thinking she was a bit... not right in the head.

Huh, so much for making new friends.

They'd probably be off away from the nuts girl as soon as they'd done the responsible thing and showed her that Tol wasn't dead and, therefore, wasn't haunting her. But she'd seen what she'd seen. Yes, she'd still felt drunk when she'd woken, a bit, but hardly at all. He'd been *there*. He really had.

Now they walked up to the reception desk just inside the Intensive Care Unit, having been buzzed in by a grumpy-sounding nurse. Cal, Milly and Mae flanked Delilah like bodyguards. They'd tried A&E first, but no one there would tell them anything. If they had no luck here either, the next stop was the morgue. That thought sickened Delilah. If things hadn't gone so badly wrong between them... If Tol hadn't stormed off and got on his bike... She couldn't help feeling like she was partly to blame.

From a few paces away, Cal nudged Delilah, then gestured at a whiteboard behind the desk. Delilah squinted at it and saw Tol's name on the patient list. "There, not dead, see?" Cal whispered. Delilah took this in, and felt relief go whooshing through her legs, almost taking them out from under her.

"That's all we needed to know," said Mae, turning on her heel. "Come on. If we're quick, maybe my dad—"

"Can I help you?" asked the nurse, only briefly glancing up from what she was writing. And yes, she did look as pissed off as she'd sounded on the intercom.

"Oh, no, thank you, we were just leaving," said Mae, over her shoulder, already heading back towards the doors.

Everyone was surprised when Delilah stood firm in front of the desk, even Delilah herself. She hadn't planned this. But suddenly she just knew what she had to do. "We're here to see Tol," she said, working hard to keep her voice steady, making sure she looked the nurse in the eye and appeared confident.

She felt Milly, Mae, and Cal shift beside her—felt their surprise.

"It's family only," the nurse said curtly. "And do you know his family because we don't seem to have any records in the system for—"

After only a second's hesitation, Delilah cut in. "I'm sorry. I should have said. I'm his sister."

The nurse's expression softened at this. "Oh. Right. Well, we'll need to go through these forms, and I'll fill you in on his condition. In private."

"That's fine," said Delilah. She could still feel her friends staring at her, but she didn't take her eyes off the nurse. "But please could I see him first? Just for a minute?"

The nurse may have softened towards Delilah, but she still had a fierce glare for Milly when *she* stepped forward too. "Of course. Only you, though," she said. "I'll be with you in a moment."

As the nurse returned to her writing, Milly touched Delilah's arm. "Are you sure you—"

Delilah swept her gaze across all three of them, willing them to go along with this. Willing them to understand. "I'm sure. Meet me out front, yeah?"

Cal nodded and, seeing that Mae was about to reply, took her by the shoulders and steered her gently away. Milly wasn't moving, though. Delilah gave her a pleading look and said, in a low voice, "I need to see him, for myself."

Milly was about to reply when the nurse looked up again, so she just held up her hands and followed reluctantly behind Mae and Cal.

Delilah took a deep breath, turned to the nurse and gave her an enquiring look.

"Second on the left," she told her. "My colleague Kate is in there. But just for a minute. I'll get those forms—do you have some ID?"

Delilah nodded, then set off before the nurse asked to see it there and then. She followed the corridor round, found Tol's room, and hovered outside, her hand on the push plate. She watched her fingers trembling and made herself take a deep breath. *I can do this*, she told herself.

Then she went in.

Tol was lying on a bed, with tubes snaking out of his mouth and nose and monitors attached to his arms, linking him to the beeping machines that surrounded him.

Nurse Kate was checking the machines and noting down the readings. She looked up and gave Delilah a sympathetic smile. "We've had to induce a coma," she said gently. "Until the swelling in his brain subsides."

Delilah nodded mutely and inched closer to the bed. Forced herself to look at his bruised, battered face. His right eye was purple and closed, just as it had been when he'd appeared to her, looming over her bed. His lip was split, badly, and sealed with a crust of dried blood. His ribs were taped up on the right side, too, where his shirt had been torn and bloody.

"Tol..." she whispered, her voice cracking.

Images of his raw aggression in the woods flooded her mind, and fear swelled inside her. Her heart pounded in her ears and she had to lean on the metal side bar of the bed, as her legs threatened to give way.

And then there was... all this. This was shocking. It looked so brutal, and so odd, as if Tol were part of the machines around him. *And, oh my God,* she thought, *he's got a tube shoved down his throat. They must have had to cut...* Just looking at it made her gag.

Completely overwhelmed, she backed away slowly on her shaky legs, fighting the urge to run. She jumped at the voice behind her. "I know it looks awful..." It was the strict nurse, now clutching the forms.

Delilah whirled round and bolted out of the room and back down the corridor. She hit the exit button at the double doors and slammed through them. At the end of the hall, she dashed past the bank of lifts and took the stairs, almost hurtling headfirst down them in her hurry. She didn't stop running until she was outside, gulping at the cool early morning air.

* * *

A little while later, Delilah sat with Milly, Mae and Cal on the grassy bank of the busy dual carriageway. Cars zoomed by, and trucks juddered past, but somehow the noise, speed and sheer power of the passing vehicles was so visceral, so real, that it was strangely reassuring. She couldn't have stayed at the hospital. No way could she have sat calmly in the café there and had a nice cup of tea, as Milly had suggested.

She'd told them in halting, breathy bursts about the coma and the horror of seeing Tol all wired up. Milly had put her arm around her shoulders as they listened.

As she'd spoken, Delilah had felt herself calm down, a little at least. Now she decided to tell them the details that she'd held back the night before. She really appreciated that they'd stuck around to wait for her. After all, they hardly knew her. She wanted them to know everything, however weird it sounded. Besides, staying cagey and closed all the way through school had got her nowhere, she realised now—if she wanted to make some real friends, she needed to open up a bit.

"There's some stuff I didn't tell you, about last night," she began tentatively. "In the woods, it wasn't just the owl... before that the trees were, well, it was as if they were whispering... and

I felt like I was being dragged down into the ground. I could hardly get up."

Milly drew in a breath, sharply. "Oh my God," she gasped. "You must have wandered into the Dark Woods."

"Oh, come on!" Cal snorted.

Delilah nodded at Milly, then stole a glance at Mae, who looked anxious. "And I saw the Twisted Tree, right in the middle," she continued. "I hurt my ankle and I had to lean on it, I didn't realise then where I was—I didn't realise that 'til halfway through last night – but when I put my hand on it..." Just the thought made her shudder. "It was like black tar seeping all through me. I felt so dizzy and sick..."

"Oh for God's sake, you were wasted off you face!" Cal protested. "Course you felt sick and dizzy, and you were lost and scared. It was your—"

"Don't you *dare* say it was her imagination," snapped Milly.

Cal sighed. When he spoke again, he avoided Delilah's eyes, even though she was looking straight at him. "I'm not saying the owl attack was your imagination. But maybe you got between it and its young, or something. I don't know." He paused, thinking it through. "And then you flung it away from yourself, in a panic."

"I didn't!" Delilah insisted, incensed. "It was like the bloody thing was possessed! It was going for my throat, trying to kill me! If it wasn't for—" She stopped herself sharply.

Cal was looking at her now, tight-lipped, arms folded. Clearly disbelieving. *You haven't heard the half of it yet*, she thought grimly.

"If it wasn't for what?" asked Milly gently.

Delilah sighed. It might as well all come out. Cal couldn't think she was any crazier than he clearly already did, after all. "It was this... mysterious force," she began, struggling for words to describe it. "Like a... hurricane of light, but not light that you could see."

"Oh right, light you can't see, *that* kind of light," muttered Cal, and Mae nudged him hard on the arm.

"The owl was going for my throat, and the force... it hurled it away from me..." Delilah squeezed her eyes shut and shook the stark images from her head. "That's how I escaped."

Cal shrugged. "Look, you were petrified," he reasoned. "Desperate. People do incredible things when they're under that kind of pressure. Maybe you threw it off you. I read about this mother, she just lifted this car right off her kid. Compared to that, an owl is nothing."

Delilah's chest tightened with sudden anger. "It wasn't me. I know it wasn't!" she insisted. Then, shocked by her outburst, she lapsed into brooding silence.

"Why are you being such a knob about it, Cal?" That was Milly, stepping in.

"Someone has to keep a grip on reality around here," Cal snapped. The two glared hard at each other, a full-on row bubbling just under the surface.

"Are you saying I made it all up?" murmured Delilah, hurt.

She directed this at Cal, but it was Mae who spoke. "Whatever happened, it's over, and she got away," she told them all, in a tone that said *discussion over*. She stood up and brushed down her jeans. "Now can we please get out of here, and on the way back can you help me work out what the hell to tell my dad? He's called me, like, twenty-five times." With that, she began to walk away.

Cal stood too and set off after her.

A moment later, Milly and Delilah got up. "Come on, let's catch up," said Milly, but Delilah put a hand on her arm, holding her back. "Milly, I swear to you, there is a Dark Woods, and there was some kind of power or force—it saved me."

"I believe you," said Milly. It was a simple declaration, and Delilah felt the one hundred percent truth in it. She thought she might cry with gratitude, but instead she managed a wobbly smile as tears brimmed in her eyes.

"Thank you," she said. "It means a lot." After a moment, she added, "And I absolutely did see Tol appear in my room."

"I know," Milly said gently. "I know you did. Look, don't worry about Cal—he's a good guy, but he's a *guy* guy. He's kind of *man make fire, man hunt woolly mammoth*. You know…"

Delilah knew Milly was trying to make her laugh. She smiled briefly but couldn't get her mind off Tol. "When he appeared in my room, his face was all bashed up, just like it is in there." She gestured towards the hospital. "How could I have made that up? It was *him*. But if he's not dead, how is that possible?"

Milly slowed a little, thinking. There were a good ten paces between them and the others now. Delilah was relieved about this—she didn't fancy hearing Cal's take on things.

"Maybe he was having an out of body experience," said Milly at last.

Delilah smiled again, then she saw that Milly was utterly serious, and she felt completely freaked out. "Out of his body *how* exactly?" she asked, heart pounding.

"Spirit-walking," Milly said matter-of-factly. Seeing the surprise on Delilah's face, she added, "I'm kind of into this stuff. I've read lots of reports of it from people who've come out of comas. Mostly, the subjects who've had these experiences say that people can't see them, though. They say they're trying to talk to their husband, or whoever, and the person has no idea they're there."

Delilah frowned, confused. "So, then, why could I see Tol?"

Milly thought about this. "Maybe you have psychic ability," she said, with sudden excitement. We could borrow some specialist paranormal recording equipment—I know this guy online… Then if you see Tol again—"

Another wave of sickness coursed through Delilah's body. "I don't *want* to see him again," she protested. "In body *or* in soul, spirit, whatever it is."

"Sorry," said Milly quickly. "I wasn't thinking. Of course you don't. And look, if you like I could stay over again tonight."

Delilah gave her a small smile. "Thanks, I really appreciate that. But I'll be okay. If it happens again, I'll just tell myself he can't hurt me. If your theory is right, and he's *spirit-walking* out of his body, he can't actually *do* anything, can he?"

Milly shook her head. "No, he can't physically attack you."

Delilah tried to take comfort from that. And Milly's explanation was the only one that made sense... Well, apart from Cal's take on it all, that she'd imagined the whole thing, of course. If it were someone else, maybe she'd think that too. But it had happened to her, and she knew what she'd seen, and felt.

Tol had been right there—and he'd felt so *real*. So, either Milly was right, or she was having hallucinations. Though horrifying, spirit-walking was a more appealing explanation than thinking *that*. And it was comforting, too, understanding that Tol couldn't actually hurt her.

Scare the hell out of her, yes. But not hurt her.

Mae turned then and called, "Come on! Do you actually *want* my dad to ground me for the rest of my life?"

Milly and Delilah glanced at each other. Delilah knew that Milly didn't want to break off the conversation either, but she wasn't ready to explain to Mae and Cal what they'd been talking about. "Sorry!" she called to Mae. Then, "Let's just keep this between us, yeah?" she said to Milly under her breath, as they quickened their pace.

"Sure." Milly gave her a sympathetic smile. "And listen, it will all be okay, you know?"

Delilah managed a small smile in return. "Thanks," she said, "I'm sure it will." But she couldn't meet Milly's eye. There were so many questions—what if Tol appeared to her again? What if he didn't make it out of the coma, *ever*? What if he *died*?

What if, what if, what if...

The truth was, she was far from sure of anything.

Chapter 5

That afternoon, Delilah was walking around the overgrown gardens of the manor house, deep in thought. Lots of different subjects swirled round in her head like coloured scarves—Tol, the owl attack, the accident, what to do about Edie, her dad's shitty attitude, her potential new friends, and what she might do with her life in general when she left the manor house.

She really did wish she could switch her mind off sometimes.

This last topic had been brought into sharp focus by the memory of the owl making straight for her throat, beak glinting in the moonlight. By the petrifying thought which had gripped her: *I'm going to die.*

But she was alive. She'd survived. Thanks to the… well, the whatever it had been.

When the shock and fear had settled, she'd been left with a new sense of… It was hard to know what to call it. Of *aliveness*, she supposed. Of *awareness* of her aliveness.

She whispered it to herself. "I am alive."

Now there was just the small question of what she wanted to *do* with her life. She wondered if Uni actually *was* inevitable, as she'd always assumed. It was just what you did, wasn't it? If you were clever enough, and you had the money, you just *should* go, shouldn't you? And if you'd jumped through all the hoops so far. Was it a bit of a waste doing A-Levels next if she didn't? But then, if going to Uni was her path, surely she'd feel it more? Wouldn't she know what subject she wanted to study, or at least in what department? Wouldn't she feel more excited about it?

If she really wanted to go, wouldn't she just *know*?

When you found your true path, you just *knew*, didn't you?

For the first time ever, she asked herself how you *know* whether you want something. It wasn't because other people thought you should want it: If that were true, she'd be marking out this garden into parking spaces for the luxury flats her *dad* wanted her to want.

She thought about the things she knew for sure she *did* want. She'd wanted her mother back, desperately, every day since the accident, but she knew that wasn't going to happen.

She'd wanted Tol.

She winced as she remembered her intense physical reaction to him. One word: *Want*. She'd wanted him so much that the thought of not getting him had made her feel physically sick. But then, he hadn't turned out to be what she'd thought. *That* was the understatement of the century. And now he was in a coma and she was in this terrifying mess, trying to make sense of a possessed owl, a scary spirit looming over her, and why the real Tol had been so furious with her when she'd said what she'd said. *I should have known.* It had been like a trip-switch, triggering such rage in him... And if he hadn't stormed off so angry he wouldn't have got on his bike and he wouldn't have crashed and...

Before she could stop it, the thought was there, front and centre in her head:

If he dies, it'll be my fault.

She couldn't *go* there, but too late, her stupid overactive brain had already arrived at guilt city.

"Yeouch!" she cried, her feet crashing hard into something solid, nearly knocking her over. As her focus flipped away from the awful thought in her head, she felt the release of its grip on her. She was perversely glad she'd hurt herself. She leaned down and pressed her hand on the object, parting the overgrown grass for a better look. It was a low stone wall, as high as the top of her ankle. Her fingers felt along a bit further. The wall snaked out in both directions.

Just then, the clunk of the back door made her look up. It was Edie. Delilah saw that she only had one arm in her raincoat. The other sleeve was inside out, trailing by her knees. She stood up and hurried over to help.

"This coat is broken," said Edie mournfully. As Delilah reached the back porch, she was suddenly filled with affection for her great aunt. She remembered the photo she'd found, of young Edie in the beautiful dress.

This frail old lady had been *her age* once.

"It's not broken," she said gently. "It just needs ..." She put her hand up the sleeve and pulled it the right way round. "There you go." She guided Edie's arm into it, and as she stooped to zip it up for her, Edie stood with her arms held out to the sides, like a child.

As they made their way onto the overgrown lawn, the wet grass squeaking beneath their feet, Delilah tried to take her great aunt's arm. "Here let me—" she began, but Edie shrugged her off, saying, "Oh, don't you fuss, I'm fine."

"Okay," she said, while thinking *Please don't slip over and break your hip and have a cardiac arrest from the shock and die.*

They walked on around the garden, and, as they neared the place where Delilah had found (and almost broken her toe on) the little wall, she crouched down. "Look at this," she said, pulling back the grass again so Edie could see.

Her great aunt peered down at the chunks of stone for a moment, completely confused. Then her face lit up. "The herb garden!" she cried. "Oh, we had everything here – feverfew, for headaches. Calendula, for cuts. Chamomile, peppermint... Lemon balm for nerves."

"Yes!" said Delilah. Now that she looked at the wall again, a vague memory was forming in her mind of running through the garden, plaits flying, ribbons undone, her arms filled with lavender. "I remember them," she murmured. She had a sudden idea. "We could restore it," she suggested. "I mean, I could organise it, get some gardeners, and you could tell me what to plant. Would you like that?"

"Oh, yes!" cried Edie. Then she looked at Delilah intensely, and her eyes were filled with sudden tears.

"Yes," she said again, "I really, really would."

"Then that's what we'll do," said Delilah. "I'll get started right away."

Smiling, Edie took Delilah's arm and placed it under hers, patting it gently, and they walked on. Delilah smiled too—Edie may not quite know why, but she was clearly excited about her idea for the garden. It made Delilah feel excited too, and like they were getting somewhere. Like the seed of some kind of relationship had been planted between them. And she felt that it might grow into something very rare, and special, and somehow magical.

* * *

Later that afternoon, Delilah was high up on the parapet of the manor house. She'd found a little door at the end of the upstairs hall which gave on to a rickety flight of stairs, and then another door out to the roof. She'd hoped that the outline of the old herb beds would be visible from there, and she'd been right.

The idea of restoring the herb garden had had such a positive effect on Edie that Delilah wanted to get started as soon as possible. She also liked the idea of using her father's credit card to fund something he'd be utterly furious about. She could almost hear him in her head, yelling down the phone, outraged.

A garden? For that batty old crone? When we're going to concrete over it anyway?

Imagining his reaction did scare her a little—well, okay, a *lot*—but it thrilled her too. She was still horrified by the way he'd talked about Edie—as if she were just an inconvenience to be dealt with. Not even a person at all, let alone his own late wife's aunt.

His daughter's *family*.

But Delilah knew that pointing out to him how awful he'd sounded wouldn't get her anywhere. He always met confrontation head on with blazing anger. If she roared, he'd roar louder.

No, she'd box clever and hit him where it hurt—his wallet.

She glanced over at the unstable gable end of the building and smiled to herself. Maybe she'd get a surveyor to come out and look at that too. Get it repaired. That would probably run into thousands. Thank you, *Daddy*.

On the subject of *scared and thrilled*, that was kind of how being on the roof felt, too. She stood a safe distance back from the edge—the parapet was crumbling in places and there was no barrier at all in one area, where a couple of the little turrets had completely fallen down.

She leaned forward and peered over—it was a sheer drop onto the craggy paving slabs that formed the path round the manor. You might hit the lawn if you were lucky. Not that *that* would make much difference.

From up here, you'd die instantly, surely?

Delilah stepped back again and carried on with her sketch, pausing only to watch a bird of prey soaring above, circling and gliding over her head as the sun began to break through the grey skies. At first, she flinched away from it, her body reacting reflexively after the strange owl attack. But she told herself firmly that whatever had happened in the Dark Woods wasn't a normal thing. It hadn't made sense at all.

Nature just didn't act that way for no reason.

She had no doubt that she'd been in the Dark Woods of local legend, whatever Cal said. The atmosphere had been sickening and strange, and she'd felt the earth dragging her down, and heard the trees whispering. Maybe the owl had been affected by the place too. By the—what would Milly call it?—*negative energy*.

But anyway—it was over now, and she'd got away, thanks

to that force of rushing power, whatever it had been. And she never had to go back there, ever. Her heartbeat began to settle and pretty soon her anxiety ebbed away and she started to actually enjoy watching the bird soar and circle. She promised herself she'd look up what it was. And she'd have to learn about herbs too, to get the garden right for Edie. Her first thought was to check online on her phone, and then she remembered about the lack of Wi-Fi. Maybe she'd find some nature books in the house.

Smiling into the emerging blue sky, she watched the bird's path as it circled in a wide arc above her. She'd already spoken to a gardener Jane had recommended, Bob. He'd sounded really nice on the phone, and he and James, his apprentice, could start in a few days. Then, even standing up on the parapet, her stomach lurching a little from the height, she felt for the first time since it had all unfolded that she'd finally landed on solid ground. A moment later, though, she was consumed by the question of how she'd ever sleep again. The dream, and then Tol in her room… Even if he couldn't physically hurt her, it had all been so terrifying. It was okay in the daytime, but once night fell would she be too scared to even close her eyes?

This is normal, after what you've been through, she told herself firmly, imagining what Milly would say to her if she were there. *You'll get over this.*

Thoughts of Milly brought her mind back to the conversation they'd had when they'd hung back from Mae and Cal. Tol himself was wired up to machines, unconscious and under twenty-four-hour supervision, so there was no way he could get to her. And even if his spirit, soul, whatever, was walking out of his comatose body, and appeared to her again, it couldn't harm her. She felt better, thinking that, and began to relax a little. She'd be okay. Everything would be okay.

Delilah managed to hold onto those thoughts and feelings all evening and, being so exhausted from the night before, actually fell asleep fairly quickly. Soon she was dreaming again. She found herself walking through the woods again, in her night dress. At first it was quite a pleasant, dreamy feeling, almost as if she were floating. Birds called across the canopy, and dappled light moved over her body as the branches above her swayed in the light breeze.

But then, a gathering realisation, a dawning, a quickening of her heart... She felt a thick rope of tension in her stomach as she recognised where she was.

It was the place where she and Tol had made out, and then fought. Her arm dropped down to her side and she began to back away, her trance-like state fading.

It wasn't *safe* here.

She had to get...

Suddenly he was right behind her.

His face was still battered and bruised, one eye swollen shut, as it had been in the hospital. He grabbed her round the waist, and she bent double sharply, hoping to free herself, but he held her tight, squeezing the air out of her. "You know nothing about me," he breathed, into her ear. Panicking, she threw herself upright, hitting his chin with her head, sending him staggering backwards.

Choking back sobs, she ran, feeling him close behind her, willing her stone-heavy legs to work. There, on the path ahead, was a door in a frame. She threw herself at it, scrabbling at the handle with fear-deadened fingers. Just as Tol lunged for her, she got through, slammed the door, and fumbled with the huge key in the lock on the other side. It was just like the one for the front door of the manor. Somehow, she got it to turn. There was a roar of rage from the other side and an animal cry as Tol slammed his shoulder into the door. Delilah held her breath, but the door stood firm.

She finally breathed out, her heart pounding right through her.

Glancing around, still dazed, she realised that she was now in the upstairs hallway of the manor house. She knew just where to go—the pull of it was so strong. Soundless on her bare feet, she tiptoed past Edie's room and her own, right to the end of the hallway. Then she slipped through the little door and up the rickety staircase, through the second door and out, onto the parapet.

She registered the cool, rough stone beneath her bare feet and the night breeze on her skin, ruffling her hair. A white owl, maybe even the same one she'd seen from her bedroom window, swooped low overhead, owning the night sky.

That inky blue. All those stars.

The beauty of it caught in her throat.

"Imagine. Being that free."

She turned towards the voice. She saw Tol, inexplicably next to her, watching the owl too. Strangely, she didn't feel scared of him, perhaps because it felt like nothing up here on the roof could be frightening. Not here in this place of beauty and freedom and perspective.

She stepped over to the parapet, to the part where the turrets had crumbled away. Though it was dizzyingly high, she felt completely safe. She extended one bare foot, feeling for the edge, then bending her toes round it. A little of the stonework fell away under her skin.

Her foot settled there, half over the edge. She shifted her weight onto it. Would the eroded stone hold her? Did it matter? Tol's words echoed deep inside her.

Imagine. Being that free.

Smiling serenely, she lifted her arms out wide.

The white owl flew low again, hooting wildly, and she felt the ruffle and rush of its wings brush her skin, startling her. She registered the cool, crumbling stone beneath her feet. The breeze on her face. The sound of the owl, hooting insistently.

It was all very, very real.

She looked down. Her stomach flipped at the sheer drop beneath her, at her foot on that edge, her body weight at its balance point, holding her, poised, between life and death.

I'm awake, she thought. *Oh my God, I'm awake.*

She shifted her weight carefully onto her back foot. As she stepped backwards, Tol was suddenly right in front of her. His face was only a breath away from hers, his arms outstretched. "Come with me," he whispered.

Delilah screamed as he fell backwards, smiling at her.

In a split second, he was gone.

"No! No!" she gasped. She willed her legs to move and stumbled back towards the roof door.

She almost ran straight into Edie, crying out in shock to find her there. Her great aunt's hair hung loose, and her long night gown billowed in the wind. She stood strong and steady, her eyes bright. And when she spoke, her voice was full and assured. "Find the Green Witch, she will guide you."

Delilah barely registered the words. "Edie!" she shrieked. "Oh my God, what are you doing up here? You have to get back inside!"

Edie looked suddenly confused again. In a wavering, little-girl voice she asked, "Do I? Why, are we going to have cocoa?"

Shakily, her heart hammering wildly, Delilah bundled Edie through the doorway. "Yes, sure—we'll have cocoa," she stuttered.

As she closed the door behind them, she stole a tentative glance back at the parapet. It was still and silent. Tol was gone.

* * *

"'Find the Green Witch. She will guide you,'" Delilah said to Milly again, after she'd been through the whole story. "That's what she said." As soon as she could get away, once Ewelina had arrived and Edie was settled in the garden, she'd shakily called a cab and gone straight to the library, knowing that Milly was working that day.

"The Green Witch?" Milly repeated. She looked so astonished that Delilah began to feel a bit silly. Maybe her great aunt had just been confused after all. But she'd sounded different than usual—so aware and certain. "I tried to ask," she said, "but she was back to her usual self right afterwards, telling me she had a tin of peaches she'd won at the school fair last week that we could have with our cocoa."

Milly smiled sadly. "Oh, the poor woman," she said, with feeling. "Dementia really is such a distressing syndrome. But look, don't worry that you can't get anything more out of Edie. If she really does know something—if there is a Green Witch— I'm sure I can help."

"I hope so," said Delilah with feeling. "I have to make sense of all this... somehow. Right now I feel like I'll never sleep again."

"Oh, you will, because if you don't you'll become psychotic," said Milly matter-of-factly. "Well, actually, the effects of sleep deprivation mimic those of psychosis – so, hallucinations, delusions, paranoia, disturbing thoughts... "

She looked up and was clearly horrified at the panic on Delilah's face. "Oh my goodness, sorry," she gabbled. "Why on earth did I say that? I was just rambling on. Me and my bloody fascinating facts. That won't happen. Actually, it's almost *impossible* to not sleep at all. You have micro-sleeps without even knowing it. Anyway, we're going to work this all out."

"I hope so," said Delilah shakily.

Milly stopped suddenly and took her hands, looking intensely at her. "We will," she said firmly, squeezing them tight. "Okay?"

Delilah nodded, blinking fast as she felt tears surging up from deep within her. "Okay," she said, choking them back. Why ever Edie said it, I can't get it out of my head now. Not after what happened in the woods, that force—"

"You think that force could have been this Green Witch Edie talked about?"

Delilah shrugged. "I don't know. But if it was, maybe *she* can help me stop Tol appearing again. Edie obviously thinks she will help me, well, 'guide' me, she said, so... If she's even real."

"Well, let's see what we can find out," said Milly. She ushered Delilah into a private area, with a table in the centre. Old books lined the walls, some tattered, many leather-bound. "This is the perfect place to start."

"Wow, it's like the restricted section in Harry Potter," Delilah joked.

"They were all donated by a parapsychology professor, in his will," Milly told her. "No one's ever read them... Well, apart from me. Aneela wants to get rid of them and have a Starbucks in this bit, but luckily Mark the manager isn't keen."

There was a small pile of books on the table and Delilah picked them up one by one and looked them over. "Ghost sightings? The occult?" She put on a spooky voice. "Beyond the veil? Mwah-ha-ha!" She glanced up at Milly. "And you believe in all this stuff?"

Milly shrugged. "Well, yeah, in just... general weirdness, I guess."

Delilah opened one of the books and read at random. "...my husband reincarnated as a dolphin..."

Milly laughed. "Well, okay, I'm not saying I believe all of it." Her eyes scanned the shelves to the left of them, and her fingers flickered over the books' spines. "Wicca. Witchcraft. Hmm."

She took down a book called *Witchcraft Through the Ages* and flicked through the chapters. "Nothing about a Green Witch. Let's try this one..."

As Milly pulled down another book, Delilah surreptitiously drew her phone from her bag and started tapping.

"Not here, either..." said Milly after a couple of minutes.

"A Green Witch works in harmony with nature and the Green Magic of the natural world," said Delilah, reading from her phone screen. "Green Magic is very powerful, and has great healing properties..." She looked up, smiling apologetically. "I put my phone on the Wi-Fi."

"Are you *trying* to kill the library?" Milly said, but her eyes were wide and her face was flushed with excitement. "So, if that's what your great aunt was talking about, are we looking for an *actual* Green Witch?" she asked. "Like, a *woman*?"

Delilah shrugged. "I guess so." She thought for a moment. "And if we are then... What if... It says Green Magic has great power. The power I felt—it pushed that owl... *thing*... away, so I had a chance to escape. Maybe the Green Witch was there and she sent this Green Magic to save me. I know I didn't imagine seeing Tol by my bed. I was awake, and he was there. I know it was all real, whatever Cal says—that, and the Dark Woods dragging me down, the owl being, you know, possessed or something. The force that saved me... Well, it could have been the Green Witch Edie's talking about, couldn't it?"

Milly frowned. "But you didn't see anyone at the time, did you? I mean, if this Green Witch was there, wouldn't she have stayed to see if you were okay? And I'm not saying it isn't true, but Edie gets confused, doesn't she?" She frowned, apologetic. "I hate to say this, but now we know that Green Witches are a thing, well, maybe there was one in something she saw on TV."

Delilah thought about this. "I don't think so. I really think it was to do with the stuff that happened to me. Maybe the Green Witch lives there in the woods, and doesn't want to be seen, or known about—like, a wild woman." She looked up and held her friend's gaze. "What if Edie knows about her from living in the manor all these years? The woods are right next to it, after all. Maybe that's why she told me to find her. Maybe the Green Witch can give me some charms or protections or something..."

She stopped talking abruptly as another librarian stepped into their section.

The woman gave Delilah a tight smile, then said to Milly, "This gentleman can't get his card to activate. Could you..."

"Coming," Milly said. When the woman had gone, she turned to Delilah and mouthed, "Starbucks lady."

Delilah grimaced and Milly smiled. Delilah thought how lovely it was that, although they'd only known each other such a short time, they really seemed to be on the same wavelength. They really *got* each other. She wished there had been someone like Milly at school. Things would have been so different then.

They headed out of the section and as they made their way back across the library Delilah said quietly, "Thanks for this. I appreciate your help. And your *support*. You know, the *not* thinking I've lost the plot."

Milly waved this away. "Course I don't. And what about tonight?" she asked.

"I'll be okay," said Delilah.

Milly smiled wryly. "*So* unconvincing. Look, call me any time. I'll turn my ringer up loud so it wakes me. Sure you're okay?"

"I'm okay," said Delilah. "Well, I will be. When I find the Green Witch."

The girls hugged goodbye. It seemed to Delilah that Milly instinctively understood how much she really *needed* that hug, because it was a long time before she let her go.

* * *

By seven, Delilah was all cleared up from dinner with Edie, and waiting for Paulina, another of the lovely carers, to arrive for the night. The one good thing to come out of the terrifying roof episode was that she'd rung Jane, told her about Edie getting up there, and straight out insisted on a carer being there every night and as much as possible in the daytime. Of course, Jane had been horrified that Edie could have been hurt and agreed to Delilah's arrangement immediately, in case this was the start of Edie wandering at night time, which was common in those with dementia apparently. And, of course, Delilah had locked the door to the roof, and hidden the key.

She'd found something that intrigued her when she went up to lock the roof door. She'd smoothed down the peeling blue cornflower-patterned wallpaper that covered it, matching the surrounding walls, and noticed that something was written on it. Smoothing it out she'd seen that it was "One", the same poem she'd seen before.

Now, she found some paper in the bureau and copied the poem out of the puzzle box lid, carefully and with attention, as Edie had clearly done, reading it as she went. Obviously it had been important to her aunt, as she had written it in two random places in the house, and so she wanted to make a nice copy. She also wanted to take her mind off the thing she'd decided to do—the place she'd decided to go—as soon as Paulina arrived.

As she wrote, she wondered whether Edie had actually composed it herself, or just written it down. She'd never known of Edie writing poetry, but then, why *would* she know? The poem was cryptic and confusing, but had a kind of quiet beauty about it, and a feeling of sense beyond the words, which in themselves didn't make sense at all.

One
What is here is there
And both are nowhere and everywhere.
Nothing is without
And all is here now.

You are that which you seek
But seeking never finds

As fighting never wins
Only giving up the fight.

You are not that which you see
In being, it cannot be.
Sound carries it, but ears can't hear it
If you can speak it, that is not it.

You are the air you breathe
And you are that which is breathed.
In the knowing that ends all knowledge
You and I cease to be.

Breathe, know, breathe, know
The silent sound is love
You are—I am
We are—One.

When she was finished, she folded the paper carefully in half and tucked it into her book, which was *Wuthering Heights*, borrowed from Edie's shelves. It could replace the scrap of cornflakes packet she'd been using as a bookmark. She heard Paulina's car in the drive—it was time. Time to return to the place she'd sworn she'd never go back to. Time to face the Dark Woods.

And so, after a quick chat with Paulina—during which she pretended to be relaxed and cheerful—she was on her way up the path that led into the woods. It seemed like the best way to start searching for the Green Witch, if she existed, as that was where she'd felt the force. She walked fast, looking determinedly ahead of herself. She was afraid that if she paused to think about where she was going, she'd turn around and run straight back to the manor.

Once under the cover of the trees, she trudged on, feeling her exhausted legs dragging and her unslept mind buzzing with scratchy exhaustion. Defiantly, she was singing a favourite song loudly to herself in her head, keeping all thoughts at bay. A few minutes later she came to the clearing where the party had been. It was strewn with crushed cans and empty bottles, some smashed and glinting in the sunlight. The earth was scorched where the fire had been. She looked again at the graffiti on some of the trees. It made her really sad to see it.

A tree was a living thing, after all.

Then she told herself firmly that the trees didn't care whether they had blue spray paint on them or not, and set off at a brisk pace again, taking the same narrow path away from the clearing that she and Tol had gone down.

She reached the tree where they'd made out and sang louder, trying to block herself from remembering their conflict, and her fear that he would hit her. It worked—at least the years of training her mind to keep thoughts of her mother's accident locked out had some benefits. *It's so lucky I'm already an expert at repressing my emotions,* she thought wryly. She looked around her and tried to feel out which way she'd gone before. She set off down a path but was soon back at the party clearing again—*if only I'd taken that one on the night it all happened.*

She had to try two other paths, both of which circled back to Tol's tree. She felt like crying with frustration and was about to give up when she noticed another path, overgrown and barely visible. It was the only option left. She stared at it. What the hell had made her take that little track when there were far better marked out paths? *Well, I was drunk, it was dark...*

She set off down the twisty little trail and soon she was there—scratched by brambles she'd kicked her way through and knee throbbing from a fall over a tree root—but there. The Twisted Tree stood in the middle of a clearing. It didn't look so scary with the dappled sunlight shining through the canopy above, and she couldn't hear any of that weird whispering. Still, the whole area was kind of sinister, and she didn't plan on being there any longer than necessary.

"Hello?" she called out hesitantly.

There was no reply.

Obviously, she told herself. *What was I expecting? A woman with a green face and a black pointy hat to pop out from behind a tree?*

No, she hadn't been expecting that, of course. But she'd hoped for something. She still *hoped* for something. "Okay, well, if you're real and if you sent that light power...force, I want to say thank you, for saving me the other night," she went on, projecting her voice as strongly as she could. "So, thank you. And... I need your help. My Great Aunt Edie said I should find you, and so here I am. Trying to. I need your protection. From Tol. Milly and I think he's spirit-walking while he's in the coma. He appeared by my bed. He was *so* angry... And then on the roof... I nearly stepped off. I could have died."

She suddenly had a vision of a family sitting just round the corner having a picnic and hearing all of this.

She fell silent, waiting, listening.

Nothing.

"Please, come to me," she called. "Or if you can't show yourself, give me a sign. Something to let me know you're real. Please. If you can hear me, use your power, and stop him appearing to me."

She held her breath, watching, waiting.

Still nothing.

Disappointment engulfed her. Even a change in the stillness of the place, a gathering atmosphere, would have been something. The force that had belted through the wood that night had been so strong, so powerful. As absolutely, definitely *real* as a hurricane. So now, back in the same place, she'd expected to feel *something*.

But there was no change at all. The breeze blew gently through the branches above her, throwing a kaleidoscope of dappled light on the mulchy, leaf-covered ground. Birds still sang, and somewhere nearby a woodpecker knocked at a tree trunk.

"Looks like you're not here..." she said, half to herself now. "Maybe you *are* just something Edie saw on TV. So I guess I'll go for a walk, then... like a normal person."

One of the paths looked especially enticing, and Delilah made her way down it, feeling tension she hadn't known she was carrying flood out of her as she left the place where the owl attack had happened.

As she walked, she kept listening and looking carefully around her, and sort of *feeling out* for anything that felt like that force, or even a whisper or echo of it. But there was nothing. It was beautiful in the woods, though, and she was proud of herself for facing her fears and getting out there. Just when she was about to double back, not wanting to get lost, she saw the party clearing up ahead and realised that the path had led round in a big loop.

A few minutes later, as she made her way down the track across the field, towards the lane, her phone rang in her jeans pocket. She glanced at the screen (she was ignoring any calls from her father for the moment) then held it to her ear. "Milly?"

"Can you come over?" said her friend, sounding breathless, excited. "I've got something to show you."

Chapter 6

Milly sent her address and Delilah called one of the local cab firms to take her there. Now, Milly was welcoming her into her studio flat. She had to quickly rearrange her face into an expression that said *charmed* and not *horrified* when she first walked in. *Run down* barely covered it. There was a smell of damp, horrible fuzzy carpet tiles and yellowing wallpaper with a wide pastel-coloured border at the top.

"Come on through," said Milly. "Herbal tea? I've got loads of different ones."

"Thanks," said Delilah. She crossed the room in four steps and peered into the ancient kitchen cupboard Milly was holding open. She chose something involving cranberry and rose, which sounded interesting, and leaned (not too hard) against the rickety worktop. She noticed that everything was spotlessly clean, and very, very tidy.

Milly lit the gas with a match and put some water in a pan on to boil to make the tea. "My kettle blew up," she told Delilah, grimacing. "I think it's something to do with the electrics in this place. It probably needs rewiring."

"You should get someone in to look at that," said Delilah, concerned.

"I know," said Milly. "I've told the landlord, but he takes ages to organise anything, and I can't afford it myself. Just the call out fee for an electrician is, like, seventy quid, before they've even done any work."

"Ouch," said Delilah. Then, tentatively, hoping Milly wouldn't be offended, or embarrassed, or anything else awful, she said, "I could put it on my credit card…"

She cringed inside. It sounded even worse out loud than in her head.

But fortunately Milly didn't say, *Oh, the lady of the manor swoops in and patronisingly throws her cash around* or anything like that. Instead, she just smiled and waved the suggestion away. "Thanks, that's really kind of you, but he will do it. He *has* to, like, legally. It should be in the next couple of weeks."

"Okay, great," said Delilah, feeling her cheeks colouring.

Milly looked intently at her. "Honestly, though, thanks for the offer. I do appreciate the support. Mae and Cal are great, of course, but, as you've probably noticed, they're pretty wrapped up in each other." She wrinkled her nose up. "Often *literally*. And I don't really know anyone else here, apart from the people I work with, and they're all so much older than me. I feel a bit out on my own sometimes. Well, a *lot* out on my own. A *lot* of the time." Then she stopped herself suddenly. "Wow, sorry, TMI. Enough with the therapy session."

Delilah smiled. "No problem. I get it," she said. When Milly gave her a questioning look, she explained about Hardcastle, the Least Emotionally Equipped Parent In The World ™, and the long holidays at school with only the housemistress and a few of the international students for company.

Milly seemed to understand that she didn't want to talk about her mum, and Delilah was grateful for that. She did step forward, though, looking very empathetic. *Please don't hug me,* Delilah silently begged her. *I couldn't stand it.*

Fortunately, Milly seemed to read this from her expression and leaned back against the counter. The water in the pan came to the boil and she turned the gas off before sloshing it into their cups. "This oven has to be replaced too," she told Delilah. "The gas hobs aren't up to safety standards. Since 2010, all gas appliances have to have a Flame Safety Device which stops the gas supply if the flame goes out, so you can't blow yourself up by accident. This one doesn't, what with it being from, like, the actual fifties."

"Wow, do you actually know everything about everything?"

said Delilah.

Milly smiled. "I just read a lot. It's a compulsion."

Delilah giggled. "What was that in, The Big Book of Gas Safety Legislation?"

Milly grinned. "I told you. It's a compulsion. Here you go." She handed Delilah a steaming mug.

"Thanks." Swishing her tea bag about by the string, and inhaling the delicately scented steam, Delilah followed Milly across to the sofa. She sat down, and Milly sat opposite her on the rug, cross-legged.

Now that her initial reaction had worn off, Delilah could see that the place was actually quite cosy, with Milly's posters of the Buddha, dolphins, dancing goddesses and the chakra system on the walls, burning incense and fairy lights giving the whole place a cosy glow. She was starting to think that it *was* probably just about big enough for one person, in legal terms anyway.

"I love your... stuff," she said, making a sweeping gesture with her arm which took in all of Milly's spiritual paraphernalia.

Milly smiled. "Thanks. It's not much, but its home. For now, anyway. So, like I said, I've got something amazing to show you." She put her mug on the coffee table (well, the *everything* table, as it was the only table in the room) then reached for a cloth bag. She emptied the library books it held onto the floor. "We were looking in the wrong section," she said, her eyes gleaming with excitement in the gentle light. "I got these from *local history*."

She'd marked the pages with post it notes.

"So, what are they?" Delilah asked.

"Look for yourself," said Milly, pushing the books towards her eagerly, like a birthday present she couldn't wait to see her open.

Curious, Delilah pulled the nearest book, called *A History of Bernhurst*, into her lap and flicked the pages until she came to the first marker. There was a black-and-white picture of a group of hippy-looking teens, dressed in sixties clothes. Milly leaned over and pointed at a paragraph halfway down the opposite page. "Read this, here," she said, her voice brimming with anticipation.

Delilah squinted at the page in the dim light. "'The teens claim to have felt a powerful force, which one described as "the spirit of nature", being sent to them by a Green Witch. They spent the whole night chanting and dancing in a woodland clearing and claim that they were joined by the Green Witch herself for several minutes, before she slipped away into the trees again.'" She glanced ahead in the text and put on a stern tone. "'The editor wishes to note that the girls' account may be unreliable due to the large volume of LSD and marijuana they had ingested.' Ooooh, naughty, naughty."

Milly smiled and opened another book. "And there's this," she told her. "From the... Well, I'm not sure when it was written, but it looks really old." She peered at the text, deciphering. "'And when they did enter unto that place called Truegreene Wood —"

"Oh my God, that's my wood!" Delilah cried.

Nodding, Milly read on. "'...the wilde woman did appear and she did make the woodland glowe with a thousand dancing lights.'"

"Amazing!" gasped Delilah. "And are there any that say, 'And she did kicketh the butt of the murderous local wildlife?' or 'And she did stoppeth some angry spirit-walking maniac from trying to make girls walk off roofs?'"

Milly looked unsure about whether to smile at this or not. Delilah had meant it to be funny but hearing the words out loud made her guts twist, and she wished she hadn't said them.

Milly saw her face and let the "joke" slide by without comment, and once again Delilah was grateful that she could read her so well. "No, it does not say that..." Milly continued, "but that doesn't mean she can't help. There are plenty of accounts of people feeling a powerful, magical force, and even reporting sightings of the Green Witch herself, stretching back over four hundred and fifty years."

"So she can't be a real woman, then. More like a spirit or a force."

"Or an immortal," said Milly.

"Is that even a *thing*?" asked Delilah. She shook her head. "Ha! Listen to me! Discussing whether the supernatural entity I'm hoping will save me from an angry spirit is herself in spirit form or physical-but-immortal. If I hadn't just been put off alcohol forever I'd want something a lot stronger than herbal tea right now."

"I know," Milly agreed. "Yes, I read a lot about this kind of stuff, but it's a whole different thing when it actually starts happening around you."

"What I don't understand is, according to your books, it seems like plenty of people have seen the Green Witch in the woods. So why did nothing happen when I specifically went there looking for her?"

Milly stared at her. "You went back to the Dark Woods? Wow, you have got some bollocks, after what happened."

Delilah shrugged. "I didn't want to, believe me, but I thought... that's where it all happened, and where I felt that force, which could have been the Green Witch. Now we've found these accounts, it seems likely that it was. I even called out to her..." She flushed with embarrassment, thinking back to standing among the trees, shouting into thin air. "But... nothing."

"It was only your first try," said Milly gently.

Delilah smiled wryly. "True. Maybe she'd just popped out to Waitrose," she said.

Milly grinned. "Oh, no, I bet she goes to the farmer's market, where it's all organic."

"Ha! Yeah. Imagine telling Cal what we've found out," she said. "I can see how it sounds—like some crazy fantasy, just some old story told around fires and in pubs until it took on a life of its own and got into people's imaginations." She tapped the cover of the nearest book. "And then into these. That first account said those girls were off their heads on drugs, after all. And the other one was so old—they thought any lone woman was a witch in those days, pretty much, didn't they? The Green Witch was probably just some local wise woman or herbalist who foraged in the woods—someone who lived, yes… if she was lucky…" Delilah paused, thinking of all the witch burnings that had no doubt gone on here as much as anywhere in England, and witch *hangings*, like in the Dark Woods story. A glance at Milly's face told her that she was thinking the same. "But someone who then died," she continued, "leaving the legend behind her. No immortal. No eternal spirit."

"But you *felt* the force," said Milly, looking crestfallen, all the wind knocked out of her sails. "You *felt* it. And you felt all the negative energy in the Dark Woods too."

Delilah sighed. "I know, and I want it to be true that the Green Witch can be contacted somehow, and can help me, but it feels like a long shot," she admitted. "And I don't know where we go from here. Like I said, I tried calling out for her in the woods, but—nothing. I'm not going to fall asleep tonight, no way, but I'll have to sometime, and what then? I suppose I can keep trying, going to the woods, but what if she never comes?"

"It's just a thought, but maybe you need to change tack," Milly suggested, hesitation in her voice. "If this Green Witch is a real practitioner of magic, you ought to be able to summon her on a non-physical level, not just by standing in the woods calling out for her. But you'd need to start with the basics first. Have you ever tried journeying?"

"I got the train down here," said Delilah, her face deadpan.

"Ha ha," said Milly, smiling despite herself. "Shamanic journeying. I did a workshop."

Delilah felt sudden frustration at this. When Milly had said *change tack*, she'd thought she was going to say something useful, like the name and phone number of an exorcist to get rid of Tol, for example.

But he's not actually dead.

"It's like meditation," Milly was saying.

"How is sitting around chanting 'om' going to help?" Delilah asked, a little sharply.

"I know, it doesn't sound that useful," said Milly, catching her tone. "But it's not all about 'om', it's about energy. If the Green Witch is really out there, in whatever form, she'll be able to operate in the non-physical realms."

"Hang on, rewind," said Delilah. "Non-physical realms? Remember, I'm new to this stuff."

"What I mean is, you should be able to connect with her energy and summon her to you."

Delilah had to admit that it made sense, as much as any of this crazy new world she found herself in made sense, anyway. "Fine," she said. "I'll give it a try. After all, there's no way I'm going back to the woods right now to try calling her again. It's dark and that bloody owl will be out, and probably have another go at severing my femoral artery—"

"Your carotid artery," Milly corrected, casually. "Your femoral is in your thigh. Femur – femoral, see?"

Delilah blinked at her.

"Sorry," said Milly, blushing. "It's all the reading. Anyway, you were saying..."

"I was saying, fine, let's go for the meditation thing. Seeing as we don't have any other ideas. But I'm warning you—I have the attention span of a gnat, and also I will probably need to pee in about seven minutes."

Milly smiled. "No pressure. Let's just see what happens."

"Oh, although...getting all mystical reminded me. I found something really fascinating at Edie's, and in the oddest place." She reached for her overnight bag and pulled out her book. Silently apologising to Emily Bronte, she folded over the top of the page she was on, slipped the transcribed poem out and passed it to Milly.

Milly took it, arching her eyebrow again. Delilah really wished she could do that. "Are you by any chance trying to distract me from helping you meditate?" she said.

Delilah smiled. "Maybe. But I thought it was intriguing." She waited silently while Milly read the poem aloud. "Wow," she said, finally looking up. "This is like a kind of Zen Koan."

"As in, it seems all contradictory, but it reveals some deep truth?" Delilah asked. "Yes, I thought that too."

"It's more that they allow you to understand the truth of yourself," said Milly. "The Koan is truth—*you're* the contradiction."

She kind of understood what Milly meant—she'd also felt that the poem contained some empirical, unassailable truth, and that if she didn't understand it, that was because of the way she was looking at it.

"Do you think Edie wrote this?" Milly asked.

"I don't know. It was certainly in her writing and it obviously meant a lot to her." She explained about finding the words scribed carefully in both the puzzle box lid and on the roof door wallpaper.

"Well, whatever it is, and whoever wrote it, I love it," Milly pronounced. "Do you mind if I copy it down for myself?"

"Not at all." She raised her eyebrows. "Maybe we could do that right now..."

"Oh no, you're not getting out of this," said Milly. "The poem talks about breathing. In fact, it talks about breathing and knowing in the same breath, so let's breathe and see if it leads us to any knowing."

"But it also says, 'If you can speak it, that is not it'," Delilah countered, "so even if it somehow makes us know something, we won't be able to actually communicate that in words."

Milly smiled. "You could do an expressive dance about it," she suggested.

Delilah giggled. "You really do not want to see that. I never fully grew into my legs and I'm the clumsiest person in the world."

"I wouldn't mind," said Milly, and something in her tone caught at Delilah, and made her wonder whether her friend was flirting with her. She didn't want to flirt back, and give her the wrong idea, but there probably *was* no wrong idea. She was probably just being playful and friendly. Delilah didn't want her mind to go off on a whole long tangent, so she returned to the subject of One. "It's so weird that I don't understand at all and yet I kind of do."

"I can see it's got under your skin," said Milly. "You already know parts without looking at the paper."

Delilah decided then and there to learn it by heart. She loved doing that with poetry—the steam train chug of John Betjeman or the sharp slap of Sylvia Plath. And with song lyrics. It gave her mind something to do instead of churning anxiously over and over, and it left her with a treasure house of apt words which popped into her head unexpectedly.

"Earth to Delilah!" called Milly, and Delilah let the room come back into focus. "Yep, time for some meditation," she added. "You could definitely brush up on being more present in the here and now."

"The cheek!" Delilah exclaimed. She got to her feet. "I assume the loo is in there?"

* * *

Soon she was sitting cross-legged on a cushion while Milly

wafted incense around her. Some kind of plinky-plunky music with no discernible tune was playing in the background. "This meditation will help you align with source energy and connect with your inner power," Milly intoned, in a hushed voice. "Breathe in... Breathe out..."

Delilah kept breathing in and out as instructed (she could manage *that*, at least), waiting for Milly to say something else. After a while, she drifted off into her thoughts, which were about Meg, one of the nice hockey girls from school. Maybe she could just go and stay with her and all of this would stop— but she doubted that furious wandering spirits were put off by distance, or fancy security systems like the one Meg's family had at their Chelsea townhouse.

She was so immersed in this that when Milly did speak again it startled her a little. "As you open yourself up to the subtle energies, you find the boundless, timeless state of *One*."

Delilah's eyes shot open. "You mean *One*, like in the poem?"

Milly thought for a moment. "Yes, it probably does refer to the same concept," she said. "I'm just repeating what I learned from my meditation teacher back in Totnes, and some videos online, by the way. Just because I know the language, doesn't mean I understand it from the inside or anything, though."

"It's like the poem is a secret code to something," Delilah mused. "Like it has something locked inside it."

"I know what you mean," agreed Milly. "But then, this kind of thing is all in The Power of Now, which by the way sold several million copies, so it's hardly secret. Then there's The O Manuscript, another bestseller. That one's massive—think how much wisdom is in there."

"Well, 'One' is enough for me to try to unpick at the moment," said Delilah. "One poem. One page long."

Milly suddenly gasped in mock horror. "Look what you've made me do! You're so good at stalling and diverting attention!"

"Two highly-honed skills of people who find it impossible

to just ask for what they want and say what they think straight out," said Delilah. Before Milly could reply she shut her eyes again. "Anyway, stop chatting to me. I'm trying really hard to focus on the subtle energies, like you said, and you keep disturbing me."

Now she was the one being playful with Milly, she realised. That was all it had been earlier, from Milly's side—not flirting at all. It was a relief, because she didn't want anything to come between them. Now the vague sense of unease lifted, she realised that, in the back of her mind, she'd been worrying about it. Worrying that, if Milly had feelings for her that she couldn't reciprocate, it could make things awkward for their fledgling friendship. It's not that she'd never thought about being with another girl, although she hadn't been, it's just that she didn't feel that way about Milly. It just wasn't like that.

She did try to think about the subtle energies, then. Even though she wasn't sure quite what that meant. She tried to see her chakras spinning all up her body like a rainbow of radiating jewels, but then lost focus and wondered if they'd make something to eat at Milly's or get a takeaway. Or even go out. Was there anywhere *to* go out in Bernhurst? Not Cal's pub, after the way he'd described it. She caught herself and came back to her breathing. It was astonishing that she could look at general loveliness on Instagram for whole hours but couldn't keep her mind still enough to just focus on her breathing for a few minutes.

"As your crown chakra opens, at the top of your head, so does your doorway to the infinite," Milly intoned, serious again now. "You effortlessly call the Green Witch to you. You breathe deep purple energy into your brow chakra, the seat of intuition, and hear the Green Witch's guidance as your third eye opens fully."

Third eye? What? Delilah stifled a giggle and opened her *two* eyes to find Milly looking hurt. "Sorry," she said, grimacing. "I know this is serious. Believe me, I know. I did try, I promise, but I think my doorway to the infinite is rusted shut." She felt a pang inside her, of not wanting to hurt Milly's feelings, and felt relief as Milly smiled and said, "It's not for everyone. And don't worry, there must be another way. We'll work something out."

Delilah straightened her legs out in front of her and stretched her arms into the air. "I know this might seem frivolous with everything that's going on but is there any chance of ordering pizza?" she asked. "It would be nice to just do something normal. You know, eat a meal, have a sleep. And on the subject of sleep, can I change my mind and stay over? I'll probably still lie awake all night, but I'd feel safer."

"Of course you can," said Milly. She looked really pleased at the prospect and Delilah remembered what she'd told her, about feeling pretty alone in Bernhurst. "And there's a pizza place on the main street that delivers," she added. "It's not actually too disgusting."

"Shall I call Mae?" Delilah asked then. "We could make it a girls' night. Try and lighten the atmosphere a bit."

"Naa, there's no point," said Milly regretfully. "She'd only be upset she couldn't come. Grounded really does mean grounded in her house, well, in her flat above the shop. Her dad's furious that she went to the party. She messaged me to say he walked her to the dance studio and home again today. She's not allowed to go out for anything else."

Hearing this, a vague plan began to come together in Delilah's mind. "I might know a way to get her out," she said, "but it will have to wait until tomorrow, unfortunately."

* * *

It wasn't until after midnight that Delilah began to doze off. The soft glow of the fairy lights, Milly's cosy duvet, and the lingering delicious smells of incense and pizza finally got the better of her and—before she could catch herself—she fell fast asleep. She woke with a start two hours later, heart pounding hard, and staring around her, at once searching for Tol and fearing seeing him, terrified to have drifted off. She registered where she was, lying on the sofa cushions, which were laid out on the rug next to Milly's bed.

She almost leaned over to shake Milly awake, as she'd promised she would do if she needed her, but she stopped herself. Instead, she focussed on her presence close by. She matched her own breathing with Milly's, and with each rhythmic inhale and exhale, she calmed down a little more.

Nothing happened, she told herself, daring to take her focus off her breath for a moment and think of Tol again. *I fell asleep and he didn't come into my dreams, and I woke up and I didn't see him in the room.*

She felt like just thinking of him might call him to her, and she glanced anxiously around, half expecting him to suddenly appear, but nothing happened. Breathing out slowly, she eased herself back down and snuggled under the duvet. She wasn't going to fall asleep again, no way. She couldn't let her guard down. She'd just lie there and listen to music. She put her headphones in and put her favourite Tori Amos album, *Little Earthquakes*, on repeat, but within minutes sleep had stolen over her once again.

And then, somehow, she was in the car. Their old Fiesta. In her child seat in the back. On that windy road. Singing along to the radio with Miranda. She was in her six-year-old's body, Blue Rabbit on her lap.

Reaching that bend.

As she worked out where she was, *when* she was, she fell silent. The vague sense of unease grew into blind panic. Suddenly the red car came round the bend, on the wrong side of the road, right in front of them. Miranda screamed and hit the brakes, throwing Delilah forward against her seat belt. Delilah flinched, waiting for the deafening bang to burst the air. For the ripple of sheer force to tear through her.

But it didn't come.

Somehow, miraculously, the cars had stopped within an inch of each other.

There was a moment of intense silence.

"Mummy?"

Nothing.

Delilah wriggled out of her seat belt and crawled half through the gap between the front seats, terrified of what she would see.

Miranda was staring blankly through the front windscreen, perfectly still. But after a moment Delilah saw the sharp little lifts of her chest as she snatched in air. Then she slowly turned her head and smiled shakily at her daughter, the smile instantly turning to choking sobs. "I'm okay, baby," she breathed. "Are you okay?"

Delilah nodded. She couldn't believe it, but it was somehow true. Miranda was saved. She reached out and touched her, in wonder. Then suddenly they were hugging, both sobbing hard with shock and relief. Delilah allowed herself to feel her mother's presence, to smell her scent, to breathe her in. On and on and on, one breath after another, and Miranda was there — alive.

Delilah pulled back just a little to wipe the matted hair from her face and something caught her eye...

Tol was lolling on the bonnet of the red car, face bruised and right eye swollen shut. He looked back at her with a merciless gaze and clicked his fingers. In a second the cars smashed together with a force that consumed everything, and the piercing scream Delilah heard was her own.

She woke at that moment and shot upright, clawing at her cover. Milly was suddenly awake and there, holding her, and she broke down, sobbing. "He was in my dream. Actually *in* it. And he... He made my mum survive and then..." Seeing that click of his fingers in her mind, she broke down into choking sobs again.

"It's okay, it's okay, it's okay," Milly murmured, as she held her tight.

* * *

Delilah had fallen asleep again about seven o'clock, despite herself, after she and Milly had been up for a couple of hours, and had talked over the dream—how real it had felt, how equally wondrous and appalling, and how Tol had been controlling it. Then they'd drunk more herbal tea, and shared music to try and take Delilah's mind off the whole thing (which didn't work but was sweet of Milly). She'd finally closed her eyes for a moment while Milly went for a shower and fallen asleep on the sofa.

She hadn't come to until late the next morning, startling awake as Milly, who was trying to be super quiet, dropped something in the kitchen area. She looked around her, heart pounding, panic beginning to grip her—until she took in the light coming in through the colourful saris that were acting as curtains and was bathed in relief.

She was awake, and Tol wasn't there.

Over some breakfast a little later, which was some kind of complicated muesli that Milly made herself, Delilah had explained her plan to deal with Mae being grounded. Milly had her doubts, but agreed that it was worth a try.

Half an hour later, the two girls were standing on Mae's doorstep, up a set of stairs at the side of the restaurant, carrying empty rubbish sacks and rubber gloves. Delilah was also holding a clipboard and at Milly's feet was a bucket of cleaning products, scrubbing brushes and scourers. Mr Huang, Mae's dad, had answered the door and was now eyeing them both with undisguised suspicion.

"We're taking part in a community project," Delilah

explained. "We're going to clean up the woodland. Scrub off the graffiti, pick up broken glass. You know, make it safe for children to play there."

Mr Huang did not look convinced. Delilah gave Milly a *help me out here* glance.

"We're putting it on our CVs," Milly said suddenly. "And we thought Mae... We thought it might look good, on her scholarship application for ADI."

"That's the American Dance Insti—" Delilah began.

"I know what it is," Mr Huang cut in. He softened a little. "Her mother and I have heard of nothing else for two years. New York..." He looked off into the sky, as if New York were on another planet, rather than just in another country.

Delilah and Milly looked at him hopefully. "Okay then," he said, refocussing on them. "But, how about getting this task force of yours to do the high street next?"

"I will suggest it to the project leader," Delilah improvised.

Mr Huang nodded slightly then turned to call Mae, but she was already racing up the hall behind him. "Thanks, Dad, I love you," she said, as she slipped past him and out the door.

Mr Huang nodded again, watching them clatter away down the stairs. "Straight back afterwards, Mae!" he called after them.

"Of course, Dad!"

An hour later, the girls (and Cal, who'd met them in the lane) were in the clearing in the woods where the party had been, really getting stuck into the clean-up job.

"There are wild ponies up here too, somewhere," Milly told Delilah, as she scrubbed at a tree. "They live up in the high woods, and on the open land. There's someone from *Wild Britain* who keeps a check on them, but they stay away from people, generally."

Delilah glanced around at the rubbish they still had to collect up, despite having already filled two black bags. "I don't blame them," she said. "'People' have ruined this place. But we're getting there. It's looking better already, isn't it?"

Milly nodded. "Yup." They shared a satisfied glance.

Mae grimaced at some unidentifiable bit of debris she'd just picked up. "This had better not be a condom... Yuck, it is." She pulled a disgusted face as she dropped it into the rubbish bag. "I didn't realise we were actually *doing* this," she grumbled.

Delilah grinned. "Got you out, though, didn't it?"

Mae was now watching Cal's muscles move under his t-shirt as he strained to pull a twisted piece of rusty metal out of the ground. "Yes it did," she said, without taking her eyes off him. "Thank you. Very much."

Amused, Delilah raised her eyebrows at Milly, who rolled her eyes in return. Then they got on with clearing up some more old cans and broken glass, Milly holding the black bag open while Delilah threw them in.

"You know, it did sound familiar, that stuff about the Green Witch," said Mae. Milly had filled her in on what they'd found out, just before they all met up with Cal, but she had clearly wanted to wait until he was out of earshot to talk about it. "I must have heard some of the old people talk about it, when I was a kid, I mean." She glanced up at Delilah. "Do you really believe there is a Green Witch living in this wood?"

Delilah shrugged. "Not like a real person, no, because the accounts of her go back hundreds of years. Milly thinks she might be either—" Delilah hesitated. Now, literally in the light of day, what had seemed to make sense in the candlelight of Milly's flat just sounded silly, but she made herself say it anyway, "that she might be *immortal* or... non-physical—like, from another, erm, plane of reality or something." She blushed furiously, hearing it out loud. She blushed even more when Cal, who obviously *could* hear, grunted in derision at this and muttered "for God's sake", shaking his head, before he recommended battle with the metal. Mae looked deeply uncomfortable at this, but Milly ignored him. "That's why I showed her how to journey," she said. "Well, tried a bit of meditation, anyway, to start with. I thought maybe she could call the Green Witch to herself if she—"

"Oh, so you've been opening your infinite chakra for her, have you?" Mae interrupted playfully, clearly trying to lighten the mood.

As Milly pulled a face at Mae, Delilah registered that, although she was still smiling, she looked suddenly flustered, but she didn't pause to think about it. She was too focussed on the Tol situation. "I couldn't really concentrate," she told Mae. "It's not as easy as you think, *just breathing*. And then last night Tol was in my dream. I was planning to confront him, if it happened again, to ask why he's doing this."

"Good idea," said Mae. "If you can get some control back, maybe all this will work itself out."

"But I couldn't..." Delilah sighed. "It was too awful. He..." She shook her head quickly—she couldn't bear to go into it again. In fact, just thinking about it made her feel like she was drowning... She glanced at Milly for help.

"He made her relive the crash, when her mum died," Milly told her. "Except he changed it and made Miranda survive, I mean, he made the cars stop just in time, before they hit each other. But then he set it in motion again." She winced.

"Oh, God, Delilah. You should have said something earlier!" cried Mae. "You poor thing. It must have been awful."

Delilah tried to hold back her emotions, but the fresh sense of loss was overwhelming and suddenly she found herself crying. Milly and Mae put their arms around her, and Cal strode across to them, concern all over his sweaty face. "Why would he do this?" she sobbed. "I know he was angry with me in the woods but that was sick. Twisted."

"He must have had a lot more problems than we realised," said Milly.

"I'm sure it was bad, but the reason it seems out of character for Tol to do this is because he *didn't* do it," said Cal carefully.

"Dreams are just dreams, and hallucinations are... *treatable.*"

The word hung in the air and Delilah looked up at him sharply.

"No. Enough," he said. "We have a serious situation here. You nearly walked off the roof. You would have *died* if Edie hadn't turned up right at that moment." He met Delilah's tearful gaze, his voice all frustration and concern. "We have to get you some help, and I'm not talking about cleansing your aura or whatever."

"Finding the Green Witch *is* the only way to help," insisted Milly, incensed.

Cal laughed bitterly. "You can't really believe all this stuff," he muttered. Then he looked at Mae. "Can *you?*"

Mae didn't meet his eye but instead flicked her hair and began to wind it around her finger, watching the orange, black and blue twist forming. She stayed silent.

Delilah felt distress clawing at her throat. "You think I imagined it all? That it was all in my head?" she said weakly. It was weird. She *knew* Cal thought that, but somehow she just desperately wanted him to simply say "I believe you" instead.

"Well, what *do* you think?" Cal asked Mae, broodily.

Mae dropped the twist of hair and shook it back over her shoulder. "I don't know, to be honest," she admitted, not meeting Delilah's eye.

"Anyway, let's ease off the man-wisdom for now, shall we?" She threw a scourer at Cal. "And get this crap off this tree."

"Yes, ma'am," said Cal, a little of his usual light-heartedness returning.

"Ignore him," Milly said quietly to Delilah, as he walked away from them. "What does he know?"

"He just cares about you," said Mae.

"Yeah," said Delilah. Hurriedly, she focussed on scrubbing the tree, so that she could turn her back to them and get control of the tears that were threatening to flow again.

* * *

Another two hours later, the friends came back down the path with three full rubbish sacks, various bits of twisted metal and their cleaning equipment. The whole Tol spirit-walking and controlling her dreams topic had been put aside after that initial conversation, much to Delilah's relief. And she was feeling steadier now, no longer on the brink of tears. Just spending time in the woods had made her feel calmer and more grounded, somehow.

As they reached the lane, a dirty white van screeched away, revealing a pile of rubbish, including a battered, ripped old sofa, dumped in the layby. Delilah was overtaken by pure rage. "Hey!" she yelled at the retreating van. "You fucking idiots!"

Milly and Mae were taken aback by her venom. Amused, Cal tried out her accent. "Farking. Faaaarking."

"Well, it's completely out of order!" Delilah fumed. "They can't just treat this place like shit!"

Milly, inspired by this, shouted, "Shitheads!" after the van too, as it bumped away too fast down the lane.

"Well, on the plus side they'll have buggered their suspension," Cal said cheerily, completely back to his usual flippant self now. He flopped down on the dumped sofa, pulled a Coke from his backpack and pressed it open.

The girls all glared at him.

"What?" he asked. He held out the can, puzzled. "Do you want some?"

"No—the—this!" Delilah gaped, waving a hand over his body, which was now lying prone on the dumped sofa. "Don't *use* it!"

Cal swigged his drink and stayed put. "Well, we can't exactly go anywhere else, can we?" He turned to Mae. "I mean, me and you can't be seen together. If it gets back to your dad that I've been within three miles of his lovely daughter, who is obviously way too good for me..." He made a slitting his throat gesture with his free hand.

Mae softened at this, perched on the edge of the sofa and cuddled into him. "You know it's true, I am *way* too good for you," she said. "He's a smart man, my daddy."

Chapter 7

That night, Delilah stayed up as late as possible, wandering around the house, reading and trying to watch TV. When she finally admitted defeat and headed to bed around one o'clock, she opened her window and gazed out, breathing in the still night air, looking at the woods. She wondered, for a moment, if the Green Witch was actually out there in the ether somehow, or if it really was just an old story which had fuelled local people's imaginations for centuries.

And Tol... She knew where his body was, but where was his spirit tonight? Was he planning to appear to her again, or to invade her dreams? What if he did something else awful, like with the car crash? Pushing the unsettling thoughts away, she put her headphones in, turned her music up loud (Fiona Apple this time) and began to pace around the room, trying to put off lying down for just a little longer.

She'd only sat on the edge of the bed for a second. The next moment, she was fast asleep, sprawled out across the covers, her head almost hanging off the far side and her hair spilling down to the floor.

A moment, or perhaps several hours, later, she woke. Horrified that she'd fallen asleep, she reached for her phone, to turn off the album she'd had on repeat. She pulled out her headphones and, for a second, there was silence. Then the sounds rushed in. Branches creaking and swaying in the light breeze, leaves rustling, a hooting owl, night animals foraging...

Her unease grew as she felt for the bed cover below her.

Her hand closed around dried leaves and gritty soil.

A jolt of panic shot through her stomach. She sat up and as her eyes became accustomed to the dark, she could see a gnarled shadow looming over her. It was the Twisted Tree. She was in the Dark Woods.

It felt so real she couldn't be sure she was dreaming. Had she somehow sleepwalked all the way up here? Then the malevolent whispering began. She staggered to her feet, fighting the ground as it began to pull her down. She tried to move but it was like wading through thick mud.

There was a screech in the tree nearby and with horror she realised that the owl was there. Before she could make herself look away, she'd spotted it among the branches. It held her gaze for a moment, and then ruffled its feathers and began preening itself. Trying to control her panic, she kept looking at it but focussed her mind on getting away from the Twisted Tree. She pulled her leaden feet up one at a time and forced herself to take step after step, as her mind writhed away from the haunting whispers, afraid to make sense of the poisonous words.

She stumbled and turned her gaze from the owl for a second, and suddenly it was swooping towards her, flapping its wings hard, flying straight at her. She screamed and tried to shield her face, but it was too late. It was attacking her eyes and she was shrieking and thrashing about, trying to fight it off. Stabbing pains wrenched through her every time its beak connected with her flesh, and blood drowned her vision.

Just as she was blacking out, legs giving way, giving up the fight, there was a low whistle and the owl immediately ceased its attack. She caught her breath and looked up in trepidation, blinking away hot blood. With her damaged vision she could just make out a figure. She knew it was Tol. She couldn't see him properly, but she could feel his presence, dark and menacing and revelling in her distress. The owl was perched on his shoulder. When he spoke, there was amusement in his voice. "You're just not *seeing* it, are you?"

The next moment, she found herself sitting bolt upright on the bed in a cold sweat. A dream, thank God. *Thank God.* She rubbed her hands over her eyes several times until she was truly convinced that they were okay. But just as she was swearing never to close them again, to go down to the kitchen right away for a strong coffee, a tidal wave of exhaustion swept over her. She lay back down and fell into a delirious half-slumber of disturbing images and strange, nonsensical thoughts—thoughts that voiced themselves over and over and would not stop, until she felt like she'd lose herself completely in that limbo between sleeping and waking.

* * *

Delilah had dragged herself down to the kitchen at first light and deliberately turned her mind to something other than Tol, terror and exhaustion. She began looking up herbs and plants for the garden in some of Edie's old books. It helped that many of the pages were marked, and that little notes had been added, like "grows well by the south wall" or "do not overwater".

She was well aware that she was just hiding from herself, her fear and her feelings with all this activity, but it was the only thing she could think to do. Going for a run wouldn't work—before the sweet release of simply running, of becoming a moving, foot-pounding breathing machine, there would be a couple of miles' worth of free-form thinking as her busy mind was let loose, and she couldn't face that. She was too scared of where it might take her.

Was Cal right? Was she going crazy?

No, she couldn't let her mind go *there* either—she got up, put the radio on loud, and started cleaning out the fridge. That's where Jane found her when she arrived for the day, and she threw herself into helping out with Edie and doing jobs around the house, only stopping for lunch because Jane insisted.

Late that afternoon, Mae called. Somehow she'd got her dad to agree to let her out, seeing as they were continuing with the "community project". Now both the girls were heading up the lane to the layby. Mae was carrying a hammer, and Delilah had a large painted sign, which she'd made that morning from bits and pieces in one of the sheds. She'd decided the wildwood needed her help—there was still a ton of metal to wrestle out of the ground, and she planned to find out about stronger cleaners to get the graffiti properly off the trees.

As they walked, Delilah told Mae all about what happened the previous night, in as little detail as possible. *"You're just not seeing it, are you?"* Mae repeated, echoing Tol's words, sending another bolt of cold fear through Delilah. "Seeing what, though? What do you think it means?"

Delilah sighed. "If I knew that... I've been going over and over it in my head all morning. Well, really trying not to. But totally failing. Still, at least the fridge is clean now. And the bathrooms. Vacuuming's done..."

Mae didn't laugh, though. Instead, she looked uncomfortable. "Look, please don't take this the wrong way, but maybe you *should* talk to a doctor about this..."

Delilah was taken aback. *Mae too, then. Doubting me.* She remembered she'd been tactfully non-committal in the woods, when Cal had directly asked her what she thought of the whole thing. Well, she couldn't blame her, she supposed. *If it hadn't happened to me, I wouldn't believe it either*, she reminded herself, in her head. And only this morning, she herself had wondered for a moment whether Cal could be right about her. About all of it. Just for a moment, but still. And she was definitely keeping any doubts to herself.

"I just mean, to get some sleeping tablets or something," Mae went on.

Delilah looked straight ahead, not wanting to meet her gaze, feeling her heart banging in her chest. "A doctor can't help me with this," she said stiffly, after a while. "No one can. No one human, anyway." She could feel Mae's concern coming off her in waves and tried to *will* her not to say any more about it.

Luckily for her, as they rounded the corner they saw Bob the gardener, whom Delilah had contacted about overhauling the manor house gardens. She'd told him about the dumped rubbish in the layby too and, true to his word, he had piled it up in his pick-up truck to take to the tip and was just getting back into the passenger-side door. She called out and tried to hurry over to the truck, but her sign slowed her down, so Mae took it from her. "I'm Delilah, we spoke on the phone," she said, reaching the wound-down window. "Thanks so much for doing this."

"Nice to meet you, love," he said warmly. "Good to put a face to the name."

Bob was in his late fifties, she guessed, with deep-creased tanned skin and a sense of fun about him. She liked him right away. "And this is Mae," she said, as her friend drew level with the truck and gave him a smile, which he returned with a nod.

Then, "Sorry to rush off," he said, "but we're already late for a job. We'll be with you Wednesday, as I said. I'll send you that plant catalogue."

Delilah smiled. "Thanks so much, that'll be great."

The engine of the pick-up truck roared into life, focussing her for the first time on the driver. She knew he must be James, the apprentice Bob had mentioned. She smiled at him automatically, politely. At first, he just gave her a carefree smile back and tipped his battered hat.

But then he looked again at her, and she looked again at him. She was as curiously struck by him as he clearly was by her. They held each other's gaze for what felt like whole minutes but was probably only a couple of seconds. Those deep green eyes, that curling dirty-gold hair, those tanned hands on the steering wheel, and a dulled silver snake ring on one finger... A snake swallowing its own tail.

Delilah felt like she was reaching for information she couldn't quite grasp.

Just as she was about to say, "Do I know you?" Bob grinned at James and he remembered himself and pulled the truck away, still stealing glances at her.

She watched the pick-up go all the way down the lane, the old sofa bouncing a little in the truck bed as it went over the bumps. When she finally turned to Mae, she found her friend doing goggly eyes at her. She shook her head, laughing. "Stop it! Don't look at me like that! I'm *so* off guys. I just... I feel like I know him from somewhere." She tried to shake it off. "He must have one of those faces."

"What, you mean *gorgeous*?" Mae teased.

"I mean... familiar." She couldn't help staring down the lane after the pick-up, that *reaching for information* feeling still strong within her, and the weirdest sensation that she already knew James, but had somehow forgotten the fact. For the whole of her life.

Mae started up the "entranced by gorgeous bloke" teasing again, so Delilah got busy hammering the sign she'd made into the ground, getting Mae to hold it steady. It read: "No dumping—by law! Offenders will be prosecuted. Please report any infringements to the police or call the Truegreen Community Project on—" Crouching down, she took the marker pen from her jeans pocket and filled in her own number. As an afterthought, she added, "Volunteers welcome."

Mae looked cynically at it. "I love your spirit, Delilah," she said, "but you aren't going to get any jolly hockey sticks community volunteers. Not round here. What you've basically just done is give out your phone number to every creepy weirdo in a twenty-mile radius who wants to ring you up and do heavy breathing or whatever. Do you want that? Because, round here, that is a *lot* of creepy weirdos."

"Yes I do," said Delilah, while secretly trying not to let this comment bother her. She knew Mae wasn't intending to be negative or put a downer on things. She'd just grown up in a place where nobody had ever tried to make a difference, or if they had, they'd given up a long time ago. She could let the place drag *her* down too, or she could try and do something to make it better. She planned to walk a few of the paths and see how much rubbish and debris was there to be cleared up, and to call the council about the metal. "You just need to have a little faith," she said then, more to herself than to Mae. Then, giving the sign one more wiggle to get it completely level, she turned her attention to the path that led to the woods. "Come on, I want to check how my trees are doing."

Mae raised an eyebrow, making the blue stud in it gleam in the sunlight. "*Your* trees?"

Delilah felt embarrassed. "Just—*the* trees, okay?"

Mae got out her phone and glanced at the time. "Oh, sorry, I can't," she said, having the decency to look a little bit guilty at least. "I thought that eco-warrior stuff was just you breaking me out of jail again. Cal's picking me up from here on Clarabelle in, like, five minutes." She couldn't disguise her glee and broke into a wide smile. Delilah couldn't feel annoyed. "Oh, to be young and in love," she said.

"You've never been in love?" asked Mae.

"Maybe I've never been young either," said Delilah. "Never felt it, anyway." She sighed. "Okay, fine, go and enjoy your disgusting happiness."

Mae spontaneously pulled her into a huge hug. Delilah hugged her back, watching the flashes of blue and orange fan out as her long hair slid back across her shoulder. She had the funny thought that the first time she saw Mae, she wouldn't have believed the feisty, all-attitude girl would ever hug her. *Punch* her, yes. But not hug her.

She decided not to hang around to be a spare part while Mae and Cal had one of their full-on snogging, arse-groping greetings, as if they'd been separated for years rather than just overnight. Instead, she just told Mae to say hi to him from her.

Then she took the path up into the woods. Rather than her usual sense of loneliness at being alone, she felt a sweetness in it. In breathing the beautiful summer air, in feeling her body work as she climbed the hill, and in hearing the birdsong in the leafy canopy above her. She soon passed by the clearing where the party had been. It looked really beautiful and inviting without all the rubbish—even the graffiti had faded a bit with all the scrubbing.

She wandered further and further into the woods, taking note of where the random upside-down office chairs, rusting bits of metal and abandoned plastic bags full of goodness-knows-what were located. The aerosols and crisp packets, tobacco pouches and drinks cans she could deal with herself, the next day probably.

After a while she noticed her mind feeling truly calm and clear for the first time since the whole Tol thing had started. Even with so much clean-up still to do, it made her happy, just being surrounded by the trees, seeing how light played on the branches and watching the patterns it made constantly moving around her. The wood was peaceful and yet vibrantly alive, a palette of greens. As she walked, she found herself noticing every single little detail of the landscape around her. The cushiony moss on some of the tree roots, the pinecones at her feet, the soft breeze on her skin, the birdsong, the craggy roughness of the tree bark.

An old rotted-out tree stump.

A stand of skinny, peely-barked silver birch trees.

A white frizz of cow parsley.

Her movement was fluid, her steps even, and she began to match her breathing to them, four steps in, four steps out. This wood was such a special place.

A fleeting thought crossed her mind, *how will I find my way back?* but somehow she couldn't seem to make herself worry about that. She was in too much of a calm place, in too much of a rhythm, to be easily tipped into worry or anxiety. It was a relief after the days before, and it was a completely new feeling, and yet totally natural.

Half an hour later, she was deep in the woods, breathing in a steady pattern as she walked, soaking up the beauty of the golden late afternoon light playing on the trees all around her. She found herself focussing on small, exquisite, unexpected things—a spider in its web, a patch of tiny pink flowers, a delicate eggshell. She began to notice a sort of golden fuzzy haze round everything, too. Maybe it was just the sunlight doing something to her eyes, but Milly would probably say she was seeing the energy fields of the trees and plants. Whatever it was, it just added to the beauty of the place.

She had a strong urge to sit down and try meditating again— but she was too worried about closing her eyes in case she accidentally fell asleep and ended up trapped in a dream with Tol again. She shook the thoughts of him away, scared they'd somehow call his spirit to her. For the first time she thought, *what the hell am I doing out here on my own?* To try and stifle her rising unease, she busied herself by setting off at a faster pace, heading uphill. She'd looked at Edie's ancient OS map in the kitchen, so she knew that this would eventually lead her to the high places where the woods gave way to open land.

The rhythm of her footsteps on the pathways she chose, working her way steadily uphill when she could, washed her anxiety away. When she'd walked for what felt like about an hour, breathing steadily and marvelling at all the small, beautiful treasures along her trail, she found herself coming out onto open ground. After a while longer, she heard something unusual, a sort of rustling noise, coming from around the next corner.

She hesitated, cautious.

Her senses were so heightened that she'd really felt as if she'd just *know* if someone else was around up here. Maybe she was wrong about that, though. In her head, she suddenly felt very alone and vulnerable again. But her body, still happy in its rhythm, kept moving her forward and she went with it, gathering her courage. She rounded the corner boldly and gasped in delight to find that the path opened out onto a wider green space, and that the noise which had alarmed her was being made by the herd of wild ponies Milly had talked about.

There were six of them in all, lined up with their bodies alongside one another in a row. They were pointing in opposite directions so that their tails could swish the flies away from their neighbours' faces. They were grazing intently, their powerful jaws munching away, teeth pulling at the lush grass.

One looked up at Delilah and she instinctively circled away, then approached at an angle. She'd ridden all her life and she knew that ponies, as prey animals, could interpret straight-lined movement towards them as a threat. "So this is where you guys hide out," she said softly. The pony who had turned to look at her at first glanced up again, and snorted loudly, making her smile. "Yes, you *are* beautiful," she told him.

She kept circling closer, and talking softly about the pony, Pippin, she'd had on loan at school. "Yes," she added, "I'm afraid it was that posh kind of school where you could keep a pony if you wanted." Then, *why am I always apologising for myself?* she wondered, and decided to try and stop doing it.

Soon she was stroking the nearest pony's nose, keeping calm and steady, but absolutely thrilled inside, thinking, *these are wild ponies and they're letting me this close*. It was like harmony in motion, and she got that beautiful feeling again, of being connected to the stream of life, to the spirit of nature. Soon, all six ponies were standing around her, making her giggle as they vied for attention. "Yes, yes, you're all beautiful," she told them, stroking their soft muzzles.

She could have stayed with them for hours, but after a few more minutes, they put their heads down again and set off as a herd, munching their way along the scrubby grass. If there *was* a flesh and blood somehow-immortal Green Witch in these parts... Well, Delilah could definitely see the appeal of living wild up here. On a lovely summer's day, anyway.

As she made her way back down, she thought about finding her way back to the Dark Woods and calling out for the Green Witch again, or even sitting down somewhere to try the meditation after all, but she was tired and hungry and wanted a bath. She smiled to herself, thinking how domesticated she was, how domesticated most people were. She'd have no idea which plants she could eat if she lived out here, or which would poison her. No idea how to make a shelter, how to tell if water was safe to drink or even how to build a fire, never mind how to light it.

Soon she was back down in the woods, walking under the beautiful green-gold canopy of branches again. She kept her breathing in a rhythm, in for four counts and out for four. She felt like she could hear every single bird call and branch creak and leaf rustle. The wood was alive—everything was somehow breathing with one united breath, and she was part of it. It felt like the poem she'd copied down, "One". When she scanned through it in her mind—she'd almost got it off by heart now— there wasn't a particular line that described how she was feeling, or anything like that. But it matched somehow, as if the same breeze blowing through the space between the tree trunks here was blowing through the spaces between the words of the poem.

Another half an hour passed and she wandered into the most beautiful clearing which she hadn't passed on the way up to the open land. She sat down to rest, still breathing in the steady pattern. She rubbed her aching muscles—your body just didn't work as well when you hadn't slept properly for days. She leaned again a tree trunk, an oak, she was pretty sure, enjoying its solid feel against her back.

Suddenly, a deer wandered into the clearing. She expected it to startle and bound away the second it saw her, but instead it looked right at her. She looked back, deep into its almond eyes. It was only young, and it looked so fresh, so *bright*, and so part of nature, so connected with everything around it. For a moment she caught hold of that feeling too, in her chest — clear, sure, instinctive.

Delilah moved her head, just a fraction, and the deer turned and bounced away through the trees. She felt honoured and dazed as she watched it go, knowing that something magical had just happened. For a moment, she'd been part of nature too. She'd felt connected to everything, felt herself as not a physical person but as consciousness, flowing through time and space. She'd never experienced anything like it before.

She decided to try meditating again. She took a drink from her water bottle and placed it down beside her. It was all she had with her—she'd found out when they did the initial clear-up that there was no signal in the woods anyway, so no point in bringing her phone.

Remembering what Milly had showed her, well, trying to anyway, she crossed her legs and closed her eyes, letting her breathing fall into a more casual rhythm, but keeping gently focussed on it. At first, she shifted and shuffled about, noticing every itch and muscle ache. But she stuck with it and after a while her body began to settle into a deeply relaxed state. Every time her mind wandered she brought it back to her breathing. When she was really clear and steady, she felt for that feeling again, that connection with everything, which Milly had talked about. She was sure she'd actually just experienced it for the first time. After a moment of reaching, waiting, listening, she found it again. Smiling to herself, she let it flow through her. Or perhaps, she felt, it was the other way around—she was a stream of consciousness, flowing through *it*.

The feeling of flow and harmony stayed with her. Her mind wandered, of course, over about a *million* subjects every thirty seconds, but as soon as she noticed, she just brought her focus gently back to her breathing. When she opened her eyes about twenty minutes later, feeling that it was time, everything looked clearer and brighter, and she could almost *feel* the beauty, saturating her eyes with soft, wet clarity, like dew. And that shimmery haze was there again, around the trees and plants, even more clearly than before. It was the best half hour she'd spent since the whole thing with Tol had started. In fact, since before then.

Actually, since before she could remember.

Her mind hadn't stopped thinking, but she'd stopped paying so much attention to the thoughts—she'd just let them come and go as Milly had told her to. And soon, the gaps in between the thoughts had got longer, and there was this kind of awareness there, that she knew was *her*. Maybe that's what the poem "One" meant by "If you can speak it, that is not it", because there was no way she could put this feeling into words. It wasn't even a feeling, and there wasn't even a word for it.

She was not the thoughts, she was the one watching the thoughts.

She realised that she'd felt this way before—while out running, on long beach walks on the annual school trip to Dorset when everyone eventually stopped chatting and fell silent, and at times where she was listening to music and got completely lost in it. But she'd never consciously realised it before, that *she* was there, the one watching the thoughts. She recalled one of her favourite songs, "Silent All These Years" by Tori Amos, and made new sense of some of the lyrics. She thought back to Tol's piercing question, which had disturbed her so much: "Who are you, Delilah?" This time, she didn't feel an emptiness, she felt a knowing.

This.

This is who I am.

It was awe-inspiring, and yet felt perfectly normal, as if she'd just noticed a limb that had been there all the time but she'd never used. It'd also relaxed her so much and given her such a feeling of grounding and safety that she couldn't resist the sense of exhaustion which washed over her, after the nights of jagged feverish half-slumber and the edgy days running on adrenaline. She closed her eyes just for a moment and in seconds she was fast asleep.

* * *

Delilah woke to find the light fading from the woods. She realised that she'd slept for hours, leaning against the tree in that amazing peaceful state. She'd woken still feeling that way and now she was completely refreshed. After a quick stretch to ease the stiffness in her neck she grabbed her water bottle and stood up, keen to get going and find her way back to the manor before it got completely dark. Jane must be wondering where she was, and Edie too, perhaps.

She only went a few paces before sensing that something was wrong. There was a hyper-real colour to everything that couldn't be explained by the dusky half-light. Then a strange, exotic bird flew past her, almost hovering in the air, its jewel-bright colours like fireworks against the browns and greens around her.

And there was something hanging from one of the trees up ahead.

She couldn't make out what it was at first, but as she drew nearer, she saw that it was a teapot, tied up by its handle with a ribbon.

Odd.

She started to feel panicky—something really wasn't right. Her mouth was dry as tinder and she unscrewed the lid of her water bottle. She tipped it to her lips then hesitated, a flash of colour catching her eye. The liquid sloshed back down again and she held up the bottle, gazing at it in astonishment—the water was a lurid pink. The bottle itself was no longer plastic, but thick glass.

That's when she understood. A deep sickening feeling made her stomach lurch.

"Oh my God, I'm dreaming," she murmured.

But how could she be? She could *feel*—feel the bottle in her hand and the ground under her feet. She was aware of the taste in her mouth and where the cuffs of her sleeves brushed her arms. She curled up her toes in her trainers, blinked her eyes. She was *here*, wherever here was. Really *here*. But she couldn't be, could she?

She sensed someone behind her before she heard the footsteps, muffled on the soft loam and leaves. Her mind dropped its struggle to understand what was going on as survival instinct took over and she held still, poised, on alert.

Did she dare turn around?

The gruff voice behind her flooded her body with terror. "Nice place you've got here." She whirled around to find Tol a few paces away, leaning languidly against a tree. She gaped at him, terrified. "The teapot's a little random," he said. "But—whatever. Up to you. You should put some protection around here, though. You wouldn't want just anyone to walk in."

Through her shock she somehow took in that his bruises were yellowing now, and that the swelling over his eye had gone down. As she stared, his mouth curved itself into a slow, wolfish smile, his eyes cruel. She stared at him, frantically trying to think of a way out of the situation.

"Why are you doing this to me?" she murmured.

"I want you to come with me," he said, as if it were obvious. "And you will, this time. You got lucky on the roof."

She struggled to control her panic. She took a few steps back, wary of him making a sudden lunge for her, but he just leaned casually against the tree and sighed. "Okay then, I'll start," he said, sounding bored. "What, do you want a glass? Ice?"

"I'm dreaming. You're not real. None of this is real," she stuttered, backing away. A few more paces and she'd make a run for it.

Tol sighed impatiently. "No, no, come on, pay attention," he chided. "That's not what you say, at all. *You* say, 'Yeah. And tonic. A slice of lemon.' And then I say, 'Oh, I'm sorry. I really must have a word with the caterer.'"

Delilah was backing off in horror, cringing away from his words. "This isn't happening," she told herself.

Tol shifted against the tree, clearly enjoying himself now. "And then *I* say..."

She turned to run and suddenly he was next to her, his mouth brushing her ear. "Come on, let's go for a walk." She screamed as he grabbed at her hand and strode off, dragging her with him. She kicked out at his legs, but he just pulled her towards him with such a force that her chest banged hard into his. Then his arm was round her neck, the bend of his elbow tight against her throat.

Panicking, struggling to breath, she wrenched his fingers back, and when they neared her mouth, she bit them. Hard. He shouted in shock and pain, losing his grip on her, and she staggered a few paces away from him. He lunged for her feet, bringing her down with a thud, and she instinctively kicked back at his face, wishing for an actual weapon.

"Oh no you don't, not this time," he grunted, dodging her flying feet. "This time you're coming with me." He loomed over her, pushing her roughly onto her back. Something glinting in the fallen leaves beside her caught her eye.

A jewel-hilted dagger.

For a moment, this astonished her—it hadn't been there seconds before. Then she remembered that she was dreaming. However real all this felt, she *had* to be. There was no other explanation. And he'd said this was *her* place, after all. Maybe she'd wished the dagger there. That kind of thing happened in dreams, didn't it?

Tol was sitting on her stomach now, his weight trapping her, holding her down by the shoulders. The feel of his body on hers was sickening. He smelled of stale sweat, sweet day-old beer and motor oil.

"This is all a dream, all a dream, all a dream," she told herself, repeating it like a wish, or a mantra. "You can't hurt my actual body."

Tol looked amused. "Your *actual* body, as you call it, might continue to live, I suppose, if you're found in time, but that's irrelevant. It'll just be an empty shell. You'll be gone. You'll be with me. And if you don't come, I'll take your friends. All three of them."

Delilah gaped at him, cold horror settling over her. "No. You can't... No..."

"Then come." His hands were over her nose and mouth, suffocating her. Shocked, she stared into his dark, malevolent eyes. There was not a shred of humanity there. Not a sliver of compassion.

He's going to kill me.

Only just holding back her panic, she forced her fingers to find the dagger, edging gently down the blade until she felt the hilt. She grasped the handle, but her arm was completely trapped, and her other arm was crushed between them, so that was useless too.

As she struggled, her head swam with the lack of oxygen, and her vision blurred into blobs of colour, until she began to flicker in and out of consciousness. When she came round the next time, she found him leaning close to her ear, whispering something she couldn't understand. An incantation. Something deep inside her, some instinctive knowing, told her that if he finished it, she would be lost forever. Dream or no dream. "Say yes... Just say yes..."

"No." In a blind panic, she gathered every last thread of

life-force left in her and managed to shift sideways, freeing the hand that held the dagger. Suddenly images were flashing into her mind—her and some girls at school, all huddled onto one bed, wrapped in their duvets, whispering after lights out. Of what Estella had told her...

She steeled herself and raised the dagger, then she brought it down with all her strength and will... towards her own heart.

Searing pain tore through her. At that same moment, she woke with a start, beside the tree where she'd sat down to meditate. Bewildered, she scrabbled across the ground, shrieking, terrified that Tol would grab her again.

When he didn't, she leapt up and looked wild-eyed around her, taking in that there was no one there. Sobbing with shock and fright, she collapsed onto the cold earth, finally understanding that she'd woken up. Her heart was pounding hard in her ears.

She got to her feet and took uncertain steps one way and then the other. She couldn't be sure now which direction she'd come from, let alone of the way back to the manor house. It was inky dark. She must have been asleep for hours because the waning moon no longer penetrated the thick canopy of branches above her.

An awful realisation hit her then. There was nothing to do now but wait for the dawn. She was terrified that Tol would appear in a waking vision at any moment. The beautiful wildwood she'd been so at one with felt seething and malevolent now, as she huddled against a tree. She stayed there for hours, trembling with cold and barely-contained panic, hardly daring to move. As dawn began to lighten the sky, she tried to pull herself together. She could see which path she'd come down, and, gathering all her courage to move from her spot, she hurried back in what she hoped was the direction of the manor in a flurry of stumbling footsteps and snatched, shallow breaths.

After taking wrong turns and having to double back three times, she finally found the path leading down to the field and almost fell through the manor house door just as the sun was coming up.

* * *

Delilah sat in the kitchen, after a long shower, with wet hair trailing around her shoulders, making damp patches on her dressing gown. The early morning sun was yet to hit the room and one of the aged strip lights flickered. It would have made her feel twitchy and anxious usually, but she felt that way already and barely noticed it. The kettle boiled and she crossed the room and picked it up, her exhausted arm muscles pounding from that one simple movement.

"Jesus!" she shrieked, as boiling water sloshed over her hand.

Couldn't she even pour water into a mug now? It was like she wasn't in control of her limbs. She knew she should run the burn under the cold tap straight away, but she didn't bother. Focussing on it, on that one physical point of pain, was actually quite comforting, compared to the blind terror she'd felt the night before. She knew that terror still lingered within her, only just kept at bay by the dawn light, ready to overtake her and leave her paralysed at any moment.

She opened the cupboards, suddenly hungry, then closed them again as the feeling ebbed away. She sat down at the table, her tea in front of her, then had to get up and pace around the room—she couldn't just sit there drinking tea like everything was okay.

Nothing was okay.

Yes, the dagger thing had worked. Thank goodness those memories had flashed into her mind, just when... She shook the thought away. Estella had once told them about being trapped in a lucid dream, desperate to wake up but unable to, for what seemed like hours. She said she'd heard that if you can hurt yourself, give your body enough of a jolt in the dream, you can startle yourself awake. In that moment, with Tol and the dagger, Delilah had remembered that sliver of information. Thank goodness it had turned out to be true.

She realised now that she must have been dreaming—lucid dreaming. She'd never experienced it before, so she'd had no idea how completely real it could seem. No wonder she'd been thrown, and thought she was in some completely other place. No wonder she'd been scared out of her wits. But what if there was nothing nearby that she could hurt herself with next time?

Next time.

The thought sent panic coursing through her again. She couldn't live like this, with this fear, without a safe place anywhere in the waking world or in sleep.

As she paced by the kitchen counter, she picked up a teaspoon, to put it into the sink. It slipped through her fingers and fell to the floor with a loud clatter. She jumped—to her, it was as startling as a sudden earth tremor. Then she found she didn't dare pick it up, in case somehow turning her eyes to the floor, even for a moment, left her vulnerable. She didn't want to glance up and see Tol standing there, as she had done when she'd woken up after the owl attack in the Dark Woods and found him by her bed, his face all bashed up, just as it was in the hospital.

As if that would make any difference, she thought again. *I have to sleep sometime, and then—nothing can protect me.*

Chapter 8

Delilah had called Milly as soon as she knew she'd be up and told her about what happened in the woods. She'd sounded so terrified about Tol threatening to take Delilah's friends if she wouldn't go with him that Delilah immediately wished she hadn't said it. Milly had wanted to come over right away, despite having to go to work, and had almost insisted on it, but Delilah had managed to persuade her that she was okay.

As soon as Milly had hung up, Delilah felt fear tear through her again, and she ended up on the tatty sofa in the corner of the room, huddled into a ball, her eye sockets pressed tightly into her knees, sobbing. All wrung out, she closed her eyes for a moment—just a moment—then opened them again and dragged herself up from the sofa.

Mae would be at the dance studio by now and she guessed that Cal would still be flat out from his double shift at the pub. She felt so completely alone that she picked up her phone and called her father. It went straight to message, in Hardcastle's own steely voice. *I am not available at the moment.*

"When are you ever?" she muttered.

"Please leave a message, or call my secretary, Kim, on 07596220181."

"I'm not calling your fucking secretary," she hissed, over the digits. There was a beep on the line. "Please call me back as soon as you get this. It's urgent." Her voice wavered and then tears broke through. "I-I can't cope..." She took a deep breath. "Look, just ring me, okay?"

Delilah threw her phone on the counter in frustration and sank back down onto the sofa in the corner of the room. She stared exhaustedly into space, her eyelids flickering shut for another moment. Then, terrified of falling asleep, she pulled herself up again, rubbing her face.

She went over to the sink, taking her glass from the kitchen table on her way, and began running the hot water. She put the glass under the tap, rinsing the rim with her fingers. Suddenly it slipped from her hand, and she moved to grab it, too late. Her fingers wrapped round it just as it hit the ceramic and smashed. She cried out, pulling her hand back as a curved piece of glass slid across her skin, scoring a line round her index finger. Blood began to pool there, then run down her wrist. "Shit!" she muttered, pressing the wound hard with her other hand, waiting for the searing pain to ease off. Then she'd have to look, to see how bad it was.

"Did that hurt?" A languid voice came from behind her.

Startled, she whirled around, her cut finger still in her mouth. Tol was standing beside the table. She tried to back away, but she was hard up against the sink, trapped. Holding down blind panic, she thought back, to sitting on the sofa, to closing her eyes that second time. She suddenly understood what had happened—she'd fallen asleep, yes, but she hadn't woken up. "I'm dreaming again," she muttered, under her breath.

As Tol regarded her coolly, she reached a hand back into the sink and closed her fist tight around the broken glass. The shards bit into her skin in several places. The pain was searing, but it didn't wake her as she'd hoped it would. The little cuts burned uselessly. "Wake up, dammit," she murmured to herself.

Tol was suddenly standing right over her, his lips by her ear, almost touching. "Come with me," he breathed.

"No!"

Before she could think, he made a sudden move towards her, and an image of him suffocating her in her dream in the woods flashed through her mind. She could almost still feel his hands on her throat.

She panicked and glanced around her.

The knife block on the counter caught her eye. She made a sudden lunge, grabbed a large steel chopping knife from it and held it out in front of her to defend herself. "Go away," she said, as firmly as she could.

She expected Tol to back off, but, "Oh, please, be my guest," he said, his smile widening. He held his hands open, inviting her to attack him.

She looked at him warily, unsure of what to do next.

"It's you I want," he told her. "But if you don't come with me, I'll take your friends first."

There was the low grumbling of an engine outside the window, and the crunch of tyres on gravel, but Delilah didn't notice. She was too horrified by what she'd just heard. She stared at him with sheer loathing. "You're sick."

His gaze burned into her. "Oh, I am so, so much more than that."

Suddenly, she had the glimmer of an idea. Grabbing the broken glass hadn't given her body enough of a jolt to wake her up. But tonight, when she'd fallen asleep in the woods, when that dagger had been within reach...

That had done the job, the last time she was trapped in a lucid dream.

Now, she held the kitchen knife against her own throat, her eyes full of fire, brimming with defiance.

Tol's own eyes shone with greed. "I knew you'd come."

"With you?" she said. "Never." She steeled herself and pressed the cold blade hard against her throat. "I'm waking up."

"What the fuck?!"

Cal had burst in and threw himself across the kitchen, knocking the knife from her hand. He shouted in her face, shaking her by the shoulders. "What the hell do you think you're doing?!"

She gaped at him. "I'm dreaming," she stuttered. "Tol's here."

"No one's here, look!" he yelled, gesturing wildly around.

Delilah looked pleadingly into his eyes, willing him to

understand. As this was her dreamscape, and he was her dream Cal, maybe he'd listen to her if she wanted him to. "He was right here!" she insisted. "You have to help me wake up, Cal! Please!"

Cal held her away from him and stared at her in obvious shock. "Fuck, is that what you think..?" he stuttered. "You *are* awake! I'm here, I'm real." He shook her shoulders hard. "See?"

Delilah was about to protest, but just for a moment she paused and took it all in.

The firm feel of his fingers gripping her shoulders.

His aftershave smell.

The backpack he still had on.

She glanced out of the window. Clarabelle was on the drive. *Real, real, real.*

Her hands flew to her neck. "Oh my God," she stuttered. "Oh my God."

Cal finally let go of her. "Jesus Christ, you nearly slit your throat open!" he shouted. "One more second and I would have come in here and—" He shook his head savagely.

Delilah broke down into tears, imagining the same *could-have-been* scene that he was.

Her body in a rag doll heap. Her eyes glassy, unseeing.

Blood everywhere.

Her legs collapsed from under her, and Cal grabbed her up then helped her into a chair. He crouched down in front of her, taking her hands, his eyes locked on hers. The fear she saw in them, fear for *her*, was so raw, it made her wince. "You have to get help," he said. "You know that, don't you?"

Delilah didn't know in that moment how to answer that, where to even start. So she didn't. Instead, in a small, trembling voice she asked, "Will you go and get Mae? I need her."

Cal paused for a moment, then, "Okay," he said. "I'll get her and bring her here. Then I'll go to the hospital, find out who we need to speak to, and what we have to do. Alright?"

Delilah didn't reply, didn't *agree*, but she appreciated the "we" more than she could ever express.

As Cal made for the door, she was suddenly anxious. She leapt up out of the chair and dashed over to him before she could think what she was doing. But then she paused. She couldn't say, *please stay, in case Tol comes back,* could she? He already thought she had serious mental health issues.

He gently led her back to the chair and pressed her down onto it. "You stay there," he said firmly. "Just stay in that chair and don't move, okay? You'll be fine. I won't be long."

He switched on the TV, found a talk show and turned it up loud. Then he took a drink and something wrapped in foil from his backpack. He put these down on the table in front of her. "You stay right there," he repeated. "Watch that, and eat this." He unwrapped the foil for her. Inside was a slightly squashed homemade cheese roll. It looked so domestic and mundane and *real*, she nearly cried.

Cal turned in the doorway. "You just stay right there," he said again. "Promise?"

She nodded. *Promise.*

* * *

Cal's bike roared up outside the dance studio. He kicked down the stand and pulled off his helmet, to hear music blaring out of the propped-open front door. He swung his leg over his bike and strode towards it. On the steps, he paused, watching Mae.

God, she was beautiful.

And smart (and smart-mouthed, which he also liked).

And so, so talented.

He watched her kick and spin around the hall, hair flying, revealing sudden flashes of blue and orange as she swooped and leapt. Sometimes, he could hardly believe they were together. That she'd chosen to be with *him*.

And Mae was a good friend too, he thought, to Milly, who'd

hardly dared say a word to anyone when she'd first arrived in town, and now to Delilah. She'd want to know right away what had happened at the manor house, he knew. And she'd want to go straight there. Of course she would.

Cal headed up the steps, but suddenly stopped again. He stepped to the side, out of Mae's vision, as she spun across the doorway. Delilah was ill—seriously ill. She didn't even know what was real anymore. He thought back to shaking her shoulders—he had pretty much felt the waves of fear coming off her. She wasn't in her right mind. She'd had a knife to her own throat, for Christ's sake. A few seconds later and he would have walked in on a blood bath. What if she got confused again and thought she was dreaming, or thought Mae was on Tol's side?

No.

He wouldn't take her into that situation and leave her there.

His mind was made up—the best thing he could do was get to the hospital and speak to someone right away. Get Delilah some help. Sure now, he bounded back down the steps, and pulled on his helmet as he straddled his bike again. As the engine roared into life, he kicked the stand up and sped away.

* * *

At that same moment, in the manor house kitchen, Delilah was picking little chunks off the cheese roll and arranging them into a pattern on the table. Every few seconds, her eyes did another sweep of the room, systematically, from one corner to another, looking for Tol.

As if that would stop him appearing.

As if he couldn't, in a split second, be right in front of her face.

Just thinking that made her squeeze her eyes shut and grip the edge of the table hard. She wanted to put on the vile trainers and run for miles and miles and not stop until she had somehow outrun herself, left herself behind. She'd promised Cal she'd stay in the chair, but not moving was making her fidgety and anxious. It had been a couple of hours now—she felt like she'd explode if she didn't do something. On impulse, she snatched up her phone and called Milly again. She'd be heading out for work, but maybe she could walk and talk... She heard ringing at the other end—once, twice, three times...

Delilah tapped her fingernails on the tabletop.

"Hi, this is Milly—" said a bright voice, and for a moment she thought it actually was. Her heart sank as she realised it was just the voicemail, and she ended the call. Tears welled up in her and spilled down her cheeks. After everything that had happened the night before, she must know she needed her. She'd assumed she'd be hanging on the phone, waiting for her call. So where the hell was she?

* * *

Milly was home, in fact. She was huddled against her front door. She'd wanted to reach for her phone, but she'd known for absolute certain that if she moved a muscle, or made a sound, Tol would find her. She couldn't actually *see* him like Delilah did. Delilah had a special gift. Well, it was turning out to be more of a curse, actually. But she could feel him, seeping through the walls, reaching out, searching for her. He was taking his time, she knew. Sniffing her out by her fear. Enjoying the strange game of hide-and-seek. When Delilah had told her that he'd threatened them all, in the lucid dream, that he'd take them instead if he had to, she'd started to feel uneasy, and with every minute that passed she'd worked herself up into more of a state.

She tried to still her pounding heart, to drop her energy right down, to imagine a cloak of mirrors around her, hiding her. She knew that it was hopeless, though. She was giving herself away by blasting out cold terror with every fibre of her being, but she couldn't do anything about it. With every breath fear was sucking her deeper in.

* * *

Cal zoomed down the dual carriageway to the hospital, slipping seamlessly into the outside lane to pass cars. Lots of people didn't *get* motorbikes, and that was fine, but to him Clarabelle was like an extension of his body. She meant freedom. Riding her, he felt fully alert, alive, connected. The road stretched out ahead, near-empty, inviting, unfurling like a ribbon before him.

* * *

Delilah had got up from the chair (sorry, Cal) and gone over to the window. No sign of Mae and Cal. What was taking them so long? She called Mae, it was past eight now, an acceptable time, and waited for the rings to begin, her back pressed against the sink, eyes scanning the room for Tol.

* * *

In the dance studio, Mae didn't even hear her phone ringing in her bag. She was throwing herself around, twisting and turning, giving everything to the music. Letting all her pent-up stress out. Cal wouldn't let the Delilah thing go—he was convinced she was having some kind of breakdown and he wanted her to agree with him—but really, she didn't know what she thought. She did know that the whole thing was freaking her out, though, and the sooner it stopped, the better.

* * *

Delilah sighed as Mae's phone rang out and clicked to message: *I'm not here right now, blah, blah, and if that's you, Dad,* again, *I really am dancing. I went early, like I said. Come check if you don't believe me. Byeee!*

Well, she can't answer her phone from the back of a bike, Delilah told herself. She checked out of the window again, then began to pace round the room.

Milly should have answered, though, she reasoned.

If you don't come with me, I'll take your friends first.

A chilling thought hit her. What if Tol wasn't here right now because he was somewhere else? What if he'd got to her friends already? Was that why Cal had been so long? The idea of any of them being hurt sent such a jolt of terror through her that she had to heave at her lungs just to get the thinnest thread of air into them. It felt like the room was getting smaller and smaller, or that she was getting bigger and bigger, like Alice in Wonderland. The walls were closing in. She felt them inching towards her, could imagine them pressing into her chest, stifling her. Soon there would be no air left at all.

She had to get out.

Now.

She scribbled a note for Mae and Cal in case they showed up. It read *With Milly.* She threw her phone into her bag and banged out into the hallway, gasping for breath. The vile trainers were there by the mat and she shoved her feet into them, using her first few steps to push her heels in properly. She stumbled outside, pulling the door shut, and wedged the note under the ancient knocker. Then she was off, pounding up the path, heart skittering, hair flying.

* * *

Mae hit the crescendo of her dance, leaping and spinning. She felt a tide of outrage at Tol, whether he was truly spirit-walking or had just traumatised Delilah with his anger to the point where all this had come on. It rushed through her, snatching all the breath from her body. Then the wave broke. She bent at the waist, her sweaty hair swinging along the floor.

A moment later, she went over to the sound system and changed the track. As she moved lyrically to classical piano, a calm descended. Her body swept across the floor, her hands and arms leading her completely now, and she went with them, her mind empty.

Overhead, one of the ancient fittings, holding a weighty metal spotlight, creaked loudly. The bolt that was holding it together had needed tightening six months before. With time, and all the base that boomed through the place, it had worked itself loose, and with Mae's fierce last track it had loosened even further. Now it was hanging by its last half spiral.

Mae moved in circles, pure grace now, pure harmony, right beneath it.

* * *

As Cal neared the roundabout for the hospital, a warning flickered across his consciousness. He tuned in, feeling out the bike beneath him. There. It was a tiny vibration. He could barely feel it, but he knew—something was up with the engine. It was probably nothing, but...

He looked for a place to pull over. There was no hard shoulder here, only crash barriers. He'd have to wait for the next lay by.

But a moment later, something juddered under him, and the bike flung itself out to the left. Instinctively, he threw himself right to keep from losing control. He swerved wildly, trying to regain his balance, registering that something was wrong with the steering.

He'd only taken his concentration off the road for a few seconds, but when he looked up a truck was suddenly right there. It must have slowed. And it was indicating. It was pulling out around, what? He glimpsed a flash of metal prongs. Some kind of tractor.

The driver hadn't seen him.

He didn't have time to slow down. There was only one place to go. He had to get around the truck before it pulled completely into his lane. He accelerated as strongly as he could, hearing the protest from the engine, feeling the juddering and resistance from whatever had gone wrong in there.

The sliver of road between the truck and the central barrier was narrowing fast. But Cal was almost level with the cab now. His foot was jammed hard on the accelerator, his body flat against the engine, every fibre of him willing the bike forward.

He was going to make it.

He was going to get through the gap.

* * *

Milly still hadn't moved. Tol's words to Delilah played on a loop in her mind.

If you don't come with me, I'll take your friends first.

She huddled by the door, mute, as still as a prey animal with a predator's eyes upon it. Tol was here in the flat now. She could feel him, getting closer, closing in.

From her position by the door, she registered that the lemongrass and rosemary phase of her new aromatherapy room freshener was coming on again. She'd bought it a few days before, and now she felt like a completely different person from the optimistic, happy girl who'd chosen it. She'd put it in the kitchen area, to mask the sulphurous smell that sometimes crept up from the sink, however much eco-cleaner she put down it, and its warm scent had filled the whole studio room. It did a lemongrass and rosemary phase, then changed to geranium and orange. The idea of it changing was that you could keep smelling the different fragrances, and not get so used to them they didn't register with you.

The cheerful, uplifting scent jarred with her now that she felt small and scared and utterly alone. Memories of the night before had come flooding in as soon as she'd opened her eyes that morning—of Mae's anger with her, Cal's frustration. Delilah looking exhausted, traumatised, *beaten*.

If you don't come with me, I'll take your friends first.

Now she felt him drawing closer.

Closer. Closer.

At some point, she'd ended up huddled by the door.

And now he was here.

She could feel him all around her, breathing her in, relishing her fear. "Tol, please leave me alone," she barely whispered. Silent tears began to roll down her cheeks. "Please," she begged.

It hadn't occurred to Milly that the new aromatherapy room freshener might mask the smell of unlit gas. Gas which had been hissing out of the stove-top hobs all night.

* * *

Delilah was running hard, her mud-splashed legs barely holding her now, as she stumbled up Milly's road. The second she'd been told at the library that Milly hadn't shown up yet, she'd just known that something was very, very wrong. She reached her door and collapsed noisily against it. As she did, she heard Milly scream on the other side.

"It's okay, it's me!" she gasped, still fighting for breath. "What's up? Open the door!"

"I can't," Milly stuttered. Delilah winced at the terror in her voice. "He's in here. If I move, he'll—"

"Milly, please, trust me. Open the door," said Delilah, more gently.

She pressed her ear to the door now and heard movement

on the other side. Then Milly was scrabbling with the latch. The door opened a crack and Delilah immediately smelled gas, as she watched Milly reach for the light switch.

"No!" she screamed, but her voice was drowned out by the explosion.

* * *

At the same moment, just as he was almost past the truck, Cal's bike jolted. Whatever it was that had broken gave way completely. The engine stalled out, Cal lost control, and with a screech of tearing metal, his bike hit it.

* * *

At the same moment, a loud cracking sound pulled Mae's focus up to the ceiling. As her eyes locked onto the huge, heavy spotlight, it hurtled down towards her.

Chapter 9

In the waiting area at the A&E department, Delilah, clutching a sheath of forms, steered Milly from the desk over to the rows of plastic chairs.

"This is completely unnecessary," Milly complained. "I'm fine."

Delilah wasn't having any of it and pressed her down into a chair by her shoulders. Milly had been given a ticket with a number on it, 114, which seemed impossibly far from 79, the number on the digital counter mounted on the wall. "There *aren't* even forty other people here," she said, looking around. "Maybe they died of waiting and got shuffled out the back door."

"I'm clearly *very* low priority," said Milly. "Not even any burns, amazingly. So I really don't think we should bother." She moved to stand up, but Delilah nudged her gently back into the chair. "No way. You heard the paramedic. You could have poisoning, from the gas."

Milly sighed. "Fine, if it makes you happy."

"It does," said Delilah firmly. "I still can't believe you didn't smell it."

Milly smiled wanly. "I wasn't thinking. I was terrified, about..." She lowered her voice in the busy room, "You know, *him.*"

I'm sorry, I shouldn't have told you that," said Delilah.

"Yes, you should," Milly insisted. "You couldn't keep it to yourself. And my new air freshener must have masked it a bit. Huh, almost killed by aromatherapy. Who would believe it?"

Delilah smiled. "Damn those evil essential oils!" she said. "But seriously, thank God you're okay."

"Thank the Goddess you pulled me out. And threw me on the ground. And then dived onto me. And crushed my ribs, but never mind."

Delilah winced. "Sorry."

"No need to apologise for saving my life," said Milly. "And have you ever considered a career as a stunt woman?"

Delilah smiled. "It was just this instinct, to protect you. I was as surprised as you were that I went all Supergirl."

"You must have the heroine gene," Milly joked. Then, seeing the look that flickered across Delilah's face, she grimaced. "Sorry."

"No, I *like* the idea of Mum having a heroine gene and passing it on to me," Delilah assured her. "From what I remember of her, she was fierce like that too. She would have done anything to protect me. And it's definitely not from my dad, that's for sure. He wouldn't save his own granny from a gas explosion — he'd be too busy running to grab his hand-made Italian leather shoes..." She trailed off, eyes focussed on the automatic doors, and Milly followed her gaze. A paramedic was pushing a wheelchair through the opening, and sitting in it was —

"Cal!" Milly shrieked.

"Oh my God, what happened to you?" Delilah cried, as they rushed towards him.

"I crashed my bike, just tore up my leg a bit, that's all," he said. His right leg was flat out in front of him, attached to a board. His jeans had been cut away. Beyond that, she tried not to look.

"This young man is very, very lucky," the paramedic told them as he backed Cal in beside a row of plastic chairs.

Cal registered Milly and Delilah's alarm. "A few cuts and bruises, that's all," he insisted.

The paramedic was stern. "Don't play it down. It'll hurt like hell when the pain meds wear off. I could have been wheeling you into the morgue on a gurney."

Then he strode off towards the desk.

Cal watched him go. "Well, he's been a bundle of laughs."

"What on earth happened?" Milly murmured. Delilah just stared at him.

At that moment the hushed, orderly atmosphere was broken by a scream as Mae came hurtling through the doors. She crossed the room in three huge bounds and threw herself at Cal. "Oh, my God, my poochie!" she cried, kissing him all over his bruised and swollen face.

A bemused look passed between Milly and Delilah. *Poochie?*

Cal winced and Mae leapt back. "Jesus, sorry!" she shrieked. She clutched his hands in hers. "Have you seen the doctor yet? Is your leg broken? Will you ever be able to walk again?"

Cal seemed to find this darkly amusing. "It's nothing, I'm fine."

"You're not fine. You're lucky to be alive," said Milly flatly.

Mae turned and finally registered that her two friends were there. "The pain killers seem to have sent him to his happy place, and he's taking all this way too lightly," Delilah added, giving Cal a reproachful look. "Milly's serious, Mae. The paramedic said he could have *died*."

Mae gaped at her in horror, then threw herself on Cal again. "Oh, thank God, baby, thank God you're okay," she muttered, running her hands over his face, through his hair. "I love you, baby."

"I love you too, baby," said Cal.

Then they started kissing like the world was about to end. Delilah and Milly exchanged awkward glances. "So, my flat exploded..." said Milly conversationally.

It had the desired effect, as Cal pulled away from Mae and stared at her. "What? Jesus, Mil-"

Mae was staring at her too. "Oh my God," she stuttered. "A spotlight nearly fell on me. I only just got out of the way... You don't think..."

"That's—I told you that place was dangerous," said Cal, enraged. "I'll call the council the second I get out of here. You should sue. You could have been killed."

Delilah had been taking all this in, a slow, disturbing realisation dawning within her too. "You *all* could have been killed," she said flatly.

"What do you mean?" asked Mae uneasily.

Delilah looked to Milly for support, and her friend took her hand and squeezed it. "Tol—he told me that if I didn't go with him, he'd take you all first. As in, kill you all."

She hadn't lowered her voice, and a woman walking past with her arm in a sling and a coffee from the machine overheard. She shot Delilah an alarmed look and gave her a wide berth.

"It was him. He did all this."

"Oh, come on—" That was Cal.

Delilah found herself backing away from her injured and shaken friends. "No," she said. "No more talking. This has to end. Now." With that, she turned and stormed off down the corridor.

"Come on, Mil!" Mae cried, and the two girls hurried after her.

"Hey, wait for—" Cal began, but the paramedic, striding back over from the desk, bellowed, "You're not going anywhere, sunshine!"

Cal threw his hands up in frustration. "Don't let her do anything stupid!" he called after Mae. "Well, you know, stupider!"

Milly and Mae caught a glimpse of Delilah's red shirt as she rounded the corner, but even without it, they'd have known exactly where she was going.

At they turned into the corridor leading to the ICU, some visitors were being buzzed in. Delilah hurtled towards them, and as the double doors opened, she barged through, to loud protest. Mae sprinted hard to reach the doors just as they were closing and managed to slip through, leaving Milly alone in the corridor.

Delilah ignored the disgruntled visitors and didn't stop to argue with the man who stomped over to the nurse's station to report her. She walked up the central passageway as quickly as she could without looking suspicious and found Tol's room.

This time she didn't hesitate.

She burst in and strode over to his bedside. She did flinch a little when she saw him. All the tubes coming out of him—connected to the machines around the bed—were a horrible sight. But then rage overtook her completely.

She reached across the bed, grabbed his shoulders, and began to shake him violently. His head flopped back and forth like a rag doll's. "Wake up, you bastard! Wake the fuck up!" she screamed, inches from his face.

But nothing. Not a flicker. She might as well have been shaking a shop dummy.

He wasn't *there*.

Suddenly Mae was behind her, shouting at her to stop, pulling her away, and all the fight went out of her. Mae gathered her into her arms as she collapsed into sobs. "Just wake up," she murmured, into Mae's hair. "Just wake up."

At that moment, a nurse burst into the room. He was furious. "You can't just barge your way into a restricted area!"

"Of course. I'm sorry," said Mae quickly. "I know it's no excuse but please understand, she's very upset. They're very… close. She's sorry. It won't happen again."

The nurse glared at them both, then stepped aside, out of the way of the door. "Make sure it doesn't," he said crossly. "Now, out!"

He bustled over to Tol and started fussing around him, straightening his blankets.

"Come on, hon," Mae said to Delilah, who shuffled along, leaning on her, disorientated, like someone being led from the scene of a crash. It seemed silly now, but she'd thought that if she could wake Tol up somehow he'd be forced back into his body. He'd be back in that hospital bed and he wouldn't be able to reach her. At the door, rage bubbled up in her again and she turned and glared at him. "You bastard!" she hissed. "Leave us alone! Just leave us alone!"

"As I said, they're very close," muttered Mae, giving the nurse an apologetic look as she steered Delilah out of the room.

* * *

Mae had taken Delilah straight to the hospital café, and soon Milly and Cal joined them. Mae moved one of the plastic chairs for him so that he could get his wheelchair alongside the table, his leg propped up on a board, sticking out into the aisle. Delilah assumed that Mae had filled them in on what had happened just then in Tol's room while she went to the loo, but she wasn't going to start a conversation about it unless they did.

There were a few patients, visitors, and staff milling around, some stopping to chat with people as they passed by other tables. Delilah heard one woman asking after another's father, and she remembered that some people would be coming here every day, maybe for months.

Will I even be alive in another month? she wondered. *Will any of us?*

They'd only known each other for a short time, but she already cared so much for her new friends and it broke her heart to see them looking so battered and bruised and scared. To know that she was the cause of it all. If she voiced that, they'd insist that it wasn't her fault—of course they would—but she knew better. If only she hadn't gone to that party. If only she hadn't gone into the woods with Tol. Hell, if only she hadn't even come to this horrible town in the first place, things would have been fine for them.

Milly approached the table and put down a tray holding four coffee cups and a selection of biscuit snack-packs. Cal reached for one but Mae slapped his hand away. "Not you, you're nil by mouth, remember?" she said sternly. "In case they have to operate on your leg." Then she smiled her thanks at Milly, took two cups from the tray and nudged one into Delilah's hands. Delilah had to take it, otherwise it would have spilled in her lap. "Here, drink this," said Mae. "And what the hell were you thinking?" She mimed a knife to her throat, fury blazing in her eyes.

Cal fixed her with a look of deep frustration and said to her, "Don't you get it yet? She wasn't *thinking* anything!"

So, Cal had told them everything too. Delilah was knocked off balance for a moment. They knew what had happened, and how Cal had found her. They knew about her confused, terrified state. About the knife. Now they were all looking at her, expectantly. "Wow, how long was I in the loos?" she said, but none of them laughed, or even cracked a smile.

"Tol was there!" Delilah insisted, putting her cup down on the table so hard that coffee sloshed out of it. "Why don't you believe me, Cal? Even now, after what just happened to you all?"

Cal just swore and threw his hands up in frustration.

Milly reached for Delilah's hand again. "I believe you," she said gently. "I always have. And you know I felt Tol's presence too, at my flat."

"Oh come on," snorted Cal. "Sorry, Mil, I've tried to be respectful of your stuff in the past, but this is—"

"I believe you too," said Mae softly.

Cal looked despairing. "Not you as well. Feeding this dangerous delusion." He glanced quickly at Delilah. "Sorry, but it's got to be said. That's what it is."

"Three freak accidents at once?" she countered. "That's no coincidence. And it would have been true, wouldn't it? If he'd killed us, I mean. He would have left no mark—nothing to show he was behind any of this."

Milly stiffened beside her and said, "Do you think he'll try again? Oh my God, tell me he won't try again..."

Delilah and Mae didn't lift their eyes from the table. Cal spoke into the silence, jaw tight, clearly working hard to keep himself from shouting. "He won't try again—because he didn't *do* anything in the first place."

Mae glanced up at him. "How can you say that? After everything that's happened?"

"What exactly has happened?" Cal half-shouted. He winced and rubbed his ribs. "Jesus, this is all really starting to hurt." The happy-place pain killers were wearing off, clearly.

Delilah thought Mae would be all love and sympathy for him, but instead anger swelled in her voice. "And how dare you not come and get me, when you'd promised Delilah you would!" she cried. "What did you think she was going to do? Stab me?"

Delilah gasped at this. "I'd never hurt you," she insisted. "Any of you."

All eyes were on Cal, accusing. "For Christ's sake, I'm not the bad guy here!" he yelled, making everyone else in the café turn and look at their table. There were a few seconds of uncomfortable silence in the room before the hum of conversation started up again.

"But you don't believe me about Tol," Delilah said quietly. "Even after what happened with your bike."

Cal folded his arms. "Bikes go wrong."

"Jesus, Cal!" cried Milly. "What is it going to take to make you believe this is real?"

"What is it going to take to make you realise you're totally deluded!" Cal shouted, silencing the room again. Then, "Fuck, my ankle fucking hurts," he grunted.

Tears brimmed in Milly's eyes. Mae glared at Cal. "Well done," she muttered.

"Mil, hey," Delilah said gently, taking her friend's hand. She cast a pleading glance at Cal. *Say something. Make this okay.*

Cal sighed deeply. Everyone had started talking again by then, but more quietly, wary of another outburst. "Sorry, Milly," he said at last. He rubbed his face with his hands, wincing as his fingers connected with the cuts and bruises. "Look, it doesn't matter what I believe," he said then. He looked wearily at Delilah. "What matters is what you believe. I believe that *you* believe all this." He paused, then he added, "Sorry, but that's the best I can do."

Seeing him so bruised and battered and exhausted, and trying so hard to help her in his own way, Delilah couldn't help but soften. "Thank you," she said. It was heartfelt.

He looked deep into her eyes. "I'm just trying to help, okay? Really help."

"I know," she told him, holding his gaze. She felt something click into place then—some kind of new understanding between them.

A moment later, a porter came into the café, wielding a clipboard. He spotted Cal's wheelchair and went over to their table. "Callan Murphy?"

"Yup?"

"Orthopaedics are ready for you now."

Mae stood up. "Will you be okay?" she asked Delilah.

"Yes, you go," Delilah assured her. "I'll be fine with Milly."

The porter took hold of the wheelchair handles, but Mae asked if she could push Cal instead. "Later, dudes," he said to Milly and Delilah, with a lazy wave of his arm. Then Mae turned the wheelchair round and set off across the room, following the porter.

Milly and Delilah watched Mae give Cal a loving squeeze on the shoulder and he reached his hand back to touch hers. Delilah was moved by the gesture—and relieved that they seemed okay with each other again.

Milly followed Delilah's gaze. "Ah, there's nothing like both nearly dying, and then being under the continual threat of imminent death to make love blossom."

Delilah smiled at that. Then, "How about you? Will *you* be okay?" she asked, giving her friend a meaningful look.

Milly shrugged. "Yeah. Well, maybe. I'm still scared witless. But I know we'll work this out, somehow."

Delilah smiled at her, surprised once again by how much respect she felt for this girl she hadn't known for all that long, and how much she trusted and cared for her. How much she cared for all three of her new friends, in fact. They didn't even feel new anymore, not after everything they'd been through together, and she couldn't imagine not having them in her life. "Come on," she said, putting the coffee cup back on the tray, "let's go and check if your number's come up yet. By some miracle."

* * *

The two girls wandered back to the A&E waiting room and Milly glanced up at the number counter. It was on 93. She sighed. "I could probably go to Venus and back and still not miss my turn."

Suddenly a middle-aged woman rushed in and launched herself at Milly. "Oh, darling, are you alright?" she cried, hugging her tight. "We came the second we heard. Dad's just parking the car. Are you okay? Were you in with the doctor just now?"

Milly frowned at the receptionists behind the desk. "They didn't have to call you—"

The woman ignored this and leaned in close to Milly, trying to inspect the whites of her eyes. Milly jumped back. "Mum! I'm fine!" After a few more moments peering intensely at Milly, until she was satisfied that she wasn't suddenly going to drop dead, she turned her attention to Delilah. "This is my friend Delilah," said Milly. "And my mum, Carol."

Delilah smiled at Carol. "Nice to meet you," she said automatically. Carol gave her a brief, tight smile in return and refocused on Milly. "You can't go back to your flat," she told her. "And after this, we're not happy with you living on your own to go to sixth-form college either. You'll have to come back home with us."

Milly looked stunned. "But mum," she croaked, "Calverdon College is the only place that does the courses I want—I'm already an hour from it living here, but I can't move back home and commute six hours a day!"

Carol drew her lips tightly together. "I'm sorry, love," she said, "I know you're very mature for your age, but at the end of the day you're only sixteen."

Delilah jolted into action, cursing herself for being too wrapped up in her own problems and not realising Milly's situation. "She can live with me," she said.

Carol looked astonished, but not as astonished as Milly. Clearly, she didn't want to ruin her chance to stay by pointing out that Delilah was only there for the summer, not in front of her mum. Her eyes said it, though—and once again Delilah found herself appreciating how well they could read each other and how close they had got in such a short time. Years and years at school and she hadn't felt as much for anyone as she did for Milly.

"I live with my aunt," she elaborated, "just out of town. She'd be more than happy to have Milly around, and I'd love the company too." She'd dropped the "great" from "aunt" deliberately, to make it sound like she was the one being looked after by Edie, rather than the other way round, and left out the fact that Edie had dementia.

"Well, that's very kind, dear," said Carol, looking at Delilah far more warmly now. "If you have room."

Milly and Delilah both burst out laughing at this. "Mum, they definitely have room."

Just then a red-faced man came through the automatic doors, barely waiting for them to open enough for him to shove his way in. From the way that both Milly and Carol stiffened, she knew that it was Milly's father. She was confused for a moment— he was white too, like Carol, and Milly was of dual heritage. "Stepdad," Milly said quietly to her, reading her expression.

Carol glanced over the girls. "Let me talk to Trev about living arrangements," she said under her breath.

Milly braced herself as he strode up to her and gave her a big hug, then held her away from him and inspected her, as her mother had done.

"She's okay, Trevor," said Carol.

"I knew I should never have let you rent that place, Mil!" Trevor blustered, his eyes bulging slightly with the sheer outrage he clearly felt. He turned to his wife. "I said to you, didn't I, Carol, if that place is up to regulations the Pope ain't Catholic!"

Milly cringed at his loudness. "Trevor, could you just—"

"Yes, you did, dear," her mum said. This only encouraged him, and he carried on with his rant. "Gassing my angel! Explosions, for God's sake. I'll sue that crook landlord's arse so hard it'll come right out of his mouth."

Delilah raised her eyebrows and Milly cringed a deep shade of red as the whole room digested that.

"You do that, Trev," said Carol approvingly.

As Milly's stepfather continued to rain curses and threats on the landlord, Delilah backed away from them, giving Milly a little wave. "I'm gonna go," she mouthed, gesturing at the door.

Milly gave her a wave back and mouthed, "Okay, and thanks," then made the phoning her sign. She'd call her later to fill her in on how things had gone with her stepdad, and if he'd let her come and live at the manor. She must be wondering what Delilah's plans were—whether she was leaving after the summer, and how that would change things. They hadn't really talked about it, she realised. *She'd* quite like to know what her plans were too, actually, although she did already have a place at a smart sixth-form in Surrey to do English, History and Spanish. And student housing there was all arranged.

As she was heading for the doors, Trevor's voice boomed out, "And how many hours have you been waiting in this hell hole? I'll give them a piece of my mind!" Something tore at her heart as he spoke, and she realised with surprise that it was anger — anger and a little bit of envy. However loud and embarrassing Trevor was being, he obviously thought the world of Milly, and he wasn't even her biological father. You'd never catch *her* father making a scene on her behalf, although he was quick enough to get shouty with waiters and people in shops, and he loved a good alpha male showdown at work. She knew this because he liked to recount them in detail during their strained, awkward lunches. He considered almost everyone else he had to deal with an idiot, and he didn't shy away from telling them so. But it didn't mean he cared. That's what had always been missing, and that's what hurt so much now, as the doors slid shut on Trevor's tirade. *Why did you never just* care, *Dad?* she thought. *Why did you never, never actually* care *about me?*

* * *

When she'd walked back round from A&E to the main entrance, Delilah didn't head for the bus stop right away. Instead, she stood outside the front of the hospital, leaning against the wall, watching ambulance workers, porters and patients come and go. Milly had said *"we'll* work this out", but Delilah knew that it wasn't up to Milly, or the others, to get them out of this mess.

It was up to her and her alone.

Tears slid down her face as she fully understood what she was saying to herself.

What this meant.

She'd just been thinking about what she'd do after the summer, for Christ's sake. But what if she wasn't even still alive by tomorrow? There was no other option: she couldn't let anything else happen to her friends. Next time, they might not be so lucky. She had to face Tol, head on, whatever the risks. Whatever the outcome.

And if she had to say yes, to go with him, then she would. Anything to keep her friends safe. And if she died? Well, she wouldn't be able to live with herself anyway, if they did.

"Excuse me, are you okay?" asked a passing woman, peering at her with concern.

Delilah startled and pulled on a smile. "Yes, I'm —" she began. The smile wobbled. She took a deep breath. "No, I'm not," she said truthfully. "I'm really, really *not* okay." She paused. Just as the woman began to look seriously concerned, she forced herself to smile. "But it's alright," she told her. "I know what I have to do now." And with that she walked away, feeling the woman watching her curiously, but not turning back. There was no turning back now, from any of it.

Chapter 10

Delilah had only stopped into the manor house for a few minutes when she'd got back from the hospital. She'd checked in with Ewelina, grabbed a quick drink of water, then she'd gone straight out again, heading for the woods. Someone had spray painted a penis right over her "No Dumping" sign, and it was surrounded by dumped rubbish. But she barely noticed as she strode past, jangled through the gate, and marched up the field towards the treeline. Now she reached the top of the field and set off into the woods, the canopy of trees enfolding her. Shafts of sunlight filtered through the leaves and the bushes around her were alive with the rustling of rabbits and squirrels, but she barely noticed.

After a few minutes, she reached the clearing where the party had been held. From there, not even breaking her stride, she walked right through the centre, over the charred ground where the fire had been burning that night, heading for the path she'd taken with Tol.

Soon, she reached the place where they'd fought. Her mind couldn't put together the two Tols — the guy she'd come out here with had been enraged, furious with her, yes — but had he really been a dark and powerful evil force? Had there been something horribly wrong with him all along, waiting to be expressed, or had spirit-walking from the coma in his half state, between life and death, turned him like this, somehow?

And why was he so obsessed with her? Yes, she'd been with him the night of the accident, but that didn't explain it. She shook her head in frustration. How could she even think that there was anything to *explain*? None of this was explicable. It was all crazy and weird and wrong and made no sense whatsoever.

But one thing was indisputable, physical fact, at least in *her* mind, whatever Cal thought: Tol could have killed her friends, all three of them. She was sure that it was pure chance they'd all escaped with their lives. Those last little odds in the moment that he couldn't control, once the dice had been rolled, had come out in their favour that time. But he was the one who'd set each accident in motion. And she was equally sure that he'd try again. And perhaps next time he'd succeed.

Unless she put a stop to all this, right now.

She leaned back against the tree he'd punched, reached out with her fingers, and felt the place where the bark was missing, flicked off by the blow. Her fingertips connecting with the smooth patch set a cascade of memories off in her head—of their fight, his fury, wandering lost in the wood, the owl attack, the dreams, being on the roof...

She took a deep breath and steeled herself. She had come here with a purpose, and nothing was going to stop her now. She rested her forehead against the tree, rubbing her fingers over the rough bark. "Come and talk to me, Tol," she called out, hearing the catch of fear in her voice. "I'm here. It's me you want. Just... come and talk to me."

But there was nothing. Only the swelling of a breeze through the branches around her, and the sound of a squirrel or something, shuffling in the bushes. Then she remembered—the words they'd spoken the first night at the party—he'd said them in her dream that time, and so maybe they could work for her, to call him here.

"You say, 'What, do you want a glass? Ice?'" she whispered. "And I say, 'Yeah. And tonic. A slice of lemon.' And then you say, 'Oh, I'm sorry. I really must have a word with the caterer.'" She turned around, and spoke loudly, boldly, an incantation. "And then it all starts."

She waited, muscles taut, eyes flicking around the clearing. But there was nothing, just the sounds of the woods at dusk. A sudden fury flooded her. "Well, come on then!" she shouted. "I'm here! I want to talk to you!" She paused... did she dare even say what was on her lips? Yes, she was all fired up with adrenaline, fury and terror now, and she'd do anything to try and get him here. She took a deep breath and let the words free: "I'll come with you, like you want me to."

She paused, listening hard, her eyes moving over the trees and bushes. Willing Tol to appear. "You said!" she cried, her voice choking with pure frustration. "I'll come—so you leave my friends alone, okay? Well, here I am! Come and get me!"

Of course, she had no idea what she'd do if he actually appeared. Or how she'd get out of whatever she'd get into... But her outrage made her reckless. "I will come with you!" she shouted, to the skies. "I will come with you!"

There was a sudden screeching sound to the right of her, and she startled, then refocused, eager. Yes, she was scared. But she was ready.

There was another screech and her adrenaline thrummed to fever pitch all through her body. But then she realised that it was only a couple of crows, fighting in the bushes. She kicked the tree hard, viciously disappointed. She'd wanted to be a heroine and take him on, fight for her friends' lives... but how did you fight smoke and shadow? Dreams and visions?

"Where are you, you bastard?" she wailed. The wave of fury broke then, and she fell to the ground and began to shake, her voice choked with sobs. "Where are you, Tol? Where are you?"

* * *

As Delilah came back through the gate of the manor house, feeling hopeless and miserable, her phone found a bit of signal again and several messages from Milly came pinging up: *Yes, I can stay! Mum and Trevor want to talk to Edie but I said she's away and they can call her soon. I'll pay you rent. My flat declared structurally unsound and unliveable by Chief Fire Officer. Mum and Trevor can bring me and my stuff now, like today.* And the final one:

Please can it be today because if I end up having to go home maybe they'll change their minds and I might never get out of there. Ever. Ever. Eveeeeeeer.

Delilah couldn't help but smile—Milly didn't *do* abbreviation. She wrote a quick reply, "sure—to all" and added two smiley faces in case that looked a bit curt. Then she put her phone down on the kitchen table and started to rummage in the bread bin. Not eating yet that day had caught up with her and she put three slices of bread in the toaster and boiled the kettle for tea while she waited. A couple of minutes later, she buttered the toast at the counter and wolfed it without even bothering to get out a plate, washed down with big slurps of almost-too-hot tea.

Once the food hit her stomach and she could think about anything else, she realised that her plan—to somehow be brave enough to try and get some sleep after the chaos and terror of the night before—was a no go. As soon as she thought about going upstairs and getting into her bed, she knew for sure that she didn't want to be in the house alone—and she was too jazzed up with adrenaline to sleep anyway.

Instead, she decided to throw on some joggers and go out for a run, maybe swooping by Milly's place to give her a hand packing up her stuff. After all, who knew when this fierce, feral energy coursing through her veins would break and leave her in an exhausted heap—she wanted to ride it while she could. And once she'd fought past the busy mind chatter of the first stage of running, perhaps she'd fall into a rhythm, drop into that calm, smooth place she often found—then maybe she'd have some ideas on how to get Tol to come to her. One thing was for sure— she wasn't going to ask Milly for help with it. She'd dragged her friends in deep enough already.

* * *

They hadn't been allowed back in the flat at first, so Delilah waited with Carol and Milly (and an ever-changing crowd of spectators) while the fire crew finished doing things with acrow props and monitoring equipment. They'd finally been given the all clear for a few minutes, with hard hats and two firemen as escorts, to see what Milly wanted to take. The plan was that the fire crew would actually pack up and bring things out themselves, to minimise the time that civilians had to be in there.

So there Milly stood, in what was left of the sitting room area, looking forlornly at her dust-grimy things, at the smashed picture frames and mirrors, the half-falling-down bathroom wall and the bowed kitchen ceiling, which was now propped up with a yellow pole. There were bits of smashed up glass, brick and china all over the floor. Carol burst into tears at that point, and Delilah gasped and murmured, "Thank God you were right by the door. Any little bit of that stuff flying past could have killed you."

They exchanged a glance—the unspoken thought passing between them—*Tol* could have killed her.

"I hope Trevor *brains* that scum landlord," spat Carol, her voice shaking. She grabbed Milly, wailing, "My little girl!" at a pitch likely to make structurally unsound things start collapsing, before being ushered out by one of the firemen. The other turned to Milly. "Well? What do you need?"

"If it's okay, please could you just bring all of it out?" There was a catch in her voice as she added, "I'm not coming back here."

Although light removals probably wasn't his job, seeing the look on Milly's face, the fireman simply said, "No problem. Leave it to us."

The neighbouring properties had been evacuated, while they had their structural checks, but a woman from a few doors down went back to her house and reappeared with a roll of bin bags, then sent her two young boys to the Spar on the corner to ask if they had any boxes. They came back grinning, balancing a stack each, happy to be allowed to cross the police tape and be part of the drama.

The six firemen formed a chain to bring out armfuls of clothes, piles of books and boxes of...well, Delilah supposed you'd call it *Milly-phernalia*. Delilah, Carol, Milly, the neighbour and her boys, and even a few of the starers in the end, helped to load it all into the car. Delilah found release in focussing on something practical and it seemed to her like the job was done surprisingly quickly.

The fire crew pulled away in their truck a short while later, reiterating deadly-serious warnings that no one enter the premises under any circumstances. Delilah and Carol had taken up the neighbour's offer to use her loo, and when they returned, Carol went to fiddle with the driver's seat of her car to make sure she still had enough leg room to work the pedals with all the boxes jammed in behind it.

Delilah wandered over to Milly, who was staring at the police tape and the boarded-up front door. She looked pale and shell-shocked, and Delilah's heart twisted for her friend. Milly's cosy, if damp and dingy, little place, the base for the new life she'd started building here—working in the library and starting sixth-form college in September—was gone, completely unexpectedly, and in a matter of hours. Putting her arm around Milly, she said, "We are going to make you the most amazing room ever at Edie's."

Milly leaned into her. "Thanks," she said. "But..." She trailed off.

"What?" Delilah prompted.

"I'm really grateful," said Milly. "But, I just can't help thinking, how long will I really be staying? I mean—"

"Well, I know I'm signed up to St Catherine's College, but maybe I'll look at the place where you're going instead," Delilah said. She kept her tone light, trying to sound normal, though she barely remembered what normal actually *was* these days. "Then we could live here, and travel there together. And even if I can't switch, Edie will be fine with you being there, she'll love it, and I can come back every weekend." Her voice wavered, losing its brightness. *I'm not even convincing myself*, she thought.

"Thanks," said Milly again. She turned and looked intensely into Delilah's eyes—Delilah had to force herself not to look away and she felt like she might scream with the discomfort of seeing such deep-rooted fear there. "But we both know that's not what I meant. Tol…"

"I know," said Delilah. "I know what you meant. I'm going to sort it out, Mil. Somehow."

"No, I told you—*we're* going to sort it out," said Milly firmly. "The four of us together. You're not alone—you've got us now."

"Thanks. I know I have. She had to look away and swallow hard before the tears came. Carol caught her eye and waved at them. Time to go. Delilah put her arm around Milly and together they walked to the car.

* * *

"Oh my God, Mil, what the hell have you got in here?" Delilah cried. They were back at the manor house, and she'd hoisted one of Milly's boxes into her arms and staggered under the weight of it.

Milly grinned at her as she stumbled past to put the box in the hall. "The Buddha and a few of the goddesses—Diana the Huntress is actually carved from marble—candlesticks, a salt rock lamp, and a pretty hefty Wiccan chalice. Or was that a rhetorical question?"

Milly's stepdad had gone to confront the landlord about Milly's *death trap* flat, so it was just Carol who helped them bring in the boxes and bags.

Milly Milly-fied her new room in a matter of hours and it

looked as if she'd always been there. They had long, hot showers one after the other — although Milly's new room was en-suite, the aged boiler couldn't handle two going at once. Delilah had found that out once when she'd tried to shower at the same time as Jane and ended up in a lukewarm trickle, and she didn't want to inflict that on her guest.

Later they shared a pizza in the kitchen, with a game show on the little TV as neither of them could face talking much. They'd planned to go into the sitting room and watch a film afterwards, but they were so shattered from the night before, and the shocking events of the day, that they'd both had to admit defeat and head to bed.

"Do you want me to come and sleep in your room?" Milly had asked, anxiety in her eyes. Delilah had almost said yes, because she could feel how scared Milly still was and knew that she was asking as much for her own benefit. But after all the people and drama, she just really, really wanted to be alone, however scary the prospect was.

They'd said goodnight on the landing with a hug and gone to their rooms. Delilah's bedroom window was thrown out wide, and an owl hooted gently outside. The bedroom door was open to the hall too, wedged into place with a folded magazine. There was no need to try and protect herself from Tol anymore.

Let him come.

She lay still, on her back, hands by her sides, and listened to her breathing. Her mind was numb, her body exhausted, her emotions ragged. The soft mattress yielded as she let all her weight drop down into it, laying there like a rag doll. She kept breathing, in and out, in and out, in and out, until it seemed that the tide of her breath was all there was in the world.

She had no sense of how much time had passed when Tol's face appeared above hers. She gasped on seeing him, but then she sat up slowly, feeling the movements of her bones and muscles, calm and deliberate. "You came," she said.

He inclined his head. *Yes.* And in that moment, he looked younger, softer. "He doesn't have long left now," he breathed.

"*Who* doesn't?" asked Delilah, uneasy. "Cal?" It was only a broken ankle in the end, but things could go wrong. Perhaps there were other, internal, injuries...

"Your friends will be fine, if you come with me," he said.

"So who were you talking about?" Delilah pressed.

Tol shook his head. "It doesn't matter now. Let's go."

Delilah didn't have to ask *where*. It was all very clear. He hadn't appeared to her in the woods earlier, but now she knew that somehow he must have heard her words, or felt the shift in her intentions. She'd invited him to come, said she would go with him.

Now he was here, and she had to make a plan, quickly.

She forced herself to focus and think it through. What to do next depended on whether this was real—him coming to her in a vision, like he did on the roof—or whether she was in some kind of dream version of her bedroom. Her mind should have been racing with possibilities, options, but his gaze was locked onto hers and instead she felt sleepy and slow. She didn't even feel the familiar fear of him creep over her—he just looked lost, lonely, and very, very tired.

So, was this a dream? Everything seemed completely real, and just as it was when she'd gone to bed. No pink water in glass bottles. No teapots hanging from the ceiling. No strange, exotic birds eying her coolly. Maybe she was actually awake, and he was a vision.

But if they *were* in a dream, would she still be able to wish things to herself, as she had with the dagger, or could that only happen when she fell asleep in the wood? Anyway, could she really look someone in the eye and stab them in the heart? Even though she knew it wasn't physically real? It would *feel* real, wouldn't it?

Actually, she was less sure of what had happened with the

dagger now that she was thinking of relying on it so completely: Had she *really* thought it there? Maybe it had been there all along, but she'd just missed it when her eyes first swept the ground. Was she sure enough to gamble her life on it? Could she even bring herself to try and kill him? Could he even die in a dream? Would he die in the real world? A human life was a human life. If he did, how would she ever live with herself?

She tried to think of another way—maybe she could plead with him, make some kind of bargain. Maybe she could get him to somehow guarantee that he wouldn't harm her *or* her friends... He was still gazing into her eyes, and everything fuzzed together in her mind. She reached for the next logical thought, but it wisped away into nothing, like woodsmoke.

"You made me an offer," he said at last. "I've come to collect."

Yes, she had done that—she'd said she would go with him. She hadn't *meant* it of course. Well, she hoped she wouldn't have to mean it. That was just to get him here—then she was going to...

What?

She was sure she'd had some kind of plan, but what had it been? Her mind was growing ever hazier and there was such a pleasant gentleness to everything after the harsh, jagged exhaustion and terror she'd been living.

Would it really be so bad, to just give up? To let go?

It would save her friends... wouldn't it?

Did she have any other choice?

"Come with me," Tol breathed.

She got up, feeling her feet connect with the cool floorboards, *one, two,* enjoying the way all the little bones moved in them. She acknowledged how well they'd served her. How healthy she'd been in general. And never hungry, never wanting. *Lucky.* She stood and Tol ushered her through the doorway, gentlemanly, following close behind. She walked slowly along the hall, breathing steadily, head high. She reached up to the ledge where she'd put the key, out of Edie's reach. Enjoying the coolness and weight of the old iron in her hand, she unlocked the door that led up to the roof.

Only when she was on the parapet did she feel even the tiniest twinge of fear. But she didn't try to push it away. She embraced it, because it was all part of who she was. All part of her beingness, right now in the moment. She felt more alive, more tuned in, more present, than she'd ever felt before—than she'd even believed was possible.

She turned to Tol, looking deep into his eyes. "And then you'll leave them alone?"

He held her gaze and nodded slightly. "It's you I want."

"Why me?" she found herself asking.

He looked vaguely amused by this. "You still don't know." It was a statement, not a question.

"Know what?"

He smiled and shook his head a little. "It doesn't matter now," he said again.

Delilah didn't question him further. He was right—it didn't matter now. None of it mattered now. He gave a little courteous nod and extended a hand towards the edge of the ledge. "Shall we?" he said, like a charming host.

Slowly, gracefully, she walked across the parapet, to the part where the little turrets had broken away. She glanced down, taking in the vertiginous drop to the paving below. She stepped forward, her toes over the edge, a little of the stonework crumbling beneath her feet.

She spread her arms out wide.

Tol smiled. "See you on the other side," he said.

She fell.

And for a moment, she was flying.

Then, just as she was about to hit the paving, she felt magnificent, beautiful life coursing through her veins, and she wanted more of it. She wanted to *live* with a feral, animal ferocity. But it was all too late.

Her body smashed against the paving...

...and she woke up.

She drew in a huge breath and sat bolt upright, eyes wide and unblinking. Her mind stumbled over her half-finished thoughts. *I'm still... It was a... I must have...* "Milly!" she screamed, then burst into tears of relief. Until she'd really thought she was about to die, she'd had no idea, no *real* idea, of how much she wanted to live.

* * *

Milly was sitting at the end of Delilah's bed, facing her, pillows propped against the footboard and the covers untucked and rucked up so that she could get her legs under them.

Even though she'd sworn to herself that she'd keep her friend, *all* her friends, out of it from now on, Delilah had been in such a state that she'd ended up telling Milly everything, including what she'd said when she went to the Dark Woods. Now something disconcerting was happening—something she hadn't expected at all—Milly was looking at her as if she were a stranger. "And what if it had been a vision, not a dream?" she demanded.

"I...I don't know..." stuttered Delilah. "I guess it would have been too late. I'd have been—"

"Dead," Milly said flatly. "And next time, who says you won't be?" There was accusation in her voice.

"Who says there'll be a next time?" Delilah challenged. "And it wasn't my fault, Mil. It was confusing, fuzzy... I couldn't think properly. You're making it sound like I did this on purpose."

"You did!" Milly cried, then lowered her voice, remembering that both Edie and Ewelina were asleep down the hallway. "You invited him to come to you. You said you'd go with him. What the hell were you *thinking*?"

Delilah felt equally frustrated, not to mention exhausted. "I know I did, but I didn't *mean* it," she hissed. "I was just trying to get him to face me on my own terms."

"Well, I still don't know what got into you," spat Milly, "and it didn't work anyway, so don't try it again, okay?"

Delilah held up her hands. "Okay! Jesus!" She made herself pause and take a deep breath. "Look, I thought you'd understand," she continued, a moment later, trying to keep her voice calm and steady. She and Milly having a huge row wouldn't help the situation, and they'd end up waking Edie and Ewelina. "In fact, I thought you were the *only* one who would get what I'm trying to do here—but..." She cast her eyes down to the coverlet and squeezed the fabric between her fingers. She thought about not saying what she was about to say, but she felt it too strongly to hold back. "You're acting like Cal," she muttered. "Like you think I'm delusional, and all this is made up."

Milly looked utterly outraged by this. "I am not!" she hissed. "I'm just scared out of my wits, Delilah. We're got no idea how to stop Tol from doing this to you, to any of us. You're getting more and more exhausted and confused. Never mind Tol, you're a danger to yourself." She sighed and shook her head, pressing her lips together. "We're completely out of our depth here."

Deep down Delilah felt the desolate truth of this, but she couldn't bring herself to say so. And anyway, Milly wasn't entirely right... "There is a way to stop this," she half-whispered. "Don't you dare talk about it," Milly said firmly. "Don't you dare even *think* about going with him. Not for one minute—"

"But then he—"

"It's no guarantee he'd leave us alone," Milly cut in. "You know that. Whatever Tol was before all this happened, he's a crazy psychopathic spirit-walking evil entity now. He's not going to keep his word—it's all just a trap to lure you in." She stared intensely into Delilah's eyes. "And you'd better not be falling for it. You're not, are you?"

Delilah looked away. She'd *already* fallen for it. She'd tried to think, but then her head had gone all fuzzy and the next thing she knew she was on the roof and what had started out as a bluff or a strategy... well, it hadn't been anymore. Barely-audibly, she said, "No."

"Do you promise me?" asked Milly, holding her two hands and squeezing them tightly. "No more trying to find him, thinking you can outwit him, because you can't."

"I promise," said Delilah. And at that moment, she almost believed that she meant it. *Almost.* "And do *you* promise not to tell Mae and Cal what happened tonight?" she countered. "I don't want them worrying any more than they already are."

Milly hesitated, then said, "Delilah, I think maybe..."

"Promise," said Delilah, urgency in her voice. "Please, Mil."

Milly sighed. "Fine, I promise. Look, I'll think about what we should do, okay? There are a couple of people I talk to online, who know about this kind of stuff. Maybe we could get an exorcist to come or something." Delilah must have looked as alarmed as she felt—weird strangers off the internet turning up to do God knows what—because Milly hurriedly added, "Not that I'm saying you're *haunted*. Not as *such*. I mean, Tol's not dead, so you can't be."

Delilah sighed. "That's how I feel though," she muttered. "Haunted." She couldn't bring herself to face death again, but she didn't feel like she was living either. She couldn't fight smoke and shadow, and there was nowhere to run to. Her friends' lives depended on her, but she had nothing. She felt completely out of options.

Chapter 11

The next morning, Delilah and Milly got a taxi up to the hospital to visit Cal—Milly didn't bring their talk of the night before up, so Delilah didn't either. Mae was already there, perched on the edge of Cal's bed, looking gorgeous as usual in skinny jeans, offensive t-shirt and worn-in leather jacket. She leapt up to hug them both as they walked in. "I got here the very second visiting hours started," she told them, then grimaced. "Dad thinks I'm at the dance studio, so I'd better go soon in case he turns up there to check on me."

Milly sat down on a chair by the side of Cal's bed and handed him the grapes they'd bought him in the shop downstairs. He cast his eyes over them disappointedly. "Oh. Out of Mars bars, were they?"

"The phrase you're looking for is 'thank you'," said Mae.

"You're welcome, Cal darling," said Milly.

Delilah felt warmth flood through her seeing the three of them sparring together again. Cal looked rough, but he was enough of his usual self to give them cheek, so she guessed that he couldn't be feeling too awful. "How's the patient?" she asked. "Apart from gobby and sugar-fixated?"

"I'm okay," he said, shifting on his pillows, and grimacing. Mae leapt off the bed, tipped him forward and began to rearrange them behind him.

"You've got a good little nurse there," said Delilah, winking at Mae.

"Anything for my baby," said Mae.

"I'm going to hold off on the bed-bath jokes," said Cal, "but please know that I am making them in my head." He paused, as if listening to an internal monologue. "And yep, you're all laughing—you think I'm hilarious."

"Wow, if you think that, the painkillers *must* be strong..."

said Milly.

Cal pulled a face at her and closed his eyes again. "Yep, in my head you two are finding me deeply entertaining, and wait—what's this? Mae is wearing a nurse's uniform..."

Mae slapped him playfully then leaned over to give him a quick kiss. He pulled her down across his chest and this turned into a full-on snogging session, which was mercifully interrupted by a nurse—and not the kind who existed in Cal's fantasies. Like the actual, proper nurse she was, her skirt was knee-length and paired with tights, even in the height of summer, and flat, sensible shoes. "That's enough of that, thank you very much," she said sternly. A look passed between Milly and Delilah that said, *ooh err strict*, but then she grinned and added, "You'll make the other patients jealous."

"Morning, Kemi," said Cal. "How's it looking for me getting out of here today? You said that maybe, after the doctor's ward rounds..."

"No, *you* said you'd like to be out after the rounds," Kemi said, sternly but with an undercurrent of amusement. "*I* said the usual stay for a fracture like yours is at least another day. And don't even *think* about getting on that motorbike ever again. The things I've seen..." She trailed off, shaking her head, and wrote something on her clipboard. Then a call-bell buzzed for another bed, so she bustled off to help.

"I'm pretty sure she only means no more Clarabelle until she's out of the garage," said Cal. But however casually he said it, he couldn't keep Mae from looking horrified. "She said *ever again!*" she gasped. "I'm always going to be worried about you riding, after this!"

"And you think I'm not going to be stressing out every time you're dancing in that death trap studio?" Cal countered. "I wouldn't ask you to give that up, and it's the same with me and my bike."

"That loose bolt took five minutes to be fixed, and all the

others have been checked over," snapped Mae. A couple of the other patients glanced over—Cal and Mae's drama was clearly far more interesting than whatever was on the TVs above their beds. "Riding bikes is just stupid!"

Delilah stood up suddenly from the plastic seat next to Milly's and said assertively, "Okay, time out, enough already. Of course you're worried about each other, with what's happened. But no fighting. You guys love the bones of each other and nobody is doing anything dangerous right this second, so, like, just live in the moment and…" Cal was looking at her with great amusement by then and she couldn't help the frustrated smile that crept over her face, "just… freaking well love each other."

Cal laughed. "Erm, isn't that what Jesus said to his disciples? 'Just freaking well love each other, dudes."

Delilah flushed. "You know what I mean—don't let this come between you. *Any* of this."

A more serious mood came over them and all the things they weren't saying hung ominously in the air. "And how are *you* doing?" Cal asked eventually.

Delilah flicked her hair back and pasted on a smile. "Good. Yeah, good now. I had a decent night's sleep at last. No… incidents." She didn't dare look at Milly, but silently willed her to keep her promise about not saying what had really happened the night before.

"That's great," said Mae. "And, you know, I was just freaking out yesterday, after what happened with the spotlight. It scared the shit out of me. But me and Cal have chatted more and, look, don't hate me but… it's true what he said, accidents do happen." She and Cal glanced at one another and he nodded slightly, willing her to go on. Backing her up. "And we do both think you should talk to someone, about what's been going on," she finished, the extremely nervous look on her face completely at odds with her brash outfit, nails and hair.

Delilah felt her breath catch. The lies stuck in her throat but she forced them out: "You know, perhaps you're right. I've been under a lot of stress lately and things have gone haywire. I'm not saying I suddenly think I imagined it all, but... well, I feel like it will get better from now on. One day at a time, but I do feel more grounded, and if I can keep getting some sleep, that's going to help a lot." *You're only lying to protect them,* she told herself.

"Good," said Mae, clearly relieved that Delilah hadn't kicked off at them. So relieved that she seemed to have swallowed it all whole, in fact.

"And you'll see someone? To help you?" Cal asked. The concern and relief on his face was heart-breaking. *You are such a bitch for doing this to them,* she told herself savagely. *Be kind,* said a still small voice inside. It was so calm and gentle, and so *absolute* that it startled her. "Yes, I will," she managed to make herself say, and decided that she actually might talk to someone, get another perspective, just to keep her promise to them. The tension in the room suddenly released as he smiled. "Great. That's such a relief."

"We've been worried sick," said Mae.

Delilah could feel Milly trying to catch her eye, but she kept her focus resolutely on Cal and Mae. Cal flushed a little. "I, erm, I talked to someone here," he muttered, "looked into what to do, you know, how you go about getting help, what's available..."

Delilah was shocked that he'd already taken action. Suddenly, she felt like she was walking on broken glass. She had to navigate this very, very carefully. "Thanks," she said at last, deciding that less was more. Safer. She had to look like she was on the right path, but not out of the woods. *Literally, in my case,* she thought. *And I really might talk to someone. Maybe.* She still didn't look at Milly, and when they left together half an hour later, she was relieved she didn't bring up what had happened the previous night. She knew now that she had to lie to *her* too.

She *wouldn't* tell her that she was planning to take matters into her own hands and attempt her own exorcism on Tol's spirit in the Dark Woods. Milly had so many occult and new age books—all carried up the stairs by Delilah and installed in her new room. All but one, anyway, which she'd liberated from the pile and stashed in her underwear drawer. She reminded herself that she was only doing this, any of this, to protect them. So she took her friend's arm as they walked along, and she lied and lied and lied.

* * *

The Twisted Tree stood gloomily nearby, etched in moonlight, and Delilah tried to stop glancing over at it. She'd never have dared walk up here alone in the dark if she hadn't been absolutely desperate. She shivered in her fleece as she lit the final candle. They were in jam jars, so they'd stay alight, and she'd brought long kitchen matches, not a lighter, so she could reach in to light them. Oh yes, she'd thought of everything. She'd only get one shot at this and she wanted it to work.

The book had been very clear about the importance of following every element of the ceremony exactly.

Now she trod the circle carefully, as instructed, wafting the crackling sage (borrowed from Milly's room, like the book) back and forth. She'd checked which way faced north, east, south and west using Edie's old OS map, and now she called in the spirits of each direction as instructed. Then she trod the circle three times, chanting the words of protection, which were set out phonetically. She hoped she was saying them properly. It would help if she knew what they meant too, or what language they were in, but that didn't seem to be mentioned anywhere in the chapter she was working from.

Then she stood in the centre, in the pentangle she'd made as instructed—with willow from the tree by the overgrown pond, bound with green string—and raised her arms to the sky. She gathered all her courage for the final incantation, which she'd written herself, following the template set out in the book. Adrenaline coursed through her, almost buckling her legs beneath her. "Tol, I call you to me. By the powers of the guardians and spirits of the unseen realms *I call you to me.* Come to me this night." She'd tried to make it sound properly magic, but now, fuelled with adrenaline, she added, "Get out here, you fucker."

She held her breath, half expecting the sky to come crashing down. Or that psychotic owl to swoop from nowhere and attack her again, as a prelude to his appearance.

But nothing happened.

He *had* to come. She'd done the ceremony—she'd followed the instructions exactly. He had to come, and then she'd do the next part—the part where she banished him from her forever. But for that to happen, he had to turn up in the first place.

"Where are you hiding, you bloody coward?" she shrieked, her heart pounding. "Come out and face me!"

But still nothing.

Overcome by a wave of fury and helplessness, she threw herself to the ground and thrashed about, swearing lavishly. Tol would keep stalking her until she walked off the roof or something until she went with him. Where to? She didn't know. Or maybe she'd just lose her mind with terror and sleep deprivation and end up in psychiatric hospital.

The ceremony was supposed to work. It was proper, actual magic. But nothing. So then, what the hell would? She was caught in an impossible dilemma. She felt all out of options for getting rid of Tol. She felt abandoned by the Green Witch, if the bloody woman even existed in the first place. She felt terrified, overwhelmed, and bloody furious.

There was so much emotion running through her she couldn't take it, and she let out a long scream. She grabbed the willow pentangle and snapped it savagely, then beat at the ground with her fists, pouring all her rage into the earth, in absolute despair. "Help me," she begged, not even sure whom she was talking to. Not the Green Witch, that was for sure—she'd totally given up on that idea. "Help me. Help me. Help me."

Still nothing happened. No powerful force swept through the trees, coming to her rescue. She didn't look up to see Tol's boots beside her head. The trees didn't whisper sickeningly, and the ground didn't pull her down.

Nothing happened on the outside, anyway. But deep inside her, the most profound thing that could have happened did. Delilah let go. She just… *let go.*

It was an act of sheer surrender. She stopped trying to control, fix or make sense of any of it. She stopped trying to work out her thoughts and feelings, or to plan what to do next.

She gave it all up.

For a moment, there was only peace, harmony, balance.

There was only *now.*

Her whole being was suspended in that moment.

It was the same feeling she sensed within the poem "One". She found herself repeating the first verse like a mantra, softly, under her breath. "'What is here is there, and both are nowhere and everywhere. Nothing is without and all is here now.'" Over and over and over.

Then, as she felt the earth and dry leaves between her fingers, and looked at her grimy, dirt-ingrained hands, she suddenly understood something. The trees weren't whispering malevolently, as they had been before, and the ground wasn't sucking her down. That was actually the *point.* These things weren't just going on all the time, for everyone to see. If they were the place would be a tourist attraction by now.

No, they were being *activated.*

Directly *activated.*

Maybe the place where Tol now dwelt, where he could be

found, was somehow *parallel* to the real world, the real wildwood. *What is here is there, and both are nowhere and everywhere. Nothing is without and all is here now.* What if it was influencing this world somehow, and was a crossover point for his consciousness?

The rhythm of the words from "One" somehow led her to another breath-taking understanding, about one of the terrible dreams he'd stalked her in. The one that didn't fit with the rest. Lucid dreams were one thing, but that was something else altogether, she saw now. This new realisation rang around inside her head, with bell-like clarity after all the chaos, high emotion and confusion. She was so desperately seeking a way in to where Tol *was* now... but perhaps she'd already been there.

Last time it had happened when she'd fallen asleep in the woods. The different dream was the one where she'd wished for a weapon and then moments later, the jewel-hilted dagger was there lying in the grass. What if that dream wasn't a dream, not even a lucid one with his actual spirit in it? What if she'd fallen asleep and somehow woken up into some other version of the wildwood? Some kind of parallel reality?

The horrible truth dawned—if she wanted to test out that theory, she was going to have to fall asleep out here. Forget sage smoke and pentangles and chanting words she didn't even understand the meaning of. She was simply going to have to fall asleep. And the thought of that was way more daunting than anything in Milly's book.

And harder too. You couldn't just fall asleep at will, could you? Especially with about three weeks' worth of adrenaline thundering through your veins. She steadied her breathing and closed her eyes, letting the wave of exhaustion that followed such a huge outpouring of emotion break over her. Letting all the broken nights catch up with her. Letting her body get heavier and heavier and heavier. She couldn't make herself fall sleep, of course not, but she could surrender to this bone-tired exhaustion, just right now in this moment... She let the words from "One" sail around her consciousness like a lullaby on an endless loop. *What is here is there, and both are nowhere and everywhere. Nothing is without and all is here now.*

There was a soft stirring close by and Delilah opened her eyes a fraction.

Tol.

There he was, as simple as that. She hadn't even fallen asleep, just sunk deeper into herself. She could have laughed — almost. She gathered herself and got to her feet. "You came," she breathed.

"No, *you* came."

So it was true. There was another place, and she'd entered it. The place where she'd been before, and where he dwelt. She'd found it by remembering, with the help of "One", that there was nowhere else it *could* be but right here and now. She swallowed down the fear that was rising in her and focused on calling the jewel-hilted dagger to her, on feeling it in her hand. She still didn't know if she'd be able to bring herself to use it, but she thought she'd feel safer with a weapon.

But it didn't come. Not like before.

The confusion on her face made him smile. Her gaze swept over his black eye, his hospital gown half-tucked into torn jeans, battered leather jacket over the top. Then a sickening thought hit her. Maybe she hadn't gone to another place at all. Maybe this was still the real wildwood. Was he actually here, in the real Dark Woods? Had he regained consciousness and left the hospital somehow?

Shit. Everything in her was screaming *run, he's going to kill you. Run, dammit!* But it was as if the connection between her brain and her legs had come loose. He moved towards her, wincing with each step. She could see the strapping on his ribs through the thin gown, and the tracheostomy scar at his throat, still stitched, raw and livid.

He was a breath away from her now, and all she could do was

gape at him. He reached up a hand that was flecked with half-healed glass cuts and touched her cheek gently. She flinched, but she didn't pull away. His touch was real, physical, and the sense of it lingered for a moment, once his hand had drawn back.

Her brain had found her legs again, and she could have run. But she no longer wanted to. Here he was, in the real world, and here was her chance to face him and finish this, for good. She was hopeful, but cautious—which of the two Tols she'd encountered was he really? Would he kiss her, or kill her?

He did neither. Instead he stroked her cheek again, looked deep into her eyes and said, "I'm not Tol."

She gaped at him, unable to take his words in. He took her by the shoulders and gently turned her round, to face the Twisted Tree. He leant so close to her ear it made her spine tingle—with lust or fear, she wasn't sure.

"There's Tol," he breathed.

She gazed across to the tree. There was the shape of it against the moonlit sky, as it had been before. But its trunk was bulkier—there were other shapes around it. She gasped and tensed as she realised that they were figures, people, tied to it. Slumped and—what? Asleep, unconscious, dead? They were bound with ivy, keeping them upright, making them almost part of the tree. Four, five... Six in all, though she could only see a sliver of the bodies of the two on the far side of the tree trunk.

So she had shifted to somewhere else.

Bewildered, heart thumping, she made her way towards the grim spectacle. The bodies were ashen, grey—an older man and woman facing her, so tightly bound to the tree that their bodies seemed to be being absorbed into it. She looked closer—no, they actually *were*. She shuddered, taking in the two girls in their twenties beside them, wearing clothes from the nineteen forties. They were bound tight too, ivy growing over their statue-like faces now, but still separate from the tree. She couldn't believe she was really seeing this. She forced herself to stumble round the trunk, to see the other two captives. An old man with scraggly grey hair had almost completely vanished into the tree bark. And Tol. Fresh green tendrils of ivy were snaking over him, his face greying but still a flesh-coloured pallor in places, a soft glow emanating from the centre of his chest.

But that couldn't be...

She turned back to where Tol actually stood, in his gown and jeans, and gaped at him. He gave her a lopsided smile, as if he'd just surprised her with a brilliant birthday present and was expecting a thrilled hug.

He said he wasn't Tol. Through her shock and horror at the scene she allowed that to process. And the fact that the tree had just been a tree, moments before.

"So, this *isn't* reality?" she stuttered.

"It's *a* reality," he told her. Then he grinned widely. So widely that the cut on his lip opened and blood began to seep out, which he didn't seem to notice. He opened his arms expansively and said, his teeth blood-sticky, "Welcome to the real Dark Woods."

Delilah's mind was racing now. She'd really gone somewhere, in those seconds when she'd closed her eyes and let exhaustion claim her. "I'm in this other wood," she muttered.

"Otherwood," he corrected. "You're in Otherwood." Blood oozed down his chin now and onto the gown, but he made no attempt to stem the flow.

"So, if you're not Tol, who are you?" she managed to ask, bewildered, "and what the hell is this?" She gestured at the macabre spectacle of the tree.

"I am the Soul Hunter," he whispered. Then he cried it out to the moonlit skies above. He shuddered with some private pleasure, then turned back to her and looked deep into her eyes. "And you are the hunted."

Suddenly, the cut on Tol's lip seemed to tear into an impossible wound. And his whole face, Tol's face, split open, completely in half.

Delilah screamed and ran. The great chasm of sickening blackness she'd glimpsed was what lay beneath the disguise, and she knew instinctively that if she let that thing anywhere near her, she'd fall into that chasm and be lost forever.

Oh my God, how to get back? He was on her heels as she streaked through the trees. *Think.* His hand clawed at her dress then lost its grip again as she twisted hard and put on an extra spurt of speed. If this place wasn't physical, then she wasn't in her body. She wasn't *in* herself.

Shit, that was the freakiest thought she'd ever had in her life.

All her focus went to her form, lying close to the Twisted Tree in the Dark Woods of her own reality. Although her mind was telling her to get the hell away from this, whatever he'd called himself, this *Soul Hunter*, and that sick display on the tree, deeper down she knew she had to run back towards it, because that was where her body lay, in the real world.

Gasping for breath, she looped round, and in the split second it took him to register that she'd changed direction, she dived out of his reach and made for the clearing again. As she approached it, she tried to remember exactly where she'd set up the stupid ceremony, and where she'd flung herself to the ground. She reached the spot, empty here, and threw herself at the earth again, the Soul Hunter close behind her.

The next thing she knew, she was sitting bolt upright and taking a long, shuddering breath. She leapt to her feet and looked wildly around her. No Soul Hunter, and the Twisted Tree was just a tree. She ran, and was surprised that her legs, which had felt like dead weights beneath her after the long, frantic chase in Otherwood, had fresh energy. Of course—here she had been, what? Resting, sleeping, in a trance? Not running from some kind of psychopathic demonic *thing* that was using Tol's form somehow.

Her legs carried her down the field and lane back to the

manor house with speed and efficiency, as if she were just out for a run as usual. Here, her body and brain weren't already flooded with a cocktail of adrenaline and terror, although just the memory of what had happened, and what it meant, was starting to take effect. Usually, she could have covered another couple of miles without breaking stride, her breath steady and rhythmic, but as she opened the front door, she staggered under aching legs and let her breath go completely ragged, no longer forcing it to stay in rhythm.

Chapter 12

Back in her room, Delilah desperately tried to think through her options. Tol wasn't a predator but a captive, his soul a hostage of some horrific evil entity, which was intent on taking hers too. She could hardly believe it, but that didn't make it any less real.

She'd been there—to that place—Otherwood. One thought crashed round and round in her head—what if Tol woke up from the coma, and his soul wasn't back in his body? What then? She had no idea—but one thing she did know was that she wasn't involving any of her new friends in this. No way.

There was a tentative knock on her door, but before she could say anything, Milly walked in. The two girls looked at one another and Milly just instantly knew something had happened. In moments she was across the room, hugging Delilah tight, both of them awkwardly twisting as they sat on the bed side by side.

"What? What is it?" Milly asked.

Delilah shook her head. "I can't- I can't tell you," she breathed.

Milly sat back and gazed at her. "But you can, you can tell me anything. I said, we'll work this out together…"

"No, we can't. I won't put you in any more danger. I have to do this on my own."

Milly was quick to pounce on that. "Do what exactly?"

Delilah sighed. So she'd have to tell her then. But she absolutely wouldn't let her get involved. Rescue Tol's soul from an evil entity in a parallel reality to the wildwood called Otherwood."

Milly gaped at her. "What the actual fuck? But Tol… Tol's the one…"

"No." Delilah climbed across the bed and propped the pillows up against the headboard then collapsed back against them with a sigh. Then she told Milly everything that had happened.

Milly listened to the whole thing in total shock. When Delilah's story had finally come to an end, she said, "So, if we don't get Tol back into his body in time then...?"

"He won't wake up. Or he will, but he won't be *there*." Delilah paused. "But Milly, there's no *we*, you understand that, don't you? I just can't risk..."

"You're not doing this alone," Milly insisted. "We'll work something out. I've got contacts, like I said. People I can speak to, who'll know what to do. There's no way I'm leaving you to walk in there by yourself. We can—"

"No," said Delilah firmly.

"But surely it's up to me if I want to risk my life, my soul..."

Delilah was alarmed. "No, it's not. It's not even a question. Leave it alone, Mil, or I'll—" She hated to say it, but she had to try and get Milly to back down somehow, for her own safety. She looked her straight in the eye. "Or you won't be able to live here after all, and we won't be friends."

Milly took a deep, shuddering breath as this hit her. For a moment it looked like she was about to say something, but then she turned and ran from the room.

"Milly, please!" cried Delilah, already regretting her words. She heard her friend's footsteps thudding down the stairs, over the flagstones in the hall, and then the front door opened and slammed shut. Shit. She was worried sick for Milly, but she also knew for damn sure that she didn't want to let her go. Not out of her life, and not out of her house. *So don't just sit there, then,* said a small voice inside her. She scrambled over the bed and rushed after her.

She caught up with Milly halfway up the lane that led to the woods, but her friend just looked straight ahead and carried on walking. "Mil! I'm sorry!" she cried. "Please stop! I was only saying that to try and protect you. Of course we'll be friends—

we couldn't not be." But Milly kept on walking, looking straight ahead, bangles jangling and long dress swishing.

They were halfway across the field up into the woods when, desperate, Delilah grabbed at Milly's arm, caught it and swung her friend towards her. They were both out of breath, half-crying, nose to nose, staring at one another. Milly's features softened, and then she leaned forward and kissed her.

Really kissed her.

It took a moment for Delilah to process, but then she pulled away, astonished. "Mil! I don't..." Seeing the anguish on her friend's face at the rejection, she added, "I'm so sorry, it was just a surprise, that's all. I didn't mean to jump away like that."

But then Milly was daring to look hopeful, and that was awful too, because she'd just set her up to be hurt even more. "I don't think of you that way," she managed to mutter, feeling absolutely terrible. "And I didn't realise you liked me like that. I'm so sorry."

Milly was looking mortified now, and Delilah couldn't see a way to put her out of her misery. Luckily Milly herself rescued the situation. "No, I'm sorry," she said. "I don't feel that way either, well, not usually. It was just, seeing you there, so vulnerable—something came over me."

Delilah knew it was a lie, that she was being offered a get-out, but in that moment she was happy to take it. Maybe they'd talk about it more later. But right now, this would help. "Okay, I understand," she said.

Milly cringed. "Can we just forget that ever happened?"

"Of course," said Delilah. "And you'll stay at the manor, right? Please. I don't want you in danger, but I can't cope without you, I know I can't." She sat down in the lush grass and Milly flopped down beside her. "Okay," she murmured.

"But you can't get involved. Please. I'm begging you, stay out of it."

At that, Milly stood up abruptly and started walking back

to the house. She was fierce now, angry even. "I'm already involved. And maybe I want to protect you just as much as you want to protect me."

"I know, Mil. I'm sorry."

But Milly didn't reply, or even look back. She just kept walking, and when they got into the house, she dashed up to her bedroom, shut the door, and locked it from the inside.

* * *

Delilah didn't even remember going down to the kitchen. She'd spent an age sitting outside Milly's door, trying to get her to talk. But she must have done, because when her mobile rang, she found herself sitting at the kitchen table in front of a cup of tea, watching it go cold. She picked her phone up without thinking and swiped to answer. She hadn't even taken in the name on the screen. Then she realised she should have left it— she didn't want to talk to anyone at all—but it was too late. "Hello?"

"Hi." Cal. "How's it going?"

She smiled grimly to herself. "Bloody awful, thanks for asking. How's the ankle?"

"Bloody agony, thanks for asking." Pause. "Listen, I didn't just call to say hi."

Her senses prickled at the unease in his voice. It made her instantly uneasy too. "Go on."

"I don't want to stir anything up, of course I don't, but it's a small town—you'll hear about it from someone else soon, and I wanted it to come from me. Tol..." He paused, and for a moment she was sure he was going to say Tol had died, his tone was so grave. "He's going to be brought out of his coma," he finished. For a moment, she was relieved—but then her stomach twisted. What the Soul Hunter had in store for Tol was worse than death.

"Okay..." she said, trying to keep her voice steady, and not betray the panic that was thrumming in her veins.

"The hospital called and when we'd had a weird conversation about the fact I was actually in here, in another department, a doctor came round and spoke to me."

Pause.

"Okay."

"They haven't been able to track down any family, so they've finally accepted me as the best contact they've got for him. They want him to see a friendly face when he comes round." His voice lowered. "Given how he left you in the woods, it's going to be none too friendly, but still, I said I'd do it... he's got no one else."

So many questions, thoughts and emotions were racing through her, but she could only actually get one word out of her mouth. "When?"

"Tomorrow."

Silence.

"Delilah? Are you there?"

But she didn't reply. Instead, she ended the call and stared out into the gathering dusk.

* * *

Delilah was in the manor house gardens the next morning, going over and over what she'd experienced in Otherwood, when she turned to see Milly approaching her, mug in hand. "Tol's being brought out of his coma today," she informed her. "Cal called last night."

Milly braced. "Oh my goodness, we have to do something — now!"

"I'm scared that if he comes round and his soul isn't back in his body, maybe he'll just... die," said Delilah, despite herself. The thought had been gnawing at her since Cal broke the news.

And she'd hardly slept all night.

"And his soul will be trapped in Otherwood for ever," said Milly. "That's awful, worse than just physical release from this life."

Delilah couldn't help smiling at that. "Oh, is that what we're calling death now, 'physical release from this life'? Makes it sound like slipping into a nice hot bath."

Milly didn't smile back. "Having your soul taken—that's like being in hell for all eternity, if hell actually existed," she said.

Delilah sighed. "I don't know what comes after this life, if anything does. Or what will happen to Tol's soul if we don't get it back in his body before he wakes up. But the fact is, we can't stand by and do nothing, can we?" She sat down on the low stone wall of the herb bed.

"We?" Milly echoed.

"Well, I can see there's no persuading you to let me go it alone." She'd thought about that while she was awake for most of the night too.

"Good, because there's not," said Milly firmly, then sat down next to her.

They both tried hard to act as if they'd forgotten about the kiss.

"If I do nothing and Tol dies, or worse, I won't be able to live with myself," said Delilah. "But I have no idea how to rescue him, and just the thought of going back to that place…"

"But now you understand what you're up against," Milly said. "And it'll be different this time because I'll be there with you."

Delilah smiled grimly. "Yes, don't remind me."

Milly tipped the rest of her tea into the herb bed and stood up. "We'd best get on with it then."

* * *

As they headed back towards the house, Jane came out to meet them. "Edie's not feeling great," she said.

"Oh, I'm sorry to hear that," said Milly.

"Is she okay?" asked Delilah, feeling a jolt of worry in her chest. It always surprised her how much she'd come to care for Edie, love her even, in such a short time.

"She'll be fine, I'm sure," said Jane. "She's just a bit off-colour, and feeling tired and dizzy. She's probably coming down with something. She's gone upstairs for a little rest."

"Shall I pop up and see her?" Delilah asked.

"She's probably asleep by now," said Jane. "Maybe this afternoon you could read to her again, though. She liked that. I know she doesn't seem to take much of it in, but it's obvious that she likes the rhythm of your voice."

"Okay then, I'll do that," said Delilah. "Something's come up now, and we have to see to it right away." She very much hoped that she'd be back that afternoon to read to Edie, and not be trapped in the Dark Woods, or, even worse, bound to the Twisted Tree.

* * *

A short while later the two girls reached the Dark Woods, sunshine streaming reassuringly through the canopy above them. A little out of breath from the long, hurried climb up through the wildwood, they made their way over to the Twisted Tree and stood looking at each other expectantly.

"So..." said Milly. "What's the plan?"

"Erm, when you said 'we'd best get on with *it*' back in the garden, it kind of sounded like *you* had a plan," said Delilah. "I took the 'it' to mean a plan. Isn't there some kind of water-tight occult ritual to get me in and out of there safely?"

"Not that I know of. I think it's as simple as—get into Otherwood and sneak up to the Twisted Tree, without the Soul

Hunter even knowing you're there. Free Tol's soul. From what I've read, I'm pretty sure it will head straight for his body, as it's all the same energy. Then come back here and get into your body."

Delilah couldn't help smiling at that. "Then go home, get kettle on, put feet up," she added. "Simple." Bravado was good. Bravado helped.

Milly smiled too. "Exactly."

Suddenly there was thrashing in the bushes to the right of them, which made them both jump. Mae came crashing out, looking hot, dusty and utterly furious. "What the hell do you two think you're doing?" she demanded. She glared at Milly. "And don't deny it, I heard the whole stupid plan."

Milly was startled almost to tears, but Mae turned on Delilah now. "Tol's soul is trapped, is that what you think? Well, if that's true, believe me, he's not worth you risking your own soul over, or your life."

"I can make my own decisions, Mae," said Delilah.

Mae kicked the Twisted Tree, hard. Milly and Delilah looked nervously at it, as if she might have set off some kind of supernatural reaction. "This is bollocks!" she snorted. "Oh my God, Cal's going to be devastated. He really believed you when you said you'd get help, you liar!"

The thought of Cal's disappointment in her twisted Delilah's heart. "I can't just do nothing—Tol's soul could be trapped forever. And I really was planning to talk to someone about all this," she added weakly. "To get help sleeping, at least. It wasn't a lie. But now I know Tol's in danger, and time's running out for him, I have to take action."

Mae tossed her hair and folded her arms. Then, very unexpectedly, she said, "Fine."

After a long silence, Delilah ventured, "What do you mean, 'fine'?"

"I mean fine, do whatever stupid thing you're doing. But I'm not leaving. And I messaged Cal when I saw you two heading up here, so he'll be here soon too. Even though he should be resting. They barely agreed to let him out."

Delilah shrank under Mae's accusing glare. "I'm sorry. He can't come up here. He can hardly walk. Tell him—"

Mae cut her off, agitated. "I came over to celebrate you turning a corner, getting help. I followed you up here, to jump out and surprise you. I thought it would be funny. I brought muffins." She gestured towards a crumpled paper bag by the bush and Delilah was so overcome with love for her friend that she pulled her into a hug. After a moment, Mae softened and hugged her back. When they broke apart, she said, "Sorry for shouting."

Delilah shrugged, and gave her a shy smile. "That's okay, you were angry."

"I'm still angry. I'm still fucking furious, actually. But I'm not having you lying to me and shutting me out again. I'll go and find some signal and call Cal. Promise you'll wait, okay? So I'm here, for whatever is going to happen. Or *not* happen, more like."

"We're not sure *what's* going to happen," said Milly. "I suppose if Delilah just sits down and tries to meditate or fall asleep—"

"Promise," said Delilah. "Just call Cal and tell him to stay where he is." Then she swayed, suddenly dizzy, and grabbed Milly's shoulder for support. "Woah!" Her legs buckled under her and her heart raced. She gasped for breath. *What the hell is going on?* "I just need... I just..." she stuttered, and then, before Milly could grab her, she fell to the ground. Milly and Mae's horrified shrieking was the last thing she heard before she passed out.

* * *

When Delilah came round, she didn't know how long later, she was still in the Dark Woods, looking up at the trunk of the Twisted Tree. "Milly..." she croaked.

"Welcome back."

She pulled herself groggily up to sitting, heart thudding. *Tol's voice. But the Soul Hunter speaking.* She winced at the horror show of trapped souls, bound in ivy to the Twisted Tree, the real Tol included. The light that glowed from his chest was fainter than before, and he looked more ashen, more like the others, the ones who had *gone out* long ago.

"How..?" she breathed.

"How did you get here?" asked the Soul Hunter smoothly. "I'm getting stronger. I pulled you to me. His soul gives off so much energy, as it fights for freedom. There's not much left in it now, but no matter. Soon I'll have a human body, and that's when the fun will really start."

Cold horror filled Delilah as her foggy brain took this in. Then he spoke again. "Well, I'll need another soul before then, of course, to power my journeys between the worlds."

Another soul...

She tried not to look at him, but couldn't keep her gaze from sliding up to meet his—Tol's form, Tol's bruises, Tol's split lip and how it had... She couldn't think about that. She felt so dizzy and sick, and her head thudded with panic. She couldn't do anything to help the real Tol, not like this. She tried to snap out of the strange state, but it was like trying to shake herself sober, and she clutched her head as another wave of dizzy sickness pounded through her.

The Soul Hunter knelt beside her and gently but firmly laid her back down again. "There. That's better. You rest now."

No...

His hand was over her nose and mouth. She stared up at him, eyes wide with panic. Her brain was screaming at her to fight, but her limbs were so heavy they refused to move. One minute, two maybe... Her eyelids fluttered, and as her eyes closed, images, graceful and fleeting, moved across her oxygen-starved mind.

Making eye contact with the deer that day. The sudden intimacy. The surprise and delight of it.

Meditating in the woods and seeing energy fields around the plants and trees.

Cosy under the fairy lights at Milly's place, her friend showing her the local history books she'd found.

The image of Milly brought her back to the present for a brief moment, and the slightest murmur escaped from her lips, under strong fingers. The Soul Hunter stroked her hair gently back from her face with his other hand and hushed her gently. But he didn't release her. Delilah slipped further away, seeing more images.

She and her friends clearing up the rubbish from the wildwood.

Meeting the ponies and stroking the muzzle of one of them.

So soft.

Like velvet.

So easy to just rest into that softness...

As she slipped away, he linked the fingers of his free hand with hers.

Her eyelids flickered, so slightly that he could have missed it — if he hadn't been looking at them, watching for that moment, so, so close now.

So delicious to him.

"By the speaking of my ancient, true name, I call her soul to the Twisted Tree," he murmured, his eyes fixed on her pale face, his gaze flicking from her now-still lashes to her blue-tinged lips. She would have looked dead already, to anyone who didn't know better.

But the Soul Hunter knew.

He had done this many, many times before, and he'd never missed the moment.

Soon, death would come. Death in Otherwood, which was what mattered.

And then he'd have her soul.

It was very, very nearly time.

He leaned down, gently brushing her hair back, his lips a whisper away from her ear. "My name is—"

A wrenching force ripped through the trees, a force of tremendous light and power. It hit the Soul Hunter square in the chest, and he cried out as he was thrown backwards. His body smashed against a tree, and then hit the ground, and his head cracked on a rock. A light breeze ruffled the trees and then all was still. Not a branch had been broken.

Now a thin stream of air made it into Delilah's lungs and stirred her consciousness. After a moment, she pulled in a huge, shuddering breath and slowly hitched herself up onto her elbows, bewildered. Her great aunt stood over her, in a flowing green dress, her long white hair loose. "Edie?" she gasped, "but..."

Edie gave her a gentle smile. "Go now," she said softly. "Our secret must be kept, as Green Witches have kept it for centuries."

Delilah stared at her in wonderment. "So it was you, saving me that night in the woods, from the owl attacking me—well, *him*, attacking me, in the owl." She glanced over at the knocked-out Soul Hunter. Black, brackish blood oozed from the back of his skull.

"Yes, that was the last time I came out to the real wildwood." Edie smiled ruefully to herself. "I used the secret gate, at the back of the gardens. My mind... Well, I haven't been myself for a while now. But something in me knew. Somewhere deep down I remembered, who I was, what I was, and I felt, that night, you might need me."

Delilah marvelled at this. "The legend of the Green Witch in these woods," she breathed. "It was you."

"And many before me, of course," said Edie.

"The accounts in Milly's books," Delilah muttered.

The Soul Hunter groaned and stirred. They both turned sharply and stiffened, all their focus on him. Delilah gathered herself and offered Edie her arm. "Come on, let's get back to the real wildwood. Quickly."

But Edie just smiled at her. "You go, dear, and, yes, hurry." She squeezed her hand and looking deep into her eyes. "I have another path to tread now. A whole new adventure."

"Edie, you're confused."

Edie ignored that. "Go now," she said firmly. "I've already set up as much protection around you as I can, to keep him from playing his games with you. It should last for a few days, so you can get some sleep, and prepare. But once Tol is woken…"

"I know, the Soul Hunter will have a body, and then… well… he'll be out of Otherwood and even more dangerous."

Edie didn't look worried though. She just smiled and tapped her gold necklace—a tiny key, which Delilah had never seen her wear before. "You'll need this. It's the key to everything." With that, she turned and strode off into the woods.

"Edie, wait," said Delilah, astonished at the way her great aunt was moving, so swift and so sure. "Where are you going? You can't just…"

Edie paused, and turned, looking right at her. Right *into* her, it felt like. Then she said, "You're going to make an excellent Green Witch."

Delilah gaped. "What?"

But Edie didn't respond. She seemed to be listening to something or someone that Delilah couldn't see. "I have to go," she said suddenly. "Now. And so do you. Hurry." She began walking again then, and in moments she had disappeared among the trees.

Delilah could hardly begin to process what she'd heard. Edie had said she'd make an excellent Green Witch. But how was that possible?

And yet.

"One" began playing itself in her consciousness. The start of the second verse now, over and over. *You are that which you seek.* But it couldn't be. She knew herself. She was *her.*

And yet.

There was no time to think through any of it right then. She lay back down, closed her eyes and tuned into her breathing. She felt the Soul Hunter's blood-sweat presence close by, but she sent all her focus to her body lying in the wildwood. She began to drop into that state, where she could slip away, and she was nearly, almost, there. She could dimly hear Milly and Mae talking, and dappled sunlight was filtering through her closed eyelids. It felt like she was swimming to them, through green-gold water.

But then suddenly, sickeningly, there were hands round her ankle, and she was yanked back into Otherwood. The Soul Hunter had dragged himself up. The gaping, bloody gash on his head made her stomach turn.

Gathering herself, she kicked out at him hard, with all her rage and fear, but his grip wouldn't loosen. She struggled and screamed, railing against him. But he was so strong, and he was winning…

Then suddenly an understanding came over her.

Edie had said that *she* was a Green Witch too.

She didn't understand how on earth that could be, but she thought about the incredible force that had roared through the woods at Edie's bidding. It was pure power, and light and love. The memory of it washed through her mind like a healing balm. Another line from "One" weaved through her — *Nothing is without and all is here now.*

Suddenly it wasn't just in her mind anymore. It was coursing through her veins and gathering in her heart. As the Soul Hunter grabbed her hips and heaved at them, it exploded from her palms, hurling his backwards and propelling her back into her body in the real wildwood. She leapt to her feet, eyes springing open. She watched Milly and Mae scream in shock and registered that, now, Cal was there too. He let out a shout of surprise, as the force continued to pour forth from her palms, sending a forceful blast through the woods, like a power surge, lighting everything up, including her friends' startled faces.

Then it subsided, and a light breeze ruffled through the canopy, then a deep stillness settled over them.

"Holy shit," croaked Cal.

Mae was looking wary of her. "Delilah, that is *you*, isn't it?"

"Yes, it's me," she breathed, feeling her feet on the ground, letting it sink in that she really was back, and safe.

"What the hell just happened?" Cal demanded, swaying on his crutches.

Delilah turned to Milly. Yes, she was looking startled, but she was smiling. "She's the Green Witch," she said.

"I can't handle this," Cal muttered. He looked bewildered, shocked, and began to swing away on his crutches.

"Cal!" cried Delilah, but he didn't look back, and he didn't stop moving, grunting and swearing with each step.

Mae was clearly torn, but Milly said, "Go with him, we'll be okay. I'll call you later."

Delilah and Milly watched Mae go round the corner. Milly looked thrilled. "So, I have about a million questions—" she began, but Delilah, urgency in her voice, cut her off. "I hate to say this, and believe me, I don't want to do it, but I have to go straight back there right now and try to fight that *thing* again. I have to rescue Tol's soul before they wake him up."

"No, no," Milly said quickly, "Cal just told us that they've delayed Tol being brought out of the coma. Apparently the swelling on his brain hadn't gone down as much as they'd hoped."

Delilah took this in. A small miracle. Well, another one. And perhaps also one that Edie had somehow influenced from...

well, from wherever she was now. "So we've got some time?" she asked.

"Yep. Cal's keeping in close touch with the doctors."

"Good, because I need to go to Edie."

Milly frowned. "Why?"

Delilah grimaced. "Because I think she's dead."

Milly was clearly stunned by this, but Delilah, already on the move, just grabbed her arm and pulled her along. "Come on, I'll explain on the way."

Chapter 13

When Delilah and Milly reached the manor house, Delilah made her way to Edie's room. She'd asked Milly to wait downstairs — this was something she wanted to do on her own. Well, she wasn't sure she wanted to do it at all, but... She took a deep breath, braced herself, and put her head around the doorway.

So it was true.

But it wasn't awful, as she'd feared it would be. In fact, Edie looked like she was sleeping. She was lying on top of the bed covers in her long white night gown, hair spread out on the pillow. Herbs and crystals were arranged all around her body. *She must have known it was time*, Delilah thought. *She must have laid everything out, and then climbed into the space in the middle and died.*

Edie's eyes were closed. Delilah was glad that she'd gone peacefully — it looked that way, at least. She hoped she hadn't felt frightened or alone. Immediately a knowing welled up from deep within her, and formed into words: *Of course she didn't, she was going home.*

To look at Edie, only the strange pallor to her skin gave away the fact that she was dead. But to feel... The feel of her — of *Edie*, had completely gone. This body, this physical form on the bed, looked like her but it *wasn't* her. Delilah was astonished by how strong this understanding was. She could vaguely remember a friend at school saying this of seeing her grandmother in her open coffin, that she wasn't "there", but she hadn't really understood what she'd meant at the time. Well, she certainly did now.

"Edie," she whispered, more to the room in general than to the body on the bed. There had been so much she'd wanted to say, when Edie had made her revelations. So many questions... But she'd have to find her own way through now. Here, the only thing she wanted to put words to was "thank you", which she whispered over and over again, to the woman who had shown her true warmth and love, and passed on her legacy. "I am the Green Witch now," she told herself again. It didn't seem possible. She'd stopped believing there even *was* a Green Witch. But it was true. Cal and Mae, as well as Milly, had seen the force pouring from her. They were objective witnesses. Otherwood was also real, and the Soul Hunter too, unfortunately.

That was when she noticed the necklace Edie was wearing in Otherwood, the small gold key on a chain, draped over her open palm. She remembered her great aunt's words, and she knew that she must take it—she'd said that the key was the key to everything. She carefully picked up the chain from the bedcover, avoiding touching Edie's hand. Her body looked like such an object now, so *not a person* that it was a little bit scary to think about touching it—as if the hand might close over hers mechanically if she brushed against it, as some final electrical signal pulsed through Edie's nerves.

Delilah put the necklace on. She looked steadily again at Edie's body, feeling a swell of love and appreciation well up in her heart. She was sure that later she'd mourn what she had lost, but right then all she could feel was gratitude for what she'd had. Having been in Edie's life, however briefly—as a bewildered grieving six-year-old after Miranda's death, and now, as a, a what? An adult, almost. A woman, feeling lost in the world, unsure of herself, overthinking everything. And a Green Witch. A *Green Witch.* She felt a strength and determination flood through her. "I won't let you down, Edie," she said to the space in the room. And then she went to wake Ewelina, and call Jane, too.

* * *

Jane had come right away and stayed all through the night.

Ewelina had wanted to stay too, but they'd persuaded her to go home and get some sleep, as she had another night shift elsewhere the following evening. They waited until morning to call Edie's doctor. In the end, she couldn't confidently determine a cause, or joint causes, of death and had to call the coroner. By mid-morning, Edie's body had been taken away for further examination. Delilah expected she would mind about this, but because she'd experienced the complete absence of Edie when she'd first seen her body, she found that she didn't. In fact, she was grateful to the doctor and coroner for taking the time and trouble to get things settled properly, and not just putting the cause of death down as "old age". She wasn't sure they'd find any obvious cause, though. It was clear to her that Edie had simply decided it was time to go and fallen asleep forever. In this world, anyway.

Delilah had moved the herbs and crystals from Edie's bed before Jane arrived. She didn't want anyone to see that the death had looked planned. While she understood that Edie had been lucid before the end, with her strong connection to the earth and her Green Witch power—that she had simply *died*—she didn't expect anyone else to see that. Leaving things as they were would have led to awkward questions.

She'd insisted that Milly go to work as usual that morning and asked her to call Mae and Cal on the way to hold them off from coming over too, just for a day. She heard her phone pinging over and over so she knew that Milly had done as she'd asked, but she couldn't focus on her friends just then. She was exhausted, and there were tasks to be done, which only she could do, it seemed. She briefly scanned the messages in case Cal had news about Tol coming out of the coma, but there was nothing on that subject, so she didn't reply to any of them. They'd understand that she needed some time.

Just after nine, she'd reluctantly called her father at his office and delivered the news. He'd had the decency to offer his condolences, at least, albeit in a stilted, robotic way that was clearly designed to prevent embarrassing crying or any display of emotion from her whatsoever. Why she took his lead and stayed stiff and formal herself, she didn't know — habit, she supposed. She wished now that she'd wept and wailed down the phone and made him as uncomfortable as possible.

He hadn't offered to come down, of course, and just when she was about to cave and ask him to, he made some lame excuse to hang up. Now she was glad he was staying in London — he'd be no help. And — she realised with a start — she no longer *wanted* him to care whether she was okay. She was astonished — when had that happened? Maybe at some point, with everything that had gone on, she'd accepted that he was never going to. That he just wasn't built that way. Huh.

Jane had walked into the kitchen at that moment and found her staring at her phone. "I was taking Edie to the dentist today," she said. "I suppose I'd better ring them and cancel." With that she burst into messy, snotty tears again, and wailed, "Oh, it never gets any easier, when one of my clients goes!"

Delilah pulled her into a hug — she felt awkward, like she should say something but she didn't know what. This had been happening sporadically all night, and so far she'd only come up with "it's okay" when it blatantly wasn't. She really wanted to have a good cry too, but somehow the tears just hadn't come. "I feel like a total robot, compared to you," she told Jane, trying to make her smile.

"You're just in shock," Jane insisted.

"Will you stay?" She suddenly felt young and small and vulnerable. "I mean, come and stay in the house? At least for a few days."

"Of course," Jane assured her.

"Thanks." Realising Jane's agency might expect her to get straight on to other work, with other overnight stays, she added, "I'll pay you, obviously."

Jane smiled. "No need for that, my love. I'm due some holiday."

Delilah wanted to give her a huge hug, but she felt like if she did she'd be completely overwhelmed with emotion. This woman, this lovely woman, whom she hadn't even known very long, cared about her. Just simply cared about her.

Suddenly panic washed over her. What about the future of the manor house? Without Edie's funds, the place really would start falling down. There was already so much to sort out as it was. "There's the gable end and that dodgy boiler..." she muttered, then realised that must have sounded strange and random. "I'll have to sell the place," she said. *Over my dead body,* she thought immediately. "Or forget college and get a job. Not that that would even touch what needs to be spent here. Or worse, ask my dad for money and then he'll make me split it into flats and I promised myself I wouldn't let Edie down and already I'm—"

"Stop," said Jane firmly.

Delilah felt instantly awful that she'd been worrying about money and repairs at a time like this. "Sorry, I should be thinking of Edie," she said.

Jane took Delilah's hands in hers. "It's totally normal to think of things like this," she assured her, "and it's a good thing you've got a practical head on your shoulders. You're going to need it. Lots of girls your age wouldn't have a clue about any of this."

"Maybe it was that GCSE in Business Studies Dad made me take," Delilah said, darkly amused. "I wanted to do Art History as my option, but no." *Ha, maybe I'll do Art History A level instead now,* she thought, feeling strangely liberated.

Jane squeezed her hands. "Don't take this the wrong way," she said, "I wouldn't say a word against your father." She paused. "Well, I wouldn't have while he was still paying my wages, but now I can speak my mind. You make sure you do what's right for *you*, love. And I mean, about what you do with this place, about where to go to college, about everything. When you're young you tend to think that there'll be some magic moment, maybe eighteen or twenty-one, where you'll just start thinking and acting for yourself, but at the end of the day there isn't. I've seen what your father can be like, and if you let him push you around now, he'll be doing it for the rest of your life." She flushed. "I'm sorry, I shouldn't have said that."

"No, no, I'm glad you did, and you were right to," Delilah assured her. "He thinks he's going to train me like a dog to follow in the family footsteps, and end up like him. But I can't be that way, I have to be me." *When I work out who* me *is, exactly,* she thought to herself. *And I will be following in the family footsteps, but Edie's. My mother's side.* The thought brought a lump to her throat. If Miranda had lived, would she have been the Green Witch now? Would they have explored it all together? She'd have been prepared for it then, when her own time came, when she was far older...

She realised that Jane was speaking to her again and tuned into her words. "What I mean is, regarding the house and the finance, it really *is* all under control," she was saying. "There's money set aside for keeping this place up, and an allowance for you, until you come into your inheritance at twenty-one. I'll make an appointment for us to go and see Christopher Grey, Edie's solicitor. He's the executor of her will and the trustee of your inheritance. He's going to look after everything for you, so you don't have to worry. I've met him a couple of times and he's a lovely man. His family solicitors have been going for... oh, generations, certainly, and your great aunt's family, *your* family, have always used them. He'll explain everything and help you with anything you need."

"Oh," she gasped, taking it in. "So it really is okay?"

Jane nodded and Delilah felt a weight lift off her shoulders, which she didn't even realise she'd been carrying. She understood how attached to the place she must have become, to have been so distressed about possibly losing it. And, of course, now it appeared that she had a destiny here, although that still felt completely surreal as she stood in the kitchen with Jane, surrounded by the washing up, so domestic and normal.

"So, okay, good—at least I can keep the place going, for the moment."

"Well, if you decide to stay here, love, yes," said Jane, pulling clothes from the dryer now and dropping them onto the scrubbed pine table. Delilah moved to help her.

"But of course I want to stay here," she said, picking up a top of Edie's to fold.

"No one would expect a young girl like you to be holed up in an old place in the middle of nowhere," Jane went on. "After college, you'll want to be off travelling, working, seeing the world, I'm sure. We'll be able to arrange something—tenants or professional house-sitters."

Delilah was about to insist that she'd never live anywhere else ever but then found that she didn't have the energy and pulled a couple of Edie's cotton dresses towards her to fold instead. This place, falling down as it was—and located right beside the world's most horrible town—was her *home* in some fundamental way that went far beyond it just being the place where she currently lived.

"Don't worry about any of that now, okay?" Jane said then, reading the exhaustion right off her face. "Look, love, why don't you go and get a nice hot shower and then maybe try to sleep?"

Delilah nodded. The feeling that she was cared for was such a balm in itself, but she could feel sleep pulling her in, nagging at her to surrender to it, so she could begin to order and process everything that had happened. Hopefully whatever Edie had done to protect her would hold, and she wouldn't have to face any encounters with the Soul Hunter. So, after lots more hugging—Jane had burst into heartfelt tears over folding clothes that Edie would never wear again—she headed upstairs.

* * *

Delilah had fallen asleep in her clothes on top of the bed before ever reaching the shower. The Soul Hunter hadn't appeared in dreams or visions, though, so whatever Edie had done to protect her seemed to be working, thank goodness.

She'd been constantly busy once she'd woken from her nap, calling Edie's friends and talking to the funeral director, doctor and Christopher Grey the solicitor (Jane was right, he was lovely, and clearly upset by the loss of Edie). She'd tried to take in the information they had given her and failed spectacularly.

Now, at the end of the long, sticky day, she sank into a deep, bubbly bath. Neck-deep in creamy bubbles, she gazed at the taps until her eyes went fuzzy. In the silence left by Edie's TV noise *not* floating down the hallway as usual, she listened to the sound of her own breath. Of the air sustaining the life in her body. Soon she was breathing rhythmically on purpose again— four counts in, four counts out. It steadied her and filled her up, somehow—like another kind of sustenance, equal to food or drink, that she hadn't realised she needed. "I am alive," she thought to herself, over and over again, like a mantra. "I am alive, I am alive, I am alive. And I am the Green Witch."

She was so exhausted from the events of the day that, when she went to bed that night, she actually fell into a deep slumber almost right away. In those few minutes before sleep claimed her, she tried to think about the Soul Hunter and what to do next. She needed help, and she desperately wished Edie were alive and lucid to impart all her knowledge and wisdom. After that, her thoughts scrambled into the nonsense they always do right before sleep sets in, and soon she had surrendered to slumber, with no idea of where to even begin.

* * *

Delilah woke early, feeling refreshed and ready to face whatever the day held. The Soul Hunter, disguised as Tol, hadn't appeared in her room or been in her dreams either. *Thank you, Edie,* she said silently. It was like a kind of miracle, the way a decent night's sleep could change things. Her period had arrived too, flowing strong and bright red, and it felt good—like it had broken some kind of tension inside her, even with the cramps.

There had been no news from Cal about the real Tol in the hospital. She was due at the solicitors' office first thing, and she'd dashed off a quick reply to Mae's texts, so she'd know she was okay, well, as okay as she could be. But as she and Jane made their way across the gravel drive to Jane's little red car, she felt a pull in the opposite direction, back towards the gardens.

Somehow, she knew it was to do with the necklace. She tried to ignore the feeling and head for the car, but it was so strong that her legs actually felt heavy, like she couldn't have taken another step forward if she'd tried. Before she could think any more about it, the words were out of her mouth. "Jane, do you mind if we leave this for another day? I just feel like I need to go..." She gestured vaguely at the gardens, and the wildwood rising beyond. She reached for an explanation that would make sense to Jane, "for a walk, clear my head, you know, before all the busyness starts again."

Jane looked surprised for a moment but then she smiled. Her smile came from her heart and lit up her whole face. Delilah knew she was fond of her, but now, with Edie passing away, she could actually feel the warmth and care coming off her in waves. "Sure," she said. "Christopher will understand completely, given the circumstances. I'll call him and rearrange. Take all the time you need."

Delilah smiled back, wanting to match Jane's warmth, to

communicate how much care she felt for her too, but her own heart felt tight and constricted in comparison. The smile went wobbly on her lips as she felt this *lack* of whatever it was—openness, perhaps—in herself. As she wandered away, she was sure that Jane must think she just wanted some time to herself to cry the tears that hadn't yet come. She wondered when she'd started actually feeling the energy of people's hearts. Maybe it was just Jane's—she radiated such warmth you could hardly miss it, after all. Or maybe it was a Green Witch thing... She'd always been sensitive to moods and atmospheres, especially if they weren't good ones, and she felt quickly overwhelmed anywhere too busy or noisy, but this was something different.

Maybe this *knowing*, this *perceiving*, whatever it had been, had been activated at the moment of Edie's death, when the Green Witch mantle must have been passed to her. Or maybe it was triggered by starting to meditate and take notice of her breathing more. Or by her dreams and seeing Tol's spirit while awake—well, what she'd *thought* were dreams and what she'd *thought* was Tol's spirit. Things like that were bound to open something up in a person, weren't they?

Whatever it was, she was being pulled along by the feeling of knowing, round to the back of the manor house, through the half-laid-out gardens. When she'd called Bob with the news about Edie, he'd been shocked, and then given his condolences, which she could tell were heartfelt. He'd offered to put off coming for a few days, to give her some peace and privacy, but she'd insisted that was the last thing she wanted. She liked his calming, earthy presence. He and James were so good to have around.

James... there was something so compelling about him. She still hadn't shaken off that strange haunting feeling she'd got when they'd first met that she'd seen him before. Well, more than that—that she already knew him. She got a little dose of it every time she looked at him, too. She knew that she was grieving, and in shock, and there was no way she was in any state to even think about guys. Just seeing James. though, digging energetically, or kneeling down, carefully rebuilding the little wall of the herb gardens, lifted her a little. When he smiled at her it made her heart glow. *See?* she told herself. *Your heart* can *glow. You're not a total robot after all.*

Before she knew it, she was making her way through the wild bit at the back of the gardens, where they adjoined the woods. It was all so overgrown, and thick with brambles, that she couldn't be sure quite where the property ended and the woods began. If she could find the fence, or wall, or whatever it was, she could find the secret gate Edie had talked about. She didn't know why she was so set on finding it, she just knew that it was really important. She thrashed through the undergrowth and looked around her. After a moment, she noticed a thin path, lined with stinging nettles, weaving its way past the thick bramble bushes, and began to follow it.

A few minutes later, she came to the old stone boundary wall of the property, which was just taller than she was, and so covered in ivy that she hadn't even realised it was there at first. To the right was a solid wooden gate, half-covered in ivy itself and bolted from the inside. Delilah made her way to it, but she didn't go through. Something caught her eye, startling her, making her gasp. It was a tiny, thatched cottage, more of a hut really, almost hidden by the wilderness. She knew at once that this was why she'd had the feeling to come to the gate—because once she was there, she'd find the cottage.

She made her way carefully over to it and tried the door. It creaked open without resistance. She leaned as far forward as she could without actually stepping over the threshold and peered in. From the tumbledown, overgrown state of the outside, she'd expected to find—what? A few mouse corpses and old newspapers? But the sight before her made her gasp in wonder. Although dusty and dirty, the place had obviously once been loved and looked after. And it was full to bursting with mysterious ephemera. Bunches of dried herbs hung from the ceiling and smeared bottles and jars full of seeds, what looked like pieces of tree bark and dried flowers stood in rows on an ancient dresser opposite the smudgy window. One of the small glass panes was broken and ivy tendrils were creeping in and taking over the windowsill.

There was also a fireplace with a sooted-up wood-burner in it, and a battered kettle on top. A few chipped teacups were lined up on the windowsill. She wiggled open one of the dresser drawers to find a knife, string and scissors, and a heap of gauze and cotton wool. A large stone pestle and mortar stood on the dresser, accompanied by a few smaller clay ones.

In each corner of the room was a beautifully sketched charcoal drawing, on now-yellowed paper, taped to the wall. A hare, a pony, a white owl and a wolf. Delilah wondered whether Edie had drawn them herself, and why they were there. Suddenly she wanted so much to ask her great aunt this simple question, and about a hundred others, that she felt the gaping hole where Edie's presence had been, the stinging *lack* of her, and found herself sitting on the dirt-ingrained floorboards, sobbing her heart out.

When the tears finally ran dry, she noticed that one of the doors at the bottom cupboard part of the dresser was slightly ajar. She felt in her pockets for a tissue and, not finding one, wiped her nose on her sleeve, smiling at it being a very un-'nice young lady' thing to do. Then she pulled the cupboard door open a little further. Inside was a collection of chipped ceramic bowls, all stacked inside one another, and a wooden box, about the size of a large shoebox.

The box had a keyhole.

Her hand reached around to the back of her neck and, before she knew it, she was undoing the clasp of the necklace, putting the key into the lock and turning it. Then she felt suddenly frightened and pulled the key out again. What if there was some kind of really weird occult stuff in there? For some bizarre reason a shrunken head came to mind. As if Edie would have a shrunken head, for goodness' sake. But still, her heart was hammering, and her hands were trembling. She knew that Edie had meant for her to open that box, and that when she did, whatever it contained, there would be no going back. And she *would* open it. But she didn't want to do it alone.

It was time to call her friends over. And tell them everything.

Chapter 14

So that's how Delilah and her friends came to be standing in the little cottage Mae had immediately named the Witch's House ("in a good way!" she'd added hastily). Delilah had invited Mae and Cal over, and together she and Milly had filled them in on everything. After seeing the extraordinary green-gold light-force shooting from her palms, Cal was still giving her strange sideways looks, which she was trying to ignore.

"Oh my goodness!" Milly had gasped, as she'd taken in the dresser and wood-burner and rows of jars and dried herbs.

"Holy shit," Mae had muttered.

"Do you have to live here now?" Cal asked.

"I think this place is more like a home office," she quipped. Then she gave him a sincere smile. "So you believe me now? About all this?"

Cal nodded slowly. "I don't have much choice, do I, after what I saw. And if this Green Witch thing is real, it follows that what you're saying about Otherwood and Tol's soul is too."

"I'm glad you're on board with it, but can you please stop looking at me like that? I'm still me, and I'm not going to hex you or anything. Not that I know how." She frowned. ""Or how to help Tol."

Mae shuddered. "Urgh, it's so creepy, to think of some evil supernatural thing inhabiting Tol's body. We have to stop it. Well, *you* do, I guess. But we'll help."

"Absolutely," said Milly brightly. She was completely in her element in the hovel, *ooohing* and *aaahing* over everything.

"This is your Disneyland, isn't it?" said Mae.

Milly grinned. "Bloody right."

"Anything you need," Cal said to Delilah. A look of deep understanding passed between them.

Milly took a dusty jar from the shelf and held it up to the

light, swirling the dark liquid inside it around and around. "Oh, wow, maybe this is a magic potion," she murmured. Cal gestured for her to hand him the jar. When she did, he took off the lid and sniffed at it. "It's just really old coffee," he concluded. "Sorry, Mil. I don't think there are any *actual* potions. It's all just herbs and stuff."

"What do you think potions are made of?" Milly said dryly.

"Eye of newt and toe of frog," said Cal.

"I don't—" Milly began, but Cal cut her off, declaiming, "Wool of bat and tongue of dog, adder's fork and blind worm's sting, lizard's leg and owlet's wing—"

"Gross," said Mae.

"For a charm of powerful trouble, like a hell-broth boil and bubble," Cal finished with a flourish, looking triumphant. All three girls just stared at him. "What? I know some Shakespeare, so shoot me," he huffed.

Mae wove her arms around his shoulders. "You have hidden depths."

Cal fake scowled at her. "That's a compliment wrapped in an insult. Am I just a hugely handsome and fit but brainless hottie to you, then?"

Mae raised her jewel-studded eyebrow. "Mainly." Then the snogging commenced and Milly and Delilah, cringing in unison, turned to the dresser. Milly reached towards one of its drawers, then paused and glanced at Delilah. "Can I open this?" she asked. Delilah nodded, taking in that they were hers now— all of this was.

Milly opened the drawer and gasped so loudly that even Cal and Mae detangled themselves from one another and came over for a look. It was filled with crystals of all different colours, shapes and sizes, lovingly nestled in faded cloth which would once have been a bright purple.

"Nice rocks," said Cal. He pulled on Mae's arm. "Now, back to the kissing." But Mae stayed put. "They're beautiful," she breathed. "What are they?"

Delilah opened the other drawer and found that this was filled with even more. "I have no idea, or about what they do or how to use them," she added wryly, "but still… awesome."

Milly looked to Delilah before lifting out a pointed, craggy crystal with a purple base that turned to opaque white at the top. "Purple amethyst," she said. "I know this one is for healing." She gestured to a clear-white crystal next. "And this apophyllite helps connect you to the spirit realms. I recognise some of the others but I'll have to get my crystal book to check the properties. They all have different vibrations and are used for specific things."

Delilah gave her a smile, relieved that at least one of them knew something about all of this. "Thank you," she said.

"I'm starting to feel like I'm at some kind of girly psychic fair," Cal said. "All these crystals and dried flowers and things. Haven't you got anything hardcore? A shrunken head or something?"

Mae clapped him on the arm and gave him a glare that said *take this seriously*, but Delilah found herself smiling. "You know, I was actually a bit scared I'd find a shrunken head in here at first, or something else horrible. That's partly why I wanted you guys to be here when I open the box."

"What box?" asked Cal.

"I've found the box that goes with this key." She gestured to Edie's necklace. "I'm hoping it will give us some kind of an answer to what the hell is going on, or a starting place at least. But I'm too scared to open it on my own."

"Well, here we are, so let's crack on with it, then," said Cal cheerily. Delilah loved how he made the atmosphere so normal, when the stuff they were doing *so* wasn't. She crouched down and pulled the wooden box from the cupboard, sitting cross-legged in front of it. This time she didn't hesitate. She turned the little gold key in the lock and opened the lid. On the top of a stack of journals and notebooks—amongst what looked like some stones or crystals wrapped in cloth—sat a cream envelope. And on it, in Edie's spidery handwriting, was one word: *Delilah*.

Cal peered over her shoulder. "Aw, not even one *tiny* shrunken head," he sighed.

Delilah smiled at this as she carefully tore the envelope open along the top edge and pulled out several pages of cream paper covered in more of her great aunt's scrawly writing. "My dearest, darling Delilah," she read aloud. Another wave of pure *lack of Edie* washed over her and made her voice go wobbly and her eyes brim with tears. She handed the letter to Milly.

"'My dearest, darling Delilah,'" Milly read. "'If you're reading this, then that means I have departed this physical life, or that I'm completely incapacitated by dementia (I'm writing this to you now, before I am utterly lost to this cruel affliction). It also means that you know who, and what, you are, because I will have made it my final act, before going into the light or, indeed, slipping into the shadows of this syndrome, to find you, wherever you are, and to tell you the truth. So now you know that you are the Green Witch, and you understand the task that lies before you. You must keep the Soul Hunter's poison at bay with your incantations, enchantments and energy webs, so that he cannot stray beyond his realm, the Dark Woods of Otherwood.'"

"Erm—too late," Cal chipped in.

"Not helping," said Delilah.

Milly just raised her eyebrows at him and continued. "'In this box you will find my meditations, incantations, Green Witch lore, recipes for remedies and my plant medicine journal. All of these may help you and inspire you on your path, but they themselves are not your path.'"

"Huh, what does that mean?" asked Delilah, feeling panicky. "Do you think I can use her things or not?"

"Course you can, otherwise what the hell are you supposed

to do?" said Mae.

But Milly frowned. "I don't know," she said, "but listen to this. Edie goes on, 'If you are looking for potions and spells, then I'm afraid you'll be disappointed.'" She paused and sighed heavily. "Well, I for one am disappointed."

For herself, though, Delilah was relieved. It was like she'd been told she was this thing, and she didn't even really know what it was. She didn't want it to be anything scary or dark, and spells and potions felt kind of like both.

"'Unlike Wicca, Green Witchcraft is not a formal path. It is the way of the naturalist, the wise woman, the healer, the herbalist. "Magic" to the Green Witch is learning to harmonise herself with nature and understanding how its forces flow through her life, and indeed, all of life. Understanding this, and flowing and harmonising with nature, is the principle work of the Green Witch.' Wow." She paused. "Oh, Edie didn't say 'wow', I said 'wow'," she added, unnecessarily.

"Go on," said Delilah, hoping that as soon as she'd heard the whole letter, this feeling of dread and trepidation might go away. It probably would when Milly got to the part about what they needed to do to stop the Soul Hunter's poison from spreading any further, and how to rescue the souls he'd stolen.

"'The Green Witch's work is carried out via her intuitive connection with the natural world. While some other forms of witchcraft operate on a system of raising and directing energy at a goal, the Green Witch taps into the subtle flows of natural energy to gently align the human world with the natural world. To the Green Witch, all of life is magical—from the most mundane to the most heightened experiences. The Green Witch holds the principles of healing, balance and harmony as her guiding lights, and focuses her loving, aligning attention on the earth, humanity and herself, with compassion and kindness.'"

"That's you, kid," Cal quipped. Delilah couldn't help but smile.

"'She carries information between the natural and human worlds," Milly went on, "'and draws her strength and magical power from this collaboration with nature.'"

"Ah!" Delilah interrupted. "This is the bit where she'll tell me what I need to do to hold back the Soul Hunter. There'll probably be some kind of ritual and—"

"'It is up to each Green Witch to hone her own practice, based on her own unique relationship with the natural world,'" Milly read on. "There are no set rules, rituals or rites."

"Doh," said Cal.

Delilah took this in. Her heart sank. "So, no, I can't use her things then. In which case, I am in deep, deep trouble. What am I going to do? I don't know anything about any of this stuff."

"We'll help you work it out, don't worry," said Mae. "And you've already found a way into Otherwood, and done magic. That powerful force you were channelling when you came back, that was intense—we all saw it."

"Yes, but I didn't do it on purpose," said Delilah. "And I wouldn't know how to repeat it."

"'Her inner light guides her way and illuminates her path.'"

Delilah groaned again. "I don't even know what an inner light *is*," she muttered. "Edie really did pick the wrong person for this path." But the moment the words were out of her mouth she felt that knowing inside her well up into words. *You don't pick the path, the path picks you.*

"'Becoming truly present, the Green Witch merges with the energy of the natural world in each magical, precious moment. In this profound state of presence, she opens to harmony within herself, shares this with her community and experiences oneness with nature. To help her on her way, the Green Witch path focusses on seven energies: Harmony, above all, and Health, Happiness, Love, Peace, Protection and Abundance.'"

As Milly read this, Delilah felt herself beginning to relax, despite not having the answers about the Soul Hunter.

This Green Witch thing didn't feel spooky or scary or dark. Harmonising with nature, being nourished by the energy of the earth—it felt like the same thing as she'd experienced in the woods, when she'd just been walking and breathing and taking in the beauty. She could do that. She *got* that. It didn't feel *other* to her, like, say, putting on a set of clothes that didn't fit or suit her. It felt natural, part of her, like throwing on her favourite summer dress. So that was something, at least.

But what about Tol, and what about the Soul Hunter? How did any of this relate to *that*? That stuff was *way* scary, and *way* dark.

Cal was obviously thinking the same, because he said, "Surely just getting in tune with nature isn't going to stop this poison Edie talked about? The Soul Hunter is already using Tol's energy, and he made that owl attack you and nearly got you killed on the roof. Messed with your head so much you... The knife." All trace of his usual relaxed humour was gone from his face, and he was full of fierce protectiveness. "Who knows what he'll do next?"

"Not me," said Delilah grimly. "And sorry if that was a rhetorical question."

"Maybe if you can bring Tol back, his soul I mean, and get it back in his body, the Soul Hunter will have to stop using his energy," Mae suggested. "Like, he'll be pushed out."

"Maybe," said Delilah. She'd thought of that too. "But I don't know how to do that." She gestured down at herself. "For a start, I know it's stating the obvious but I'm physical. So how do I even begin? We're talking about Tol's *life* here, and I don't have a clue where to start. I'm *so* out of my depth with this."

She looked at Milly for answers, and reassurance, but her friend grimaced and said, "Let me finish the letter. There might be something more specific." She glanced at the paper again and found her place. "'I'm sure you're thinking that you'd like to have some clear instructions set out for you to help you enter

212

Otherwood and do all you need to, to keep the Soul Hunter's poison at bay.'"

"Too bloody right!" Cal snorted.

"Wait," said Delilah, hanging onto a little thread of hope. "Maybe she's going to give me some...Something, at least. A starting point."

"Maybe," said Mae. "I mean, there has to be *something*. Doesn't there?"

Milly continued reading as the other three listened intently. "'You'd like me to instruct you to use this herb, or that crystal, say this incantation and take that elixir, call on this power animal, and the essence of that particular tree. But it cannot be. The Green Witch's path is entirely personal, and is created intuitively in the moment, by the current Green Witch and her alone. Please trust me when I tell you that this letter contains everything you need to know to facilitate your journey. Once you have found your way into Otherwood, your next steps will become clear to you. You will intuitively know how to work your own magic to keep the Soul Hunter safely contained within his realm there. In the past, we haven't always succeeded, and we've been hunted and killed in this world too. Many of our beloved antecedents, the Green Witches who came before us, gave their lives in the fight.'"

Milly paused and stared at Delilah, looking utterly sick. Mae and Cal were silent.

"I could die," she breathed. "I could die doing this. And I've got no one to pass the magic on to. What would happen then?" Sudden panic gripped her. "I don't want to die."

"You won't," said Mae, but there was no conviction in her voice. "Okay look, the fact is, you might. But I can see that you have to do this. It's your destiny."

"I wish I could do it for you," Cal muttered.

Delilah, eyes shining with tears, nodded towards Milly. "Carry on."

"'This letter is the map, but it is not the territory'," Milly read. "You must explore that for yourself, and come to your own conclusions, in the now, and the now, and the now. And you must have courage, my dear, and know that you never walk this path alone. With all my love, forever, Edie.' And that's it," Milly said, refolding the sheets of paper and handing them back. "Sorry there's nothing more... specific."

Feeling completely lost, Delilah took her time sliding the letter back into the envelope, to gather herself. She placed it back on the stack of notebooks and journals and closed the lid. "'Once you have found a way into Otherwood'," she quoted mournfully. "But how do I do that? Once I fell asleep, and once I—well, maybe I did fall asleep, but it felt like I just kind of zoned out for a moment and then there I was. And last time I was dragged there, in some weird state where I couldn't function properly. There's no way I can rescue Tol like that. And there's nothing at all in the letter to help me."

"I know. It's shit," Mae snapped. "And this situation with the Soul Hunter is way more urgent than the letter implies. Edie's saying he's already contained in his realm in Otherwood, held back by her Green Magic, and you just have to find your own magic and keep him there. But we know he isn't. He's using Tol, and trying to kill you..."

"But remember, the letter was written a while ago," said Cal. "It must have been when the Soul Hunter was still safely contained. Edie said she couldn't keep up the magic, the enchantments or whatever. Perhaps you have to keep renewing it or he gets out. Maybe that's how he managed to get out into the owl, and take Tol's energy over."

Delilah laughed despite herself.

"What?" asked Cal.

She shook her head. "No, nothing. It's just, hearing *you*, say stuff like *that*. It's going to take a bit of getting used to, that's all."

Cal smiled for a moment. "Tell me about it." He pulled out his phone and checked the time. "I'm on shift in twenty minutes," he said, frowning.

"You're working?" gasped Milly.

"There's no one to cover me."

Seeing the look on Delilah's face, he added, "I don't think I should go, though. I'll ring in and say I forgot I've got an outpatient's appointment at the hospital. They'll just have to be short-staffed."

Delilah was really tempted to let him do that. In fact, she felt so lost and confused just then that she actually wanted to grab hold of all three of them and never let them out of her sight again. But instead she forced herself to say, "No, you go, it's completely fine. I need some time anyway, to try and get my head round all this and work out what to do. You're meant to be working this afternoon, too, aren't you, Mil?"

"Oh no, I couldn't just leave you to deal with all this," Milly insisted.

"No, really, go," Delilah said, "you'll get in trouble if you don't. And anyway, I can't take it all in right now. This whole thing—it's so huge. And this," she gestured at the letter, "this wasn't what I expected at all. In fact, maybe I need to *not* think about it for a while, and just let it settle in instead." She turned to Mae and Cal. "But I'll call you when I need you. I promise."

"Well, you'd better," said Cal.

"Is there anything we can do to help with the arrangements for Edie's funeral?" asked Milly.

"Thanks, but it's all organised, apparently," said Delilah. "Her solicitor told us that her funeral has been organised and paid for, and all her paperwork is in order."

The unspoken question—*did you inherit the house?*—hung in the air. No one wanted to be so crass as to ask it, but of course they were all thinking it.

"Yes, apparently it's mine," said Delilah, in answer to the

silence. "Unstable end wall and all."

"Well, we can help you with anything," said Mae. "Whether it's spell-casting or structural engineering, we're here for you."

Delilah smiled. "Thanks, you guys. That means so much to me, you have no idea. And I guess I don't really need to say this, but... let's keep this to ourselves, yes?"

Well, they all agreed on that.

"Come on then, this witch has work to do," she said, shooing them towards the door. Milly and Mae launched themselves at her at the same moment and enveloped her in a huge hug. Cal hesitated, but Mae pulled him in, and almost *over*, and they all held him up as he struggled to get steady on his crutches. "We're with you," said Milly.

"A hundred and ten percent," said Cal. "Well, that's an impossibility, but you get what I mean."

Delilah laughed dryly. "Looks like I'm going to have to get used to dealing with impossibilities."

* * *

Delilah saw her friends off in a taxi soon after, insisting over and over that she'd call them if she needed anything and let them know the *second* she came up with a plan. Her brain was so completely stuffed full and churning with everything that had happened, she knew there was no way she was going to get into the calm, clear space she needed to truly understand what to do next. So much information, and yet, she didn't feel that she had any firm answers at all. And the letter hadn't even mentioned "One", as she'd hoped it would when Milly had started reading. She wondered now if it was even connected to Edie being the former Green Witch, or to any of this. Maybe it was just a poem that Edie had liked enough to write everywhere.

Perhaps a cup of tea would help—that was the British answer to every crisis after all, and maybe it worked for supernatural emergencies too. As she made her way back towards the manor, she passed James and Bob, kneeling in a large patch of newly turned earth. "Working hard, I hope?" she teased.

"We could always do with a hand," came Bob's quick reply. "I mean, if you're not too busy with the funeral arrangements."

"It seems to be all taken care of," she said. "But I can't." The Soul Hunter wasn't taken care of, and Tol's soul was out there, trapped in the Dark Woods. What if the doctors decided that today was the day? Cal had promised to give her any news of the medical team making another attempt to bring Tol out of the coma as soon as he got it, and it could be any time. There was so much to think about, try to find out, prepare…

"Are you okay?" asked James gently. "It must have been such a shock, Edie passing on so suddenly. Looks like it's just catching up with you. Maybe you should go in and sit down. I could put the kettle on."

Delilah barely heard him, and, just as an overwhelming sense of panic threatened to engulf her, she managed to focus on the still, small patch of calm in the centre of her chest. She took a deep breath and felt her feet solid and steady on the earth below her. In that moment, she realised that gardening was *exactly* what she wanted to do, to get her body moving while her brain mulled everything over, and let it sink in. Getting her hands in some soil would really ground her. And it wouldn't be a bad thing to be close to James either. They hadn't even had a proper conversation, just smiles and waves and polite remarks as she went by or when she brought tea for them both, but he really was… Well, he had a beautiful energy about him that made her feel, just, *good*. And those green eyes…

Pull yourself together, she told herself firmly, feeling guilty and insensitive and generally like a terrible person. *There are far more important things going on right now.*

Ten minutes later, there she was, kneeling in the herb beds, turning the new compost into the soil with a trowel. She was working close to James, but the upbeat banter he and Bob had going had helped her skate over that initial awkward moment (okay, awkward *several minutes*) of being so close to him. James had knelt down beside her, and her heart had leapt and her cheeks flushed red, but thankfully he'd pretended not to notice. She'd busied herself with emptying the compost bag over her patch of ground, to buy time to compose herself.

Bob had offered her some gardening gloves but she'd politely refused. Every instinct in her wanted to push her palms into the soil, to feel it around her fingers. As she did, she felt as if her body were releasing some of its left-over stress and tension, letting it drain into the earth itself. She paused for a long moment, lost in this release, just allowing it. She felt James notice, but he didn't say anything about it and neither did she.

If she looked weird, well, *so what*?

Everything that had happened had really put things into perspective.

She realised that she was no longer having those constant thoughts about what other people might think of her, and the ways in which she could try to control what they thought. At school, she'd always been apologising, trying to explain herself, a ball of anxiety if she thought that one of the other girls had a problem with her. Now a lot of that had dropped away. Not all of it, of course, but she felt a new calm, a new steadiness. Maybe it was the Green Witch in her, the energy, the power, whatever it was, taking root already...

When she glanced up after a while, hands still in the soil, she found James smiling at her, like he understood that strong, deep connection to the earth. He was a gardener, after all. Soon the compost was all turned into the soil and they began to lay out the plants, in the places where holes would be dug for them. It was fun, referring to the original garden plans Edie had found for them, bless her heart, and passing the plastic pots to one another. After a while, they all stepped back, looking for the harmony and balance in their layout, and adjusting things here and there. Delilah wished that Edie could have been out there with them. Now it would be her memorial garden.

"The lemon balm should go in there," James was saying. Still miles away, Delilah unthinkingly reached out to pick up two lemon balm plants from the rows of little pots of different herbs, before James could point out to her which it was. "It's that one," he said as he gestured to it, but she was already lifting it, and their hands touched. A spark leapt between them. She could feel his energy, the essence of who he was. He was swirly green calm with a depth of heart, and a warming tang of humour.

"You know your herbs then," he said.

Delilah looked down at her hands in surprise, at the pots of lemon balm cupped in them. She didn't remember picking them up. And she wasn't quite sure how she knew they were lemon balm either, as the individual pots weren't labelled—they'd come in crates of twenty-four from an organic wholesaler. "Seems like I know this one anyway," she said, then found herself adding, "lemon balm for nerves."

"That's right," said Bob, who was riddling the stones out of the soil nearby.

Delilah studied the rows of pots, speaking as she pointed each herb out. "Feverfew for headaches. Calendula for cuts. Chamomile, oh all sorts—inflammation, asthma, fevers. Peppermint for stomach problems."

"You're quite the young herbalist," Bob remarked.

She felt a pang of loss, remembering what Edie had told her in the garden, about the different herbs. She'd been the Green Witch all along. *And I am the Green Witch now*, she said to herself in her head, letting it settle in. It frightened her—the bigness of it, the responsibility. But mostly she savoured it. Now she had this piece in place she could see that she'd always been reaching for some kind of missing part of herself, or for something *more* in the world around her. She'd never been able to work out why people seemed to be happy, or at least *okay*, with just *this*. With just the physical see it, hear it, smell it, taste it, touch it life. With the idea that this was all there was.

She'd never been able to feel God in the church services they'd been to with the school, or when she'd tried to pray—she'd hoped to, but never had. She realised now that she'd assumed she wasn't *okay with just this* because she was somehow damaged after what had happened to her mum. Now she knew that, in fact, she'd been yet to unlock some fundamental part of herself. And now that she had, she couldn't wait to explore it—even with the terrifying shadow of the Soul Hunter looming over her. Even with the risk to her life, and the responsibility for Tol. And what about all those others, bound to the Twisted Tree, ashen and fading? Was it too late for them already?

There were many more herbs laid out now for planting, and, as Delilah glanced over them, she was astonished to find that she knew them all. She felt suddenly shy, though, with James' intense gaze on her, and she didn't go through them all aloud. "I stayed here when I was little," she told them. "I remember this garden brimming with herbs."

"And it will be again," said Bob. "These may look like a scrappy little lot of specimens at the moment, but they'll grow up, fill the space out, and they'll love the soil here. You just watch…"

"Everything will flourish again," said Delilah, feeling the words in her bones.

Bob looked astonished. "Exactly," he said. "Have you ever thought about becoming a gardener?"

"You've got the feel for it," James said, and Delilah had to look away from his sincere green eyes before the big red flush that was creeping up her neck rose to her face and completely embarrassed her.

She let it fade for a moment, then smiled at them both. "I'd be a bit of a fair weather one, I'm afraid—running for cover the minute the rain started. You wouldn't see me at all between November and April."

Bob laughed heartily at this then went back to his work. James caught her eye, and they shared a moment of connection. She could feel the question in his look, and she knew that he felt her answer, that he understood.

There was just one word in her eyes.

Yes.

Yes, to James. Yes, to life. Yes, to the new path set out before her. The experience of facing Edie's sudden death, and the fact she might not come out of this fight for Tol's soul alive, made her want to grab life and live, live, live.

Chapter 15

The next morning was sun-soaked and balmy, and Milly and Delilah revelled in it as they made their way up to the woods. Delilah had slept again, with no visitations (she'd silently thanked Edie again for protecting her from the Soul Hunter, however temporarily) and she was finally starting to feel like her old self, even with the shock of Edie's death. Well, more like her new self, actually. She barely recognised the nervous, buttoned-up girl who'd arrived at the manor so recently, with her collection of smart heels and zero clue about who she actually was.

Mae was doing a stock-take at the restaurant with her dad, and Cal had an outpatient's appointment at the hospital. Both of them had offered to come too, but Delilah had insisted that she and Milly were just doing some initial exploration, not marching in to take the Soul Hunter on or anything dangerous. Cal had commented that it was all dangerous, then had promised to keep them posted about Tol's situation. The doctor had now told him that it would be a couple more days at least before they attempted to bring Tol out of his coma. This had been such a relief to Delilah, and to all of them—she had a little more time to work out what the hell she was supposed to be doing.

Delilah was wearing her favourite cotton dress, yellow with tiny blue flowers, and Milly was in a vest top and long boho skirt thing, her bracelets jangling as they walked. They had a small bottle of water each, but Delilah's was half-gone already and she was wishing they'd brought more. Who knew how long they'd be up there.

She slowed her pace a little and dropped into a continuous breathing rhythm, four counts to breathe in, four to breathe out, matching her footfalls. Milly sensed the change in her and slowed too, timing her steps with her own continuous breathing. After a while, Delilah's whirring thoughts slowed and she started to actually look around her as they walked on up the path, sometimes having to go in single file where it narrowed, or where brambles and nettles grew high at the edges. She watched the sunshine shimmering on the leaves in a kaleidoscope of patterns, and felt the light breeze on her skin, soothing and cooling. The mossy ground was soft beneath her feet and she was soon so completely absorbed in the present moment that she forgot she was looking for anywhere in particular at all.

A while later, far higher up in the woods, they came into the clearing. "This is the place I wanted to come back to," she told Milly, who started a little at her words, as they had been walking in silence for so long.

"I can completely see why," Milly said. "It's beautiful. It feels... enchanted, somehow."

"This is where I sat down to rest and meditated—and ended up fighting with the Soul Hunter in that dream. Well, I realise now it wasn't a dream," she clarified. "I somehow went through from this clearing to a parallel one in Otherwood, the one with the teapots and hummingbirds, where my water was pink. I realise now that that's why the Soul Hunter said, 'Nice place you've got here' when I saw him there." She grimaced. "Before he, you know, tried to kill me. I thought I had to find a way to get into his realm, that's why I went to the Dark Woods before, but that's too dangerous—he can pull me in and mess me up, totally control me. I won't have a hope if I go in that way."

"So you think if you go from here you'll be safe?" asked Milly. "Well, I mean, none of this is *safe*, obviously..."

"At least I'll have a chance. I think this is my place, my link between the real wildwood and Otherwood. The Soul Hunter has his and the Green Witch has hers." Referring to herself as the Green Witch gave her a sudden thrill and a strong sense of power and destiny. Unfortunately it was swiftly followed by total overwhelm. "Seriously, how am I going to *not* fuck this up?"

"You won't," said Milly. "This seems instinctive to you. I mean, even before you knew who you really are you were drawn here and felt the urge to sit down and try meditating. See, I told you it isn't all about chanting 'om'!"

Delilah smiled wryly. "Okay fine. Meditation is awesome," she said.

"So, what do you feel like you should do next?" Milly asked.

Delilah snorted. "Because I'm supposed to just *know*? You're the expert on this stuff."

"Maybe when you woke you did something to activate the magic," Milly suggested. "You know, by accident, and got transported to Otherwood."

Delilah smiled at this. "No, sorry to disappoint you once again, but all I did was meditate then fall asleep then when I woke up it seemed like I was there right away."

Milly pulled a face. "This real-life magic isn't as good as Harry Potter."

"Ha ha," said Delilah. "I just hope it works when I try again, without the falling asleep part. I can't promise I can do that to order when I need to so it's not an option we can rely on. I can't even be sure I can do the zoning-out thing that happened that other time. So... no time like the present, I guess."

"No time *but* the present," said Milly.

"You're so wise," said Delilah. "To think, all those hours I spent online looking at shoes, I should have been learning about balance and harmony and all things magical. You should be the Green Witch, not me."

"Huh! No thanks," said Milly. "Sorry, but what you've been through has been terrifying so far, and it's only the beginning."

And it might soon be the end, thought Delilah. But she kept the idea to herself as she settled herself in the same place she'd done before and closed her eyes. She felt silly with Milly watching her, but on the other hand she didn't want her friend to look away for a second. It was such a comfort to know she was there.

She took three deep breaths and let them out slowly through her mouth, and then allowed her breathing to settle into a gentle, rhythmic pattern, drawing in each breath to fill her lungs completely and then slowly letting it go. She allowed her thoughts to come and go, just watching them rather than getting involved, as Milly had taught her. When she did get engrossed in them, she returned to watching them as soon as she realised that she was tangled in some memory or imagined future event or conversation.

Just simply acknowledging the "what the hell are you doing?" soundtrack in her head seemed to really help calm it down, and soon she was breathing in her pattern again, feeling the gentle breeze on her face, aware of her body as an energy system, whirring with life. She dropped deeper into the meditation, forgetting anything but her breathing and her body as the instrument through which the air flowed in and out.

Soon she had the feeling that her flowing breath was part of something vast and universal, part of the pulse of all life. It felt like the air was breathing her, rather than the other way round. A beautiful sense of harmony and peace descended upon her and she spent what was probably (she couldn't really tell) a few minutes just *basking* in it.

Then, experimentally, she moved her fingertips and wiggled her toes and slowly began to stretch. It didn't feel like anything had happened, and she definitely hadn't gone anywhere. But she couldn't get upset about that right now, in this delicious state. Her body was so wonderfully heavy and relaxed that it was another minute before she opened her eyes.

When she did, she found that Milly wasn't there.

She got to her feet and glanced around the clearing. "Milly?" she called, feeling her heart start to pound. Milly had promised not to take her eyes off her, let alone actually *leave*. Where the hell had she gone? She thought that maybe she'd popped behind a tree for a pee, but that didn't make sense. She wouldn't have missed a second of this.

A brightly coloured bird flew across the clearing at that moment and hovered right in front of Delilah's face. As she registered that it was a hummingbird, her mind told her—at the same moment—that it couldn't possibly be. You didn't get them in this country. As two more zoomed overhead, jewelled wings beating so fast they seemed to vibrate, her heart began to pound in her chest. Then something caught her eye across the clearing, hanging from a tree, tied on with a blue ribbon. She peered at it. It was a tea pot. As she looked more closely among the branches, she spotted another, and another. "Oh my..." she gasped. She glanced down at her water bottle.

It was somehow full again, and made of thick glass, and the contents were bright pink.

"Milly!" she screamed, fear overtaking her. But only her echo replied.

She tried to stay calm and take some deep breaths, resisting the urge to scratch at her skin or throw herself hard at the nearest tree to try and wake herself up, reminding herself she wasn't asleep anyway.

It really happened, I'm really back here.

She'd wanted to come here, but now she was finding it hard to control her fear.

She whirled around, expecting the Soul Hunter to suddenly appear in Tol's form, like last time. She began searching around for the jewel-hilted dagger, but it wasn't there.

And then it was. Right at her feet. The emerald jewels of its hilt glinting in the dappled sunshine. As she gazed at it, a staggering realisation hit her. *I just thought it here.*

Suddenly a whole slew of ideas poured into her head: What if she'd created the teapots and the hummingbirds and the dagger by default last time, without even realising she'd been doing it? She'd always loved hummingbirds—if she ever got a tattoo, that's what she planned to have, on her shoulder. And the teapots and pink water in its odd bottle, like a Drink Me potion. Who knew if it even *was* water anymore? These things had made her feel like Alice in Wonderland last time, as they did now. What if she'd picked up on the otherness of the place, the falling-through-the-rabbit-hole feel to it all, and had the thought about Alice but barely registered it, *then* seen the pink water and the teapots, after she'd thought them there?

So, was this it, as she'd hoped?

Was this really her place in Otherwood?

Immediately, she just knew. *Yes it is.*

She recalled what else Tol had said—well, not Tol, she now knew, but still—that she should put some protection on it. She could almost see him leaning languidly against a tree, face battered, ribs broken, telling her, *You wouldn't want just anyone to walk in.* She pushed the image of him—lazing against *that* tree just there—away, in case thinking it somehow summoned him.

Protection. But what? How?

Maybe Edie's things would be a starting point.

She remembered how she'd brought the dagger here, by intensely wishing for it, and then she did the same with Edie's wooden box from the Witch's House. Maybe there would be something in Edie's journals to help her. She thought hard of the box, but nothing appeared and just as her stomach was sinking, she took a step back and her ankle knocked into something solid just behind her.

She swore in surprise then turned and crouched down, hurriedly opening the box. Or some parallel, non-physical version of it, anyway. The letter was right at the top, just as it had been before, and beneath it was Edie's pile of journals and notebooks, and some crystals. She pulled the crystals out and unravelled the cloth around them, watching them fall onto the mossy ground.

One was apophyllite, the crystal Milly had said was for connecting to the spirit realms, and she instinctively knew she wanted to use it, and just where she wanted to put it. She dashed across the clearing and dug a little hole with her hands, then placed it there at the bottom of an oak tree.

Then she ran back to the crystals. She surveyed the small pile, eight or so, on the ground. But none of the others seemed right, *felt right*, not like the apophyllite had. She remembered what Edie had said in her letter, that she'd need to find her own way…Trying to stay calm, she picked up the crystal she felt most drawn to, a small green chunk. She felt the energy of it. "It's like this but…" She didn't have the words to describe the energy of the crystal she needed, but she could feel it all through her body. She let this feeling grow and radiate, and she infused it with the same strong intention she'd had about the box, the sense of drawing it to her. She looked up at the pile of crystals again and to her astonishment found that there was one extra. It was black rather than green, a similar-sized unpolished chunk to the one of Edie's that felt most like it, and when she picked it up she knew immediately that it was right. She'd used Edie's crystal to help her find the feeling of it, but this one was hers alone.

As she hurried to the tree on the opposite side of the clearing and pushed the black crystal into the earth, she could already sense the feel of the next one she needed. It had a whole different tone to it, a faster vibration than the earthy black one. She turned and crossed to the trees to the left of her and made for one at the edge of the clearing, realising that she was defining four points, two pairs of opposites, like the points on a compass.

As she moved, her foot felt something hard and she stooped to pick up a clear, pinkish rough-hewn crystal about the size and shape of her little finger. Yes, it had exactly the same feel she'd just felt before it had come to her. For a moment her anxiety about the Soul Hunter gave way to pure thrill—she'd called this to her by feeling the *feel* of it. She moved swiftly over to the tree and placed it in the earth beside its trunk, between two thick roots.

Then she was running to the opposite side of the clearing, feeling the feel of the fourth crystal so strongly that she had no doubt it would come to her. She slowed and crouched low to pick it up—when she noticed it just ahead and put it into its place by the tree she'd been heading for. Four crystals. Was that enough? Was that all she was meant to do?

Not all...

Instinctively she made her way to the centre point of the clearing, kicking her shoes off and connecting with the earth beneath her feet until she could feel the point where the energy lines the four crystals were making crossed. She closed her eyes and breathed in deeply, pulling all four very different crystal energies into her body. She breathed them up, up, into her heart and there she weaved them together into a ball of golden light. She allowed this light to flow, on a stream of her breath, down her arms and out through the palms of her hands. She opened her eyes and gasped to find that she could actually *see* this light.

She held her arms out and willed the light to spread all around the clearing, sending it to every tree and stone. "As the new Green Witch, I claim this place," she found herself saying. "May only peace and harmony dwell here." She'd imagined that she might say something about protection, and keeping the Soul Hunter out, and also try to do something about him invading her dreams while she was at it. But that hadn't seemed right. By invoking only peace and harmony, she knew that he would not be able to enter. Focussing on keeping him out, she somehow knew, would be the quickest way to summon him here. The intention for peace and harmony in itself, and the combined vibrations of the crystals—all just *hers* in the way that Edie had explained—would mean that he could not enter, nor anyone or anything else unless invited by her.

She revelled in the beautiful golden-green light pouring through her, closing her eyes again to savour its deliciousness. Then she heard Milly calling, from far off, and, without thinking about it, she gave more space inside her to the pinkish crystal, letting the vibration of that one amplify—filling the extra space, changing the mix of energy she was flowing. Then she let the new mix of energies go, flowing to her heart and out through her palms. She felt a rushing sensation that pushed her head back slightly, as if she were moving at high speed.

When she opened her eyes again, she was back in the physical clearing with Milly fussing over her, relieved and concerned at once. "I didn't know what to do," she said breathily. "I knew you weren't asleep, but you were so still, and ten minutes went by and... Anyway, what happened?"

Delilah smiled a slow smile, still feeling the beautiful energies of her own four interweaving crystals, one of which was the same as Edie's, mingling within her, held in the glorious green-gold light. She knew this light was the basis of the Green Magic. "I've just been back there, to my place in Otherwood," she said shakily, "and it was fucking awesome."

Of course, Milly was a crackling ball of excitement after that and, on the way down from the woods, she made Delilah tell her every single detail. As they walked back through the manor house gates, Milly said, "Oh, actually, I *do* wish it was me. You're so lucky."

Delilah felt trepidation settle over her. Despite the incredible experience in her Otherwood clearing, she didn't feel lucky at all. *She* was the one who had to go from her beautiful, magical clearing to the Dark Woods, and face the Soul Hunter, survive it and come back with Tol's soul.

* * *

An hour later, Delilah had packed Milly off for her shift at the library, with promises that she wouldn't do anything either *cool or stupid*, in Milly's words, without her. Now she was standing in the Witch's House again, the drawer full of crystals open before her. Hunting through them, she soon found the four she'd placed in her clearing in Otherwood. These weren't literally the same ones, the size and shapes were a little different, but they were the same kinds, and held the same energy. She took a picture on her phone and sent it to Milly, to find out what they were, then wrapped them carefully in some cloth and put them into her pockets.

She was about to start going through Edie's journals in search of help with the task before her, when she found herself looking at the sketches of animals in each corner of the room, wondering why Edie had put them there. The hare, pony, wolf and owl. They couldn't just be for decoration—you wouldn't put something across a corner like that unless it was for a reason. Maybe they were Edie's familiars. But there weren't *actual* wolves in the woods, so they couldn't be—although perhaps there had been once, long ago.

Suddenly an image of the colourful hummingbird hovering in front of her in her clearing in Otherwood came into her mind. She gasped. Of course, they were helper animals, guide animals. She remembered that a friend at school, Jenna, had had a set of oracle cards on power animals, and that sometimes they'd draw a card to see what they got. Delilah couldn't even remember which cards she had picked now, and it hadn't felt meaningful at the time, just a bit of fun. But she'd always loved hummingbirds, and if she was supposed to have four power animals like Edie did, she felt that the small, jewel-bright bird *must* be one of hers.

She glanced at the pictures again and couldn't tear her eyes away from the owl once she'd looked at it. It was just like the white owl that had brought her back to awareness on the roof. It felt *hers*, as much as the hummingbirds in her Otherwood clearing. Could she have the white owl as a power animal, even though Edie had it too? She thought about the crystals—one of them had been the same as Edie's, and so she supposed that one of the animals could be too.

She looked at the pony again and thought of the beautiful wild ponies she'd seen in the high woods that time. She loved them, for sure, but a pony didn't feel like one of her power animals. She felt about in her consciousness, but no other animal presented itself, and she didn't see any flashes of anything in her mind's eye. She knew now how to feel a definite "yes" inside herself, and called a halt to her mind, which was parading every animal she'd ever heard of in front of her focus, to a stream of "no, no, no" feelings from her deeper consciousness.

That wasn't the way she wanted things to come to her. It felt like trying too hard. She wanted to be in the flow and just know the feel of the thing, as she had with the crystals. She'd felt that flow, and that "yes", with the hummingbird and the owl, and she was happy to wait until she could feel that deep "yes" about the other two—if, in fact, she needed to have four. She was starting to get a feel for what the Green Witch path was about. It was founded on intuition and allowing space for her deep knowing about things to come through, and on being able to feel it when something resonated with her. Drawing strength from the earth and filling herself with light and following her hunches…

As she relaxed into that flowing feeling, she found herself turning to the wooden box. She unlocked it and carefully lifted out the pile of notebooks and journals. This set off a wave of grief for the loss of Edie and, close behind, a wave of gratitude for having known her. She started to open the notebook on the top of the pile, planning to look through them all systematically from front to back, absorbing all the information she could about the path of the Green Witch. But just as she was about to open the first book, she stopped herself. That was the way she'd learnt to do things at school.

But this was different.

This was about allowing herself to be guided to the right information, rather than pushing forward, taking lots of action to search for it. *That 'trying' feeling again,* she thought. *Huh. You're told to try and try, but perhaps trying isn't always as helpful as I've been taught.* Then, as if in response and clarification, she heard herself think, *There's more ease in allowing than trying.*

She walked over to the scrubbed table and spread the books out, falling into her rhythmic breathing again. This wasn't something she could do with her logical mind—she was beginning to understand that. It was something she needed to do from the inside out, from feel and intuition. *Don't try, allow.* Relaxing, flowing with her breath, she put her hand over each book in turn.

As she moved her palm to hover over an old, tattered notebook, its cover adorned with pressed bluebells, she felt a jolt of energy. She picked up the book without hesitation and let it fall open at the centre, then instinctively turned two pages back.

On the left-hand side were the underlined headers Harmony, Happiness, Health, Love, Peace, Protection and Abundance. Delilah remembered these as the seven energies for a Green Witch to focus on, that Edie had written of in her letter. On the right were the fruits, flowers and essences which were associated with them, like frankincense and orange for Happiness, and lavender, white sandalwood powder and jasmine for Harmony. She felt especially drawn to violet, for Peace, and knew that would be important to her somehow.

In another notebook, which looked about fifty years old, she found a list of trees and their magical qualities. Milly had told her the names of the four trees she'd marked with crystals in Otherwood—Delilah had pointed them out to her in the real-world clearing—so now she could look them up. She felt that those trees were somehow *hers* too, like the crystals and the power animals. Not *hers* as in she owned them, of course, hers as in they were aligned with her energy and purpose. Milly had said they were yew, oak, rowan and hawthorn. And Delilah had jokingly said, "Don't tell me, you read a lot of tree books."

Edie's notes, her handwriting spidery even as a young woman, told Delilah that hawthorn was a magical tree associated with journeying to Otherwood and protection on both sides of the gateway. Oak was for courage and wisdom. *Well, I'll certainly benefit from both,* she thought wryly. *GCSEs did not exactly prepare me for this, after all.* Yew was for journeys into other realms. Rowan was for change and transformation.

Delilah typed these pieces of information into the notes section of her phone, intending to put them into a notebook later, along with the names of her crystals, when Milly got back to her about what they were. When she wrote this up, she'd be creating her *own* Green Witch journal—the first of many.

If she survived her showdown with the Soul Hunter, that was.

She let herself flow from journal to journal, dipping in and out, taking in Great Aunt Edie's writings about charm bags and magic balms, staves, flower wreaths and herbal remedies, poring over them way into the night. It was a completely different kind of learning, like nothing she'd ever experienced. It was an absorption, a remembering, a reactivating. Rather than making her tired, the more she flowed with it, the more alive and invigorated she felt.

Hours later, the natural flow began to ebb, and finally she knew that the session was over. She put everything away carefully and, at just after two o'clock in the morning, she began walking back to the manor through the gardens. The moon, just past full, was still bright, and she could easily walk without a torch once her eyes adjusted. She wandered over to the vegetable plot which Bob and James had turned their attention to creating, now that the herb beds were finished. She caught her breath as she saw a figure in the shadows. Whoever it was looked up, hearing this snatch of air. "It's me, James," came a voice. "Sorry, I didn't mean to scare you."

"What the hell are you doing out here at this time?" Delilah gasped, feeling her heartbeat banging in her ears.

"I couldn't sleep," he said simply. "Erm, you seem to be coming from the woods...?"

She smiled. "Oh no, I just took a walk in the gardens, because I couldn't sleep either." It was only a tiny little lie, and there was no way she was getting another innocent person involved in all this—especially not beautiful James.

"I think it's the bright moon," he said. "I'm the same every month. Is that why you—"

"No, no werewolf tendencies in me," she said quickly, keeping things light. Not adding that tonight might be her last night on this beloved earth. "But what are you doing in the veg patch?"

"Planting carrots." To her snort of surprise, he added, "Which is less random than it sounds, I promise you. The third period of the moon cycle, between the full moon and the last quarter, is just beginning, and it's the perfect time for planting root crops. According to Bob, anyway. He likes things done by the old ways. He didn't specify that it had to be done under the *actual* moon in the middle of the night, but I was up and there was nothing on TV, so I thought—"

Delilah grinned. "You thought you'd come and plant a few carrots. As you do."

He heard the invitation to flirt in her voice and took it. "It's not just carrots. I'm not *weird*. I've got beetroots as well."

As they'd been speaking, Delilah had moved closer and closer to him. Now she could see his face clearly, washed in moonlight. He looked back at her with the same open gaze. "You're beautiful," he said suddenly, then added quickly, "I mean, not the way you look..."

Delilah raised her eyebrows. "Charming."

"Well, of *course* the way you look, but I mean *you*. *You* are beautiful." He sighed. "That went well then."

The flow state she was still in, and the threat that faced her, combined to make her bold. "No, that did not go well," she said. "But this will." She stepped towards him and put her arms around his neck, gasping as she felt her whole body release at the touch of him. At his honey-flowing energy. And then she kissed him, long and slow, and he kissed her back, and the feeling was so exquisite, filling every cell of her being with pure delicious sweetness. No more carrots were planted that night, or beetroots either, for that matter.

Chapter 16

Delilah stood in her bra and knickers, hair wet from the shower, in front of her wardrobe. The doors were flung out wide and she was looking over her cotton dresses and checked shirts. Cal had called at nine thirty, waking her from the few hours' sleep she'd grabbed — once she'd finally managed to tear herself away from James.

They're bringing Tol round, it's scheduled for three o'clock this afternoon.

The call had shattered the happy haze she'd been in since her time spent in the Witch's House, and in the moonlit garden.

Time had run out.

It was now or never for Tol.

And for her.

What *did* you wear to take on an evil spirit in another, parallel, realm of reality? She felt like putting on armour, or a bullet-proof vest, but it was her soul that was at risk, not her body, and nothing could protect that.

A flash of green between two floral dresses caught her eye and she pulled their hangers apart to reveal a stunning dress. She swore loudly in surprise. That hadn't been there before. Edie must have slipped it in without her noticing, just before she died. She pulled the dress out and held it up to the light. It was absolutely beautiful, with intricate beading which seemed to be made from tiny crystals, and ivy leaves embroidered on the elbow-length sleeves and bodice. She glanced over at the picture of Great Aunt Edie which had fallen out of the airing cupboard that day when she'd first arrived, and which was now propped up on her perfume bottles. It was the same dress. She gasped, remembering that it was also the same dress Edie had been wearing when she'd appeared to her in Otherwood.

She took it carefully from the hanger and slipped it over her head. Seeing herself in the mirror made her catch her breath. She had to admit it looked absolutely gorgeous. And it fitted perfectly. Even though her logical mind was telling her that wearing it in the woods would get it dirty and possibly torn — like that mattered compared to the life and death task she was facing — she knew it was the right thing. The darkening sky outside foretold an oncoming storm, and a rain mac and wellies would have been more sensible, but then, if she started going down the road of thinking about what was *sensible*, she wouldn't have the guts to do any of this. She slipped on a pair of ballet pumps and headed downstairs. Milly, Mae and Cal would be arriving soon.

She'd thought about sneaking off early and doing this without them, to keep them safe from any risk, but the simple fact was that she was too scared. She really felt like she needed them, and now she understood that, although *she* was the Green Witch, they were all in this together. And anyway, they were already at risk. She'd sent a cab to go round town and collect them — she was paying, she'd told them, no arguments. She was surprised by how assertive she seemed to have got, and they had been too. They'd be arriving soon.

She picked up the small bag which held the four crystals and her water bottle, the same one she'd had with her both times in the clearing when she'd entered Otherwood. There was no point taking her phone — there wasn't any signal up in the woods. Her plan was that she'd know by the look of her water, or the pink liquid that replaced it, whether she was in Otherwood or not. *I'm sure the teapots and hummingbirds will be a bit of a clue too,* she told herself wryly, but still, it felt good to have a link, a reference point in both worlds.

She made her way down the stairs and along the front hallway. She often avoided looking at the pictures of her mum on the side table there, finding it too painful, but today she paused and took them in. "I love you," she breathed. Then she shook away the tears that had sprung into her eyes, took a deep breath and fixed her focus on the door. She walked out and turned back to look at the manor house, *her* manor house, holding the image of it in her mind, making sure she really had it. Just in case...

She pretty much walked right into James as she turned around.

"Hey!" he said cheerily.

"Hi," she said.

They both moved towards each other, then hesitated and drew back.

"Shall we just skip the awkward bit?" Delilah suggested.

James grinned at that. "Yes, let's. Nice dress by the way."

"Oh, thank you." Delilah looked down at herself and had to admit it—she looked good. Just then a cab pulled up at the gates and Mae sprang round from the other side and began helping Cal out with his crutches. "I'm going into the woods, with my friends. There's a... *thing* we need to do." She thought quickly. "Photography. For Milly's project. Hence..." She gestured at the dress. "But I'll come and find you, when I'm back." *If I'm back*, she thought, the smile falling from her face.

James took her by the shoulders and looked deep into her eyes. "Be careful," he said gravely. "And come back."

She blinked at him, astonished, for a moment certain that he knew what was going on. But that was impossible. That would mean he knew about all this, and who she was. And of course there was no way he could. He must have caught an expression on her face that she'd tried to disguise—a sense that there was a more serious side to what they were doing than she'd admitted.

The cab pulled away. Her friends were coming towards them. "I've got to go," she said hastily.

"Okay, see you later then," he said, far more casually. Maybe she'd read too much into his words. Maybe he just had an intense, protective side to him.

She took a few steps away, but he gave her such a long, slow beautiful smile—his green eyes glinting with mischief and fun—that she walked right back to him, threw her arms round his neck, and gave him a lingering kiss. When they broke apart, James put his forehead to hers and said, "Hello."

"Hello," she replied.

She did move away then, letting go of his hand at the last possible moment, and hoping with all her heart that it wasn't actually *goodbye*.

* * *

Delilah and her friends set off up the lane, heading for the woods. "Yes, apparently I am kissing James now," she told them, before they could ask. "It started last night when he was here planting carrots." Seeing her friends' questioning looks, she added, "It's a moon thing."

"Oh, of course," said Milly. "Just past full moon is the time to plant your root veg."

"*Of course*," said Cal. "I totally knew that."

"The point is not carrots," said Mae. "The point is, are you two together now?"

"I don't know," said Delilah, "but we're meeting later, if there *is* a later."

"Of course there'll be a later," Mae insisted. She was her sassy self today, clearly meaning business, and Delilah was glad of it.

"Have you—" Cal began.

"Cal!" squealed Milly, "that is between the two of them and none of your business!"

Cal blushed, which was very cute and endearing on someone so unshaven, leather-jacketed and borderline scary-looking. "I didn't mean that!" he protested. "That's you with the dirty mind, Mil! I meant, have you told him? About all this?"

"No," said Delilah. "I almost did, but it was nice to, you

know, just feel like a normal girl for a while. Maybe I will, though, in time. If there *is* time."

"Which there will be," chimed in Milly.

"And the kissing," Milly breathed. "Was it—"

"Amazing," Delilah finished, breaking into the wide grin she'd been trying to keep off her face since walking away from James. She, Mae and Milly did a kind of squealy huggy dance thing which made Cal roll his eyes and shake his head.

"I *knew* you were appreciating his gorgeousness, when you first saw him in the truck," said Mae. "Nice dress by the way."

Delilah smiled thank you, and Cal said, "Excuse me, his *gorgeousness*? May I remind you that you are *my* girlfriend?"

Mae cuffed him playfully. "I can't help having eyes in my head," she said. "She," she jabbed a finger at Delilah, "was trying to give me some line about only staring at him because she felt like she knew him from somewhere."

"I *did* feel that," Delilah protested. "I still do, though I can't place him, and when I mentioned it last night, he insisted he doesn't know *me*...I just did *also* register the gorgeousness."

The four friends' mood changed at they made their way up the field and into the woods. They had to take it slowly, with Cal struggling to get over the gnarled tree roots that sometimes criss-crossed the path. "Is there some kind of plan?" he grunted, as he shook off a bramble branch which had wrapped itself around his right-hand crutch. "I feel like we should have weapons or something, although I know that's pointless." He waved the crutch in the air. "I know it's like, 'Give Tol's soul back, or I'll *meditate* you into tiny pieces!'"

Delilah smiled at this, but it made her feel like crying too— Cal still trying to be funny when so much was at stake. The little sliver of normality it gave her for a moment just made the whole thing seem even more scary and alien when it faded. She pulled herself together—she had to be the one to take charge here. "There's kind of a plan," she said, "and kind of not. I know that isn't very helpful. I'm intending to drop through into Otherwood via my clearing and try to get to the Soul Hunter's realm, the parallel Dark Woods. It should be the same route as in this world. Beyond that, I'll be making it up as I go along."

"*Not* reassuring," muttered Cal.

"What shall we do if you go all scarily still again?" asked Milly.

"I probably will," said Delilah. "But please leave me. Whatever's going on, I'll know you're there with the physical me and that you've got my back."

"I wish there was more we could do," Cal said, his voice tight with frustration.

"Believe me, what you're doing is everything to me—I couldn't do it at all without you," Delilah insisted. She stopped and looked at them in turn. "Any of you. I don't know how I can ever show you how much you mean to me."

The girls were about to get emotional, so Cal joked, "You can pay us in home-grown veg, now you've pulled the gardener," and swung off at a pace.

The path up to the clearing was narrower, and they had to walk along in single file. Delilah, at the front, made her way carefully along, holding the dress up so that its hem couldn't brush the ground.

When she reached the clearing and entered the ring of trees, she couldn't help feeling lit up inside at the sight of it, the feel of it, despite the daunting task before her. The carpet of grasses, mosses and ferns was soft and dry. The trees that ringed it were majestic in the darkening sky. The air was warm and slightly muggy, the coming storm enhancing the woodland smells.

"I know this is the least of our problems, but it's going to tip down," said Cal.

"You're right, that *is* the least of our problems," said Mae. She turned to Delilah and asked, "Is there anything we can do?"

Delilah shook her head. "I don't think so, thanks. I'm not

even sure what *I* should do. I'll just get quiet and see what I feel."

"Good luck," said Milly, suddenly lunging at her and hugging her fiercely. Delilah hugged her back, finding herself holding on for dear life. When they finally pulled apart, Mae hugged her too, almost knocking the breath out of her. And then Cal did, just as ferociously as the girls, even with only one arm — since he could only let go of one crutch as a time.

Then her friends withdrew to the edge of the circle of trees.

It was time.

Delilah slipped off her ballet pumps, dropped her energy down, and tuned into the clearing. And into her own breathing rhythm. After a few minutes, she was moved to walk around the edge of the circle of trees. She walked round four times, each time placing one of the crystals beneath a tree, in the same way that she'd done in Otherwood clearing. She knew now from Milly that the other three were labradorite, Lemurian quartz and kyanite. Then she stood in the middle of the circle, feeling out with her feet for the place where the crystal energies crossed and amplified. When she found it and felt the energy pulse through her it almost took her breath away. It felt just as powerful as it had in Otherwood. She took the water bottle from her bag too, her marker, and dropped it at her feet.

As the energy coursed through her, she turned to the oak, where she'd placed the first crystal both here and in Otherwood. She and Milly had worked out the directions, and she'd been surprised to find that the trees she'd chosen faced due north, east, south and west respectively. She hadn't understood the significance of this at the time.

But she did now.

She could feel it.

The essences of the directions, the four elements, the trees, the crystals and her helper birds, well the two she knew of, anyway, would all come together to bring her the blend of energy and power she needed for her journey to Otherwood.

Once she'd called them in.

She closed her eyes and drew in a deep breath. For a fleeting moment she felt a bit silly, and then the momentum of what they were doing, and how much it mattered, overtook her. She raised her arms high above her and faced the oak. "I call on the energies of the north, the oak, the earth and white owl to give me courage and wisdom on my journey, and in my life always." She took a deep breath in, right to the depth of her being, and then let it go slowly.

She turned to the east. "I call on the energies of the east, the air, the hawthorn tree and hummingbird to keep me present and free, on my journey and in my life always." She took another deep breath, let it out slowly and turned to the south. "I call on the energies of the south, of fire, of snake," —she intuitively knew this was her third power animal, even as she said it—"and of the rowan tree, for transformation, on this journey and in my life always."

She turned to the west. "I call on the energies of the west, of water, the yew tree and the deer," she said, as an image of the deer looking at her in the clearing flashed up in her mind, "for healing, and for trust, on my journey and in my life always."

She took another deep breath, drawing all four of the crystal energies, now infused with the elemental, directional, tree, and animal energies she'd called in too, up on their stream of green energy through the core of her. They mingled together and filled her heart, and from there, her whole being. As she breathed out, the air flowing from her on a stream of this powerful energy, she said, "And so it is." She'd seen that phrase written at the end of incantations in Edie's journal, and saying it just felt right.

Then she sat down, careful to stay right on the place where the crystal energies crossed, and closed her eyes.

This time there was no wandering mind, or thinking she'd fallen asleep, or long wait. It just happened. A moment later, when she opened her eyes, she was in her clearing in Otherwood. Her friends were no longer there, and her water was now pink, the bottle made of heavy glass, just as it had been both times before. The green-jewelled dagger was in the grass beside her and instinctively she picked it up and tucked it into the cord around the waist of the dress. Now she wasn't panicking, as she had been last time, she could tell that she was in another reality. There was a whole different texture to the place. The clearing sparkled with life force, with nature's energy, and she felt seen by it, and known.

Welcomed in.

The emotion hit her like a wave, and she wasn't ready for it at all. She found herself curled up in a ball on the grass, sobbing and moaning, letting all of the left-over anxiety and fear from what had happened with the Soul Hunter pour from her and into the earth below. And the shock and grief of losing Edie. And the burden of who she was, and what she had to do, and how completely unprepared she felt. She cried, and rocked, and screamed and yelled, and strange noises came out of her as tension held deep in her muscles released and cleared away, sometimes making her jolt forwards or gasp with sudden, powerful movements.

For a long time, she was lost in the momentum of it all, hardly aware of herself and yet completely focussed on her body, letting it do what it needed to do, letting it channel all the stuck and repressed emotions out of her and into the earth. And all the time she felt held by the ground, by the woods, by the trees around her and also by that place inside her where the feeling of connection with the green energy was held too. That place was in her heart and was at the heart of her.

When she finally focussed back on her breathing, she felt a few drops of rain on her face. She came to a stillness and opened her eyes. The feel of the air had changed. It was now heavy and ponderous with the gathering storm. A breeze was blowing up, chasing the mugginess away. Her jewel-bright hummingbirds flitted around her, and then took shelter in the trees.

Suddenly, the sky lit up with lightening, and then, a few seconds later, thunder rolled and boomed. It sounded far away, but she still got to her feet. She silently thanked the clearing for holding her and supporting her, and took one last look at her hanging teapots, which felt strangely comforting now. Then she made sure the dagger was secure in her belt and set off on her journey.

The woods outside her clearing were the same as the ones in the real world, and she soon found the series of small paths which led from there to the Dark Woods. She'd never gone directly there from her clearing in reality, but she instinctively seemed to know the way. It was raining harder now and lightening flashed across the sky. She hesitated when she reached the throng of trees which were whispering malevolently, just as they sometimes did in the real world, her stomach lurching.

The sight of the souls bound to the Twisted Tree tore at her heart. Most were completely ashen, almost vanishing into the tree bark—so grown over with ivy that they'd almost become part of the tree. And there was Tol, the only one with a faintly glowing ember of light at his chest.

Her fingers closed around the handle of her dagger, and she ran through her plan in her mind. She'd slip into the Dark Woods unseen, free Tol's soul, and hope that it was somehow magnetically drawn back to his body, as Milly's theory went. If it didn't, she'd have to try and take him to the hospital somehow—she reasoned that if the Soul Hunter had taken Tol's soul from there to here, she could take him from here to there. But how—she had no idea. It wasn't much of a plan, granted, but it was all she had.

She took a deep breath, grounded her bare feet deep into the earth, called forth all her courage and stepped into the clearing. Well, tried to. The moment her foot touched the ground beyond the tree circle, a searing pain shot through her body, making her shriek and leap backwards. It was as if there were an invisible electric fence holding her out. She pulled herself together, squeezed her eyes shut and took another run at it, but this time the pain zapped through her so forcibly that she was thrown backwards and landed hard on the ground. She gulped at the air, too winded to sob at the pain throbbing through her, as bright and sharp as if someone had sliced a gash right across her chest.

"In your world that's called breaking and entering." The voice made her shudder with cold terror. She looked up to find the Soul Hunter, still in the form of Tol, leaning against the Twisted Tree, regarding her with casual interest. "If you want to come in, you only have to ask."

Delilah stumbled to her feet and steeled herself. The Soul Hunter gave her a slow, wolfish smile and made an expansive gesture with his arms, inviting. She took a tentative step towards the invisible boundary, keeping control of every animal instinct in her body that shrank from pain. She forced herself to step across the invisible boundary, flinching. But nothing happened. She stepped again and again, willing herself forward.

"You're letting me in," she said, trying to keep the tremble from her voice. "You're just *letting* me walk in."

He shrugged. "Of course. I was expecting you."

"Who are they...?" She gestured at the pitiful, macabre figures bonded to the Twisted Tree.

"My souls," he said, proudly. "I can become any of them — in this world at least. I would show you my true face, but I don't have one. Or if I have, I've forgotten it. It's been so, so long, you see. Centuries. Millennia, possibly. None of them work in your world anymore, only here. Except Tol's, of course."

Delilah winced at this. *They're all dead in my world*, she thought. *But their souls are trapped here. And he's talking about them like cars that won't go any more. Sick.*

247

"They haven't functioned for a long time," the Soul Hunter was saying. "That's why it was so delicious to add Tol to my collection. It gave me a new lease of life and a way out of Otherwood, into physical reality. Your world is *so*..." he rubbed his fingers together, searching for the words. "Well, it's the texture of it, isn't it? It's exquisite."

She startled as, suddenly, he was right beside her. She planted her feet firmly. She wouldn't step backwards, wouldn't give up her ground. "The see it, hear it, taste it, touch it *reality* of it," he whispered into her ear, making her stomach flip over in disgust. "That's why I'll be ready when he wakes up. Ready to make my move. Get myself a permanent base in your reality. I've almost forgotten how much fun it can be in the physical world, those hags have kept me here for so long. But then the last one went crazy and I took my chance."

"Edie didn't go crazy, she had dementia," Delilah said stiffly. "And she's not a hag." She wanted to scream at him for talking about Edie like that, but she made herself keep her temper. She needed a cool head to work out what to do next.

"And then you—your fear, all that energy—gave me even more power," he said. "Enough to play with all kinds of things—gas stoves and engines and loose bolts..."

"I'm here now, so leave my friends out of this," Delilah stuttered. "This is between you and me." When he didn't respond, she went on, "You knew what I was all along. That's why you came after me in dreams and appeared in visions. It was never anything to do with Tol and what happened between the two of us in the woods, was it?"

The Soul Hunter laughed softly. "No, nothing to do with that at all," he said. "Although I saw your little altercation. Well, sensed it. His fury drew me out of the Dark Woods, I came riding on it like a wave, as my owl. So delicious. I can do that, you know, when the energy is strong enough. Nothing like as good as actually having a human body, but still. That's why I was with Tol when he crashed the bike, after I visited you in the Dark Woods, of course." He licked his lips. "He was so, *so* angry with you."

Delilah shuddered at the memory of the owl screeching, lunging for her throat, but forced herself to stay silent, not to rise to the bait.

"So, I was there, riding his anger, *and* all his self-loathing," said the Soul Hunter conversationally. "Exquisite mix, don't you think? Well, you would know." He gestured towards Tol's form, bound to the Twisted Tree. "You're two of a kind. You're as bound up inside as he is to that tree. Well, you were." He looked her over with relish. "Now you've got a taste of the Green Magic, you're getting a bit of the wild about you."

Delilah bit her lip, refusing to give him the satisfaction of a reply.

"I have to admit, it was convenient that you were already frightened of my new... persona," the Soul Hunter continued. "It made things more fun."

Despite all her resolve to stay quiet, Delilah found herself shouting at him. "You could have killed my friends! You destroyed my sanity, and you almost made me walk off the roof! And slit my own throat!"

"Exactly. Fun."

Just then, Delilah instinctively knew that it was time to take action. She focussed inside herself and found the feeling of the mingled energies she'd created in her clearing. She drew them up, on a stream of green-gold light, until she thought her heart would burst—breathing the ball of light and energy bigger and bigger and bigger in the centre of her chest.

The Soul Hunter watched, amused. "Been learning some magic tricks already, have you?" he asked mildly. "I'm impressed. I thought you'd still be stumbling around in the dark at this point."

"More like basking in the light," she said, as she let the

green-gold light energy go. It coursed through her in a powerful stream, poured from her palms and hit the Soul Hunter in the chest, knocking him backwards. The light pulsed into him, and a strange unearthly scream came from the depths of his being.

The light continued to pour from her, and she kept her focus on it, ignoring her horror as he writhed on the ground beside the Twisted Tree. His eyes were pleading with her now, all his gloating gone. The sight of him still scared her, but she held onto her courage and didn't stop pouring the green-gold light onto him. *Into* him. A terrible shriek escaped from his lips, opening up the split again, sending blood dripping onto the soft earth. But she didn't stop. Soon he was slumped, unconscious.

Dead, maybe?

Was that too much to hope for?

She'd never felt so alive, so empowered. But she couldn't be complacent, and she had to hurry. Tentatively, giving him a wide berth, she made her way over to Tol and wrenched at the ivy tendrils that grew over him like a living prison. One came away, then another. His eyes flicked open for a moment and he looked at her. The faint ember at his chest glowed a little brighter. "It's okay," she breathed. "I'm going to get you out of here. You're going to be okay. It's all going to be okay." And for the first time, she began to let herself believe it.

But then suddenly her body convulsed hard, and she gasped, feeling as if she'd been punched in the stomach. What the hell was that? She steadied herself and focussed back on freeing Tol. But another convulsion came, and she was thrown backwards. If felt like someone had picked her body up and hurled it like a rag doll. She landed hard. Suddenly her white owl was flying around at the edge of the circle of trees, screeching and flapping its wings wildly.

"Oh my God, what's happening?" she cried out. Instinct overtook her and she just knew that she had to go with her owl. Right now.

But Tol...

She whirled around and hurried towards his bound-up body, pulling her dagger to try and cut the ivy, to free him faster.

But then she felt every single fibre of her being resound with one single word.

Run.

With an anguished look at Tol's bound soul, she left the Soul Hunter in a tangled heap on the ground and ran as fast as she could after her owl.

She hardly felt her bare feet connecting with the leaf-scattered, stone-strewn earth as she raced along, dodging branches and brambles. Her owl flew above her, slightly ahead, screeching as if its lungs would burst. She just wasn't fast enough... She had to get back to the clearing *now* but she wasn't...

Her body gave another huge jolt, as if she'd been kicked in the stomach, and she stumbled and fell, winding herself, getting a mouthful of dirt. She staggered to her feet and noticed a doorway, in the middle of a path to the right of her. It was so well-hidden she hadn't seen it on the way to the Dark Woods. And if she hadn't fallen just now, just there, she wouldn't have seen it at all. She wondered where it led to, as she began to run again, keeping her owl firmly in the centre of her vision, spitting out dirt. Then she took in the significance of the door being there. This wasn't the real world, it was Otherwood. And in Otherwood there were doors in the middle of woodland pathways, and daggers could appear, and green-gold power-light could shoot from her palms and in that case perhaps...

She turned her focus upwards and imagined her heart, her soul, melding with her owl's. Almost before the intention was fully formed, she was looking through her owl's eyes, soaring through the rain-sodden wood, expertly gliding past tree trunks. For a moment she was lost in the pure thrill of it.

The delicious freedom.

Then they were at her clearing, and she imagined herself

running along the ground looking up at her owl and the next instant she was doing just that. She threw herself down in the spot right in the middle, took a glance at her pink water in its thick glass bottle, and closed her eyes, forcing herself to take a slow, deep breath, despite the urgency she felt inside. As her body convulsed again, she opened her eyes and just caught a glimpse of her plastic water bottle and its clear contents. Then she felt a blinding pain in her head as a leather biker boot kicked her right between the eyes. Seeing stars, she swallowed down the vomit that had risen into her throat and tried to sit up.

Tol was standing over her, his ribs bandaged, his leather jacket over his hospital gown, jeans pulled on underneath. He held Mae tight round the neck, a knife to her throat. Her eyes were wild with terror, but defiant, even now. Cal was nearby, angry, and anguished. Milly lay sobbing in a heap. Delilah felt so desperate for all of them that she thought she'd die on the spot. She felt for the dagger at her belt, but it wasn't there in this reality.

"I've told them if they try anything, she's dead, and that goes for you too," Tol said gruffly. His voice was scratchy, and Delilah realised this was from lack of use and perhaps also the breathing tube which had been down his throat in the hospital. So strange, the things you thought of, in times like these, your brain working at lightning speed. Three o'clock. That's what the doctors had said. They should have had hours yet...

"Let her go," she said, trembling so much she could hardly get the words out. Her body ached all over and her head and right leg throbbed. All those convulsions she'd felt—each one must have been a blow, as he tried to bring her back.

Bring her back...

"But you were *there*," she stuttered, not understanding. "In Otherwood... I..."

"You thought you'd defeated me?" he asked. "Well, I admit that you raising Green Magic was... unexpected. It caught me off guard. Who knew you'd come so far in such a short time. Fortunately, you're a long way from being able to channel that power in any meaningful way in this world, or you might actually become a problem for me. The thing about being multi-dimensional is that I can be, you know, here and there. And in between—in your dreams, in visions, liminal spaces." He shrugged Tol's shoulders hard and his ribs crunched sickeningly. "But I do like being mortal. I might bring my whole self here, who knows."

Delilah ignored this. She fixed him with a steely glare. "Let Mae go, take me instead."

Just as Mae cried, "Delilah, no!" the Soul Hunter sighed dramatically and said, "I thought you'd never ask."

He threw Mae away from him like a discarded toy and she collapsed, sobbing, onto Cal. In that split second, Delilah tried to run, but he grabbed her. Tol's powerful hands clamped around her arms.

She was suddenly filled with a blind fury. How *dare* he do this? To her friends. To those souls trapped in the Dark Woods. To Tol. "You fancy being mortal?" she yelled. "Well, see how you like this!" She bent double suddenly, pushing the full force of her body into his still-broken ribs.

The Soul Hunter howled with pain and surprise, and she took advantage of this to kick his shin hard and knock the knife from his hand. As she ran from the clearing, shouting that she'd get help, the last things she saw were Cal hurling himself onto Tol's body, crutches flying, and Milly scrabbling in the grass for the knife.

Chapter 17

Delilah ran until she was gasping for air and her legs were so wobbly she couldn't go on without stumbling. She vaguely registered that the hem of the dress had ripped at some point and a big chunk of fabric was completely missing, leaving her right leg exposed, the bare flesh flashing in her eyeline as she ran. If she went directly downwards from here, she could join the main path that ran through the wood and get back to the manor. Then she could call an ambulance and bring James and Bob back to help. She wondered if Cal still had hold of the Soul Hunter. She desperately hoped that Milly had made it to the knife.

She crept out of the undergrowth onto the main path and began to hurry along, stumbling and staggering now on her trembling legs in the near darkness, rather than sweeping along at a smooth jog as she'd planned.

A faint noise in the distance began to grow louder, and the uneasiness in her stomach spiked. She picked up speed as the growling, guttural sound drew closer. Then all at once she knew what it was, and her breath caught in her throat.

An engine.

Suddenly the path was flooded with light, and the roaring noise felt sickeningly close. She willed her legs to go faster, refusing to let herself look back, instead glancing left and right to see if she could fling herself off the path. But the bushes to the sides of her were thick and high. She screamed as she felt the sheer power and brute force of the thing behind her, heard it kicking up the dirt and bringing down low branches.

Tol's motorbike.

Well, *a* motorbike. She guessed his own had probably been a write-off.

Cal must have lost hold of him. Her stomach lurched. Oh,

God, Cal… All of them… What if…

But all thoughts left her mind as she stumbled and almost fell. He was going to mow her down.

And then what?

If she was still alive after that, it wouldn't be for long. Pure cold terror gripped her. She felt like she was only just beginning to know herself, and…

It was over.

She turned and blinked into the headlights as the bike roared towards her, churning up leaves and slipping on the uneven mulchy ground. Even as she knew the futility of the gesture, she raised her hands above her head in surrender.

The motorbike didn't stop. Tol's body, hunched over it, didn't waver.

Ten more seconds and the bike would hit her. She could make that twelve, fifteen if she ran fast. She turned and sprinted hard. She'd take it all, every extra second she could get of beautiful, rich, precious *life*.

The next moment, she was aware of a huge commotion in the dense bushes to her right.

Then suddenly they were there, beside her on the path.

The wild ponies.

Delilah didn't hesitate. She caught the eye of the closest one as she ran alongside it, seeking a connection. She felt it join with her and then, in one swift move, she vaulted onto its back. She clung onto its mane as it galloped away at full pelt with her, flanked by the others. Fear, thrill and chaos seemed to exist within her all at once. There was distance between them and the bike now, but it wasn't stopping.

The ponies were fast, but the bike was faster.

Delilah was flooded with panic again and urged them on with everything she had.

The bike was gaining on them. Everything inside her railed against the ponies being hurt, but there was nowhere for them to divert to. They rounded a blind corner on the path, the bike at their hind hooves like a rabid, raging predator, and Delilah screamed to see a fallen tree blocking the way straight ahead of them.

An image of the ponies' bloodied, broken bodies flashed in her mind, but then, with a great leap, the two in the lead were jumping over it, and then her pony, and the others too. Instinctively, she folded forward, her fingers curled tight around his mane, her thighs and knees closing against his sides. They landed, flanked by the other three ponies, and Delilah bounced on his back then caught her balance and her breath as they shot off at a gallop again.

It was only when the earth-shuddering smash rocked through her that she thought about the bike. She glanced back to see both Tol's body and the bike flying through the air. Then she focussed forwards, and let the ponies take her far away. When the path narrowed, the ponies dropped into a canter, then a trot, and soon they were walking, picking their way through the undergrowth, sure-footed even in the densely wooded gloom.

After a while, Delilah could see the light marking the edge of the field, and her ragged heart leapt. She stilled her pony, and the others came to a halt with him. She slid down and hugged him fiercely around the neck. "Thank you," she said into his mane, half sobbing with relief and gratitude. She turned to the others, so beautiful, so powerful, and so, so brave. She thought her heart would burst. "Thank you."

Then, suddenly, lightning struck nearby again, and thunder rolled around them. The ponies bolted off at a gallop—making for the higher woods and the open land beyond, Delilah realised. She watched them go, hooves flying, tails whipping—it was pure instinct in motion.

Then she turned to the light coming from the field and began to make her way towards it. There was no way she was going back to try and help Tol. It wasn't even Tol. It was just his body—Tol was bound by ivy in Otherwood. And anyway, what if she went back and Tol's body wasn't badly injured? What if the Soul Hunter grabbed her again?

Suddenly, a white owl swooped above her, hooting, startling her. She was sure it was the same one she'd seen from the parapet, and from her window. She understood on some deep level that what she'd suspected was true: This white owl was connected to her white owl in Otherwood, the owl whose consciousness she'd blended with, to allow her to become one with it, and fly.

She got steadily closer to the light as she picked her way down the narrow path, moving as quickly as she could. Then she was there, at the tree line, by the field. The main path down was further along, far to the left of her. Here, she was almost at the manor house. She planned to stride straight out across the field, taking the most direct route down to the lane. She'd have to climb the fence, but she could run all the way back and she'd be able to call for help within minutes. She stepped out onto open ground.

For a sweet second she felt the spacious freedom of it. Then, suddenly, Tol's body lurched out of the trees to her left. His arm was mangled and hung at an odd angle, and his nose was bloody and broken. There was a deep gash on his forehead. His mouth grinned at her, teeth red with blood from his lip, which had re-split, spit oozing.

She screamed and ran, but the Soul Hunter was too fast for her.

He lunged at her, Tol's one still-strong arm clamping around her throat.

She tried to scream again, but Tol's hand was tight over her mouth, the salt taste of sweat on her tongue.

Her mind registered that somehow, incredibly, the Soul Hunter had walked Tol's body away from the smash with the log. And found his way to the treeline. A human would have known to stem the bleeding—would have been kept down by the pain. But the Soul Hunter wasn't human, and he didn't seem to care what happened to his 'precious' mortal vessel.

There he'd watched for her, waiting, like a hungry wolf.

"How did you get away from Cal? Did you hurt my friends?" she demanded, heart pounding with fear at the answer that might come.

The Soul Hunter wasn't even listening. He was looking at the exposed bloodied flesh of Tol's arm with mild interest. "Human bodies," he breathed, into her ear. "Sweat. Tears. Skin on skin. All that... blood. Delicious. I've ruined this one, I can see that. But I'm strong now. Now I'm here, I can easily get another."

"You're sick!" she spat.

"*You* drove me to this," he said. "You only had to give your consent—that was all. It would have been... exquisite." He paused, seeming to savour this thought, then his expression soured. "Now it will be, well... unpleasant."

Delilah barely took this in. She gave a sudden gasp as the Soul Hunter drew a gleaming knife from inside Tol's jacket. She jerked away but he was too quick for her and he hauled her tighter against him and pressed the blade firmly to her throat.

Delilah's survival instinct overrode her shock. She let all her muscles go and dropped back on the Soul Hunter, creating a few millimetres between her skin and the blade. Then she powered upright again, bent sharply double, and lashed out a heel to kick him hard in the shin at the same time. He cried out in surprise and broke his hold for a moment—just long enough for her to drop to the ground.

He leapt on her like a panther lunging for its prey, all power and instinct despite the injuries, the knife held in his right hand. When she saw it coming at her, she too acted on pure instinct and flipped her legs up, twisting them in mid-air and kicking his wrist hard. She stared in near disbelief as the knife was flung from his grasp.

But the fight was far from over.

The Soul Hunter made a sudden move to pin down her torso. She rolled away at the last moment and leapt to her feet. In that split second, she was torn between wanting to run for it and not wanting to risk turning her back on him.

Fight or flight.

Before she could decide, the Soul Hunter was on his feet, next to her in a heartbeat, pushing her down again. They rolled on the soft ground, scrabbling and grunting. Delilah tried to dig her fingernails into his eyes, and he twisted his head away, grabbed her hair and pulled it so hard that a chunk came away in his hand. She howled in outrage—it hurt like hell.

She spun around in his grasp and brought her knee up between Tol's legs. Connecting with the contents of his jeans made her wince, but it had the desired effect. The Soul Hunter shrieked and bent double.

And he let go.

She sprung up and there was no hesitation this time.

Run.

One pace, two, three—she willed her wobbly legs to carry her forwards. But then strong fingers locked round her arm, yanking her back. She struggled, feeling for a weak spot, a place where she could fight against his hold, but fury fuelled him now, and he clamped Tol's body around hers like a vice.

She tried to steady her panicking mind and scanned her body again, bucking her torso and shaking her shoulders, testing his boundaries. But they were unbreakable. Suddenly his hand was clamped over her nose and mouth, suffocating her. She squealed and tried to pull in a breath but found that not even the slimmest sliver of air could reach her lungs.

She really let go to panic then.

In her mind, she was thrashing and flailing, but her limbs barely moved in his strong grip. She glanced up and around, going dizzy, the shadowed treetops rushing in circles above, racing into a blur of black against the inky blue sky.

Suddenly, a white, feathered missile came hurtling out of the trees, screeching wildly. *It's that owl again,* she thought. Her vision fuzzed over and her body grew limp. *My owl.*

In one fluid motion, the Soul Hunter laid her gently on the ground, but he didn't take his hand from her face. Not until she had stopped breathing. Then he gently linked her fingers with his. He took his other hand from her nose and mouth, but she didn't draw in a sudden, huge, gasping breath, like a drowning girl breaking the surface of the water. It was too late for that. She lay still, her hair fanned out around her.

His voice was low, intoning. "By the joining of our palms, her power flows to me." He grasped her hands more tightly, as Tol's hot blood made their skin slippery. "By the speaking of my ancient, true name, I call her soul to the Twisted Tree." Licking his bloody lips with relish, he leaned over her and whispered. "My name is—"

Delilah's owl screeched, swooping across the sky above them again. She gathered what little strength she had left. *I am the Green Witch now,* she affirmed to herself. *As above, so below.*

In the last moment before death stole over her, she intended her consciousness upwards, out of her body, and joined with her owl, feeling the ground rush away from her in a swooping arc.

The Soul Hunter abruptly stopped his whispering and stared at her face, first uncomprehendingly, and then in disbelief. He shook her shoulders violently. "Oh no. Oh no, you don't!" he roared, enraged.

He dropped her to the ground like a ragdoll and closed his eyes for a moment, focussing. A bird, all sharp beak and talons, its merciless eyes gleaming, swooped low above him. It was his malevolent owl from the Dark Woods. Tol's body slumped on the ground as his consciousness soared into it.

Delilah was soaring through the wood, marvelling at the wonder of being in the owl, even more tangible in the "real"

world, than Otherwood. And the wonder of still being alive—
still being the Green Witch. The broader part of herself, the part
that was pure positive energy and had been long before her
physical life, was completely connected and one with the owl.
Was the owl. And the other part was still Delilah, but the best of
Delilah, the joy, the loyalty, the laughter, the kindness…

There was only eternity and the present moment. There
could be nothing in between, because the two were one. In that
moment, she understood every single word of the mysterious
poem, "One". More than that, she *was* the poem.

She was swooping and soaring, rejoicing at the strength of
their shared wings and the skill of their flight—when the Soul
Hunter's bird came tearing through the trees towards them.

At first, Delilah responded in harmony with the owl's
reflexes, as a creature under attack. The owl's body swerved,
dipped, then soared upwards, getting a height advantage to see
what this sudden invasion was all about. Then Delilah really
looked through her owl's eyes and recognised the malevolent
gleam of their attacker's gaze—the gaze of the Soul Hunter.

Attuned with her owl's animal instincts, they swooped again,
then hurtled off across the sky, trying to shake the pursuer.
They twisted among the trees, doubling back suddenly,
rocketing high and dropping low—but they couldn't lose the
Soul Hunter's bird. Suddenly, a vast tree trunk loomed before
them, and Delilah felt everything in her owl, and everything in
her*self*, react with a sharp swerve to the right.

Unbalanced in the air, they tumbled for a moment, wings
flapping wildly, searching for the lifting air current again. It
was only a few seconds—but it was all the time the Soul Hunter
needed. The bird swooped down onto Delilah's owl, talons
outstretched. Delilah let out a gasp of pain, released through
the white owl's throat as an agonised shriek—a razor-sharp
talon bit deeply into its feathered body.

Then, in a flurry of wings and beaks and talons, the two

birds locked in a bloody battle. Delilah's white owl shook off the Hunter's bird, and flung it far across the sky with one beat of their powerful wings. But, moments later, it was diving back towards them again—its beak aiming for her owl's eye. Delilah could sense the unnaturalness of this attack scrambling her owl's own instincts and, although they flinched away at the last moment, it wasn't fast enough. The murderous beak sank into the neck of her owl, and Delilah felt the sickening release as blood spurted from the wound, and shared in the panic coursing through her owl's body.

It was bad.

With the evil bird still hanging onto it with its savage talons, her white owl hurtled to the ground. As it ploughed into the dry leaves, Delilah was forced back into her body. It was like putting on some kind of suit—her consciousness slipped down her arms and into her hands like gloves. She pushed herself up to sitting and, with every fibre of her being, she drew in a deep, juddering breath.

Her focus slipped down to find her feet and wiggle her toes, and then, using a jolt of energy from her solar plexus, she flicked her eyes open.

She got up, steadying her breathing. She grounded herself and began to focus. "It's my time now," she murmured. "I am the Green Witch." She instinctively knew what to do as she closed her eyes and began to draw the green-gold energy up from the earth, melding with all the vibrations of her own personal crystals, trees, and power animals, swirling with the power of the four elements and directions.

Close by, she heard Tol's body stirring, and the screech of the Soul Hunter's injured bird as it tore away. She registered that he'd slipped back into the human form he'd stolen, but she stayed where she was, weaving the energy.

She didn't see his eyes open. His gaze on her motionless figure. Him hauling himself to his feet and stepping across to the place where the knife had landed. Him reaching into the undergrowth.

As Delilah stood, gently pulling the energies up and weaving them into one swirling green and gold ball of power at her heart, a thought for her poor owl tried to form in her mind. But before it could take hold, she gently focussed all her attention back to her energy. Right now, this had to be all there was.

One focus.

One stream.

One complete harmony of intention...

One.

The Soul Hunter in Tol's body stooped over for a moment, and when he straightend, the knife was in his hand—its blade sharp, lethal. He began to make his way, slowly, towards her.

The green-gold energy was swirling faster now, and growing by itself, far beyond the confines of Delilah's physical body, far and wide and tall and deep.

It was like exquisite music—the music of nature in harmony.

She flicked her eyes open, and everything swam before them in shimmering lucid beauty, including the Soul Hunter, who stood only steps from her, his eyes gleaming with bloodlust.

He drew his elbow back sharply, about to thrust the knife up under her sternum.

At that moment, she drew all the swirling energy back into herself and focussed with a depth of clarity she'd never known before. She directed it with her mind, and it came pouring out through the palms of her hands, strong and steady.

It was as powerful as the force which had saved her from the owl attack in the Dark Woods. As strong as Edie's own magic. The leaves on the trees rustled with the resonance of the blast, branches straining, but not one was broken.

All the force was focussed on the Soul Hunter. It pushed him hard, backwards, flinging the knife into the bushes. And it continued to flow over him, and then *into* him, as he scrabbled on the ground, pinned down by its power.

He fought for a few more seconds before it overwhelmed him completely. Then he keeled over, his head hitting the soft ground, his eyes disconcertingly open. The expression in them was serene, and he was still. There was no question that the Soul Hunter was gone from behind those eyes.

As the power swirled away, Delilah was left staring at Tol's body, gripped by a mix of relief and horror. Then she remembered her owl and rushed to it. She dropped to her knees and cradled it in her arms. Clasping her hands around its bloodied, broken body, she focussed the now gently flowing stream of Green Magic into it. They shared a look of deep connection, and then the life went from it. "No, no, no!" she sobbed.

Someone was running through the trees, shouting to her, and soon she vaguely registered Milly holding her tight. "Thank goodness we found you!" she cried. "Are you okay? What the hell happened to *him*?"

Delilah forced herself to wrench her gaze from her owl and focus on Milly. "Cal and Mae…" she croaked.

"They're fine," Milly assured her. "Well, they'll be okay. He got hold of me and there was a fight over the knife. Cal protected me and he's hurt. Mae's with him. When the Soul Hunter got away I went after him—I knew he'd be coming for you. Thank goodness you're okay. Tol, though…"

Delilah laid the owl gently on the ground and got to her feet. "Go to the house and call an ambulance. Get James and Bob to come and help." Milly was just gazing in horror at Tol's body, so Delilah added, "Now, Mil! He's losing a lot of blood. There's not much time." As Delilah hurried away into the woods, Milly called out, "I will, but where are you going?"

"To bring Tol back."

* * *

Delilah burst into her clearing. She took in the sorry state of her friends in one glance, as she ran to the centre to sit down. There was a nasty knife slash across Cal's right arm. Mae had it wrapped tightly with a piece of his shirt and was holding it high in the air, pressing with all her might. "Delilah, you're okay, thank God!" she shrieked, when she saw her.

"I am, but Tol's not," she called. "Can you get Cal down to the field? An ambulance is coming. I have to..." She didn't finish the sentence. She closed her eyes and took a deep breath, grounding herself into the earth, steadying her breathing.

Although she was all jangled up, her body was still pulsing with the green-gold energy and when she opened her eyes, she found herself in her clearing in Otherwood with her pink water in its heavy glass bottle. She leapt up, and before she'd even finished thinking it, her Otherwood white owl was there. She almost cried, looking at it, remembering the mangled form of its brave counterpart in her own reality. She began to run and, with the owl flying overhead, she lifted her consciousness up into it. Soon she was one with it, flying through the wood.

They reached the Dark Woods quickly. When she saw the Twisted Tree, she dropped her consciousness down, shifting back into her own body, and felt her feet hit the ground. The Soul Hunter was still where she'd left him, seemingly unconscious, on the ground. Who knew how quickly he'd recover? She swallowed her fear and forced herself to focus on Tol. The life was ebbing from his physical body with every second. She drew her dagger, now in her belt again, and hacked at the ivy holding him. "Tol, wake up!" she hissed, shaking him. "You have to come with me."

His eyes opened a fraction and he looked blearily at her "Delilah?" he croaked.

She nodded, hacking at the ivy, and pulling him away from the tree. Supporting his full weight took all her strength and she couldn't hold him up and walk at the same time. "Tol! Wake up!" she hissed, as his head lolled to one side. "Can you walk?" She released him and he staggered a couple of steps.

She waited for *it* to happen, the part when Tol's spirit magically flitted off to reunite with his body, to become whole again. But he just stood there, swaying and disorientated. If there was a way to do it—which there must have been, the Soul Hunter had spirited him away from the hospital after all—then she didn't know what it was. She sighed heavily and hitched his arm over her shoulder. "Come on, then—looks like it has to be the old-fashioned way," she grunted, staggering under the weight of him.

She half-dragged him out of the Dark Woods, grateful that whatever protections the Soul Hunter had lifted to allow her in had *stayed* lifted. She planned to deal with Tol and then come back for the others, liberating them one by one from the ivy bonds that held them. Maybe they were dead in the physical world, but their souls could be freed, to go wherever it was that souls went. But would she have to take them herself too? And *where*?

She froze as she heard a groaning and stirring behind her. Her heart began to pound in her chest and her mind raced. Stay and fight for the other souls now or get Tol to safety? It was a wrench to leave them, but she knew what she had to do. If the Soul Hunter got hold of her, both she and Tol would be lost forever, the Green Witch lineage would be broken, and the other souls would be trapped for eternity.

Swearing to herself that she'd come back for them as soon as she was properly prepared, she began to drag Tol along. His feet twisted underneath him, and her legs buckled as his full weight slumped onto her. She knew there was no way she could drag him all the way to the edge of the field in Otherwood, the place where his body lay in the real world—not in time anyway. Unbidden, an image of the wild ponies flashed into her mind. And this was Otherwood—different laws applied. She willed them to her, and in seconds they came pounding out of the trees. She heaved Tol, face-down, onto the back of the one she'd ridden in the real world and vaulted on behind him.

Then they were off, galloping through the wood. She hung onto Tol with all her strength, his limp frame threatening to slide sideways and fall under their thundering hooves. The pony seemed to sense when this was about to happen and slowed just enough to allow Delilah to rebalance Tol, and herself. It was as if she and the pony shared one mind, one consciousness. The other ponies galloped ahead of them, pushing back branches and trampling brambles, to give them as smooth a passage as possible. Her owl flew overhead, silent and agile.

Soon, Delilah could see the light at the edge of the field, and a moment later they were there. "Woah!" she cried, and the ponies came to an abrupt halt, causing Tol to slide off and thud onto the ground. As they trotted off into the woods, she knelt down beside him. Panic engulfed her. How could she get him back to his body? And what about herself, *her* body—that was in her special clearing. She didn't know whether she could even move between the worlds from any other place than that. And even if she managed it, she couldn't be in two physical places at once. That was an impossibility, and who knew what would happen to her. She realised she hadn't thought this through... *That* was an understatement. What the hell was she supposed to do now?

Her owl was flapping its wings wildly, it's screeching tearing the sky, and as she looked up at it, a shimmer in the air caught her eye. It was like a reflecting pool, and in it she could make out the vague shape of Tol's body, with Milly bent over it. Trembling, she shook her own Tol hard. He groaned and opened his eyes again. "Delilah," he murmured, grabbing at her arm.

"Yes," she said, forcing herself to squeeze his hand reassuringly, even though the sight of him still frightened her.

"Tol, listen to me. You need to go back to your body. You need to wake up. You're not in the hospital anymore, you're in the woods, and you're badly injured. If you don't get back and fight for your life, your body will die."

He gave her a look of utter bewilderment. She was about to give in to complete panic when she remembered to calm herself and listen to the whispers from her intuition. Somewhere, deep, deep down inside her, she trusted that there was a part of herself that knew exactly what to do. A moment later, a sense of knowing stole over her. "Tol, listen to me," she said firmly. "Imagine your body, okay? Imagine you're lying in the woods, on the ground. You're hurt all over, but especially your arm. Milly is with you. Can you see her?"

Tol's eyes flicked upwards and then gazed at something only he could see. "I see her," he murmured.

"Okay, good," she said. "Look at her. Keep your eyes open and keep looking. Can you feel your arm? Does it hurt?"

Tol winced. "It hurts like hell," he groaned.

"Now go," she told him. "Go right there, into that pain, keep looking at Milly. Is she looking back at you?"

Tol nodded, and suddenly, with a huge rush of energy, he was sucked up into the glimmering reflection above them. She gasped at this, then lifted her consciousness into her owl, and soared away.

* * *

Returning to the clearing, Delilah had sat down in the centre of her circle of trees. She'd glanced at her pink water in its heavy glass bottle, steadied her breathing and closed her eyes. She'd opened them in her real-world clearing and set off as fast as she could for the manor. She'd seen the blue flashing lights from the lane through the treeline before she'd even reached the field and she came out to find Tol being loaded onto a stretcher by two paramedics. A third was helping Mae get Cal down to the ambulance waiting in the lane, his arm now bandaged and strapped tightly to his chest. Milly, a foil blanket round her shoulders, followed behind. When Delilah caught up with her, she just stared blankly at her for a moment before recognising her. "Is it...? Is he...?" she croaked.

"He's back in Otherwood, and Tol's back in his body," she hissed, careful to keep the paramedic with Tol from hearing.

Milly was equally careful to keep her voice low. "We're saying Tol broke out of the hospital and crashed his bike again." She winced. "Well, Adam's bike. Cal's going to have to break the news to him."

Delilah looked incredulous. "And they're buying that?"

Milly shrugged. "They said coming out of a coma can have some strange effects, so yeah. And seeing as he was on his bike when he lost consciousness... they said he could have been confused and returned to the thing he last remembered doing. The doctors hadn't brought him round yet. That was still set for three o'clock. But he came to by himself, got up and escaped from hospital. They're all baffled about how that could possibly have happened, you know, medically speaking. So, if the ambulance guys mention it look baffled too."

"Baffled, got it," said Delilah. "I can do that. Sounds like we'll be okay. I was scared they'd have the police involved."

Milly winced. "Me too. I've still got no idea how we'll explain Cal's arm, but I threw the knife far up into the bushes. We'll have to get rid of it properly later."

Delilah put her arm around her friend. "Come on, let's catch Mae and Cal up," she said. Together the two girls hurried down the hill and the paramedic had to stop while they all hugged and then Delilah promised him that, yes, she was the only other one of them in the woods, and no, she wasn't injured and hadn't been anywhere near Tol and his bike accident. The blood on her dress was from Cal's arm, she'd explained, thinking quickly.

She said she'd gone for help when he cut it on a sharp old bit of metal in the ground, and then got herself lost. Cal caught onto the "sharp old bit of metal" story and confirmed it.

"It's terrible, what's happened to this place," the paramedic muttered. "People have dumped all sorts here, and the graffiti's awful. Time was these woods were safe for little ones to play in. Families had picnics here, kids made dens, all sorts."

"These woods will be like that again," Delilah assured him, with a confidence that surprised even her. "We'll make sure of it."

"Well, good," he said, "it's you youngsters who need to be taking action. It's your world we're wrecking. Just take care, though."

"We will," said Cal solemnly.

"Good. No more nasty injuries."

"So, why are you dressed like that?" the paramedic asked Delilah suddenly, as they carried on down the hill.

She looked down at the torn, bloody tatters of Great Aunt Edie's exquisite green dress. "Because I am the Green Witch," she said, feeling the power of the words coursing through her. "In a play," she added hastily, seeing the man's surprise. "It's a play I'm in. I came straight here afterwards. Should have changed. Clearly."

Up ahead, another paramedic called to the man supporting Cal, and Delilah took his place as he ran to help load Tol into the ambulance.

"I hope he'll be okay," said Cal.

"Me too," said Delilah. "I mean... shit."

"What if he remembers what really happened, when he wakes up?" asked Milly.

"He won't," said Delilah, catching that new sureness and confidence in her voice again. It felt like part of her now. "He wasn't *there* until I brought him back. All he'll remember is you being with him and the ambulance. Maybe me talking to him, too, when I was in Otherwood."

"You brought him back," said Cal. He gave her a broad grin, and she felt in her bones just how safe and supported his easy-going Cal-ness made her feel.

"And *you* came back," added Mae. Delilah shared a warm smile with her friend.

"I did," she said. "I came back."

"You are the Green Witch," said Milly.

"I am the Green Witch," Delilah repeated, and however inappropriate it seemed at that moment, she wanted to laugh and dance around and sing her heart out. Cal was hurt. Tol was in a critical condition. The Soul Hunter didn't have a place in the physical world, or a physical body, but he was far from defeated, and his captives were not free. But if there was one thing she'd learnt from all this, it was to live in the moment, and to dance anyway. "I am the Green Witch," she said again, feeling the thrill and joy of it, of knowing who she really was and feeling every inch her authentic self. "I am the Green Witch!" she shouted.

The paramedic, now beside the ambulance, turned and gave her a quizzical look.

"In the play! And you know, all the world's a stage!" she called out, and they all broke into deeply inappropriate laughter. Then Milly looped her arm around Delilah's waist and together they made their way across the lush green grass.

Epilogue

Delilah sat at the sunny writing desk in the morning room at the manor, answering letters of condolence from Edie's far-flung friends. The funeral had been a quiet affair at the Natural Burial Centre, as per her great aunt's wishes—Jane, the other carers and a few friends from the town were the only guests in attendance, along with Delilah and her friends.

People had commented that Edie's death had been unexpected, and of course Delilah had nodded along, but inside she understood instinctively that Edie never wanted a long drawn-out future shadowboxing with dementia. Her great aunt had passed the mantle of Green Witch on to her, and then the small part of her eternal being which was physical had slipped the bonds of this life. She'd known it was her time to go. She'd prepared.

Delilah's father first expressed undisguised glee at Edie's sudden death, but it had soon been replaced by outrage once she'd informed him that she'd be staying at the manor permanently. She'd asked Milly to stay on too, of course, and her friend had eagerly accepted. She'd also invited Mae and Cal to move in, although Cal, for all his jokes about "wanting the East Wing", had decided that he'd rather stay in his little room above the pub than in her "spooky old house". And however much Mae complained about her protective father, she still wanted to stay at home to be close to the restaurant, so she could help out as much as possible. Delilah knew she'd have to find a way to make the place work financially in the long term, but according to Edie's solicitor, *her* solicitor now, she didn't need to think about anything like that just yet.

She sealed the last envelope for her great aunt's friend Lily in Colorado and picked up a new piece of watermarked blue writing paper. She paused for a moment, pen held against her lip. And then she wrote:

Dad,

I thought nothing would happen here the whole summer, but I couldn't have been more wrong. I have been lost. I have been afraid. I have stood in the heartbeat between life and death.

But that's all over now. And yet everything has only just begun.

I have made some true friends. I have found out who I really am — or perhaps I just remembered. And I have found a place to belong. I'll be following in the family footsteps, but not quite in the way you imagined.

She smiled to herself, remembering the action day they'd held that Saturday, cleaning up the high street. She'd thought it would just be her, Mae and Milly scrubbing at spray paint and picking up litter, with the still-injured Cal on tea-making duty. But a whole crowd of volunteers had turned up to help, including James and Bob. Cal had even helped Mae's dad and some other volunteers paint over the graffiti on the front wall of The Chinese Chippy — heroically hanging onto one crutch, although he and Mae hadn't quite gone as far as revealing they were together yet.

So thank you, Dad, Delilah wrote. *Thank you for teaching me to be weak, because it made me ask for strength with all my heart. I know you won't understand any of this letter, and maybe I won't even send it, but that doesn't matter. What matters is that I understand it. I understand it all now.*

She glanced up at the sudden sound of James' laugh. He and Bob had finished the vegetable beds now and were making headway on the rose border. She hadn't told him what had happened in the woods, with Tol and the Soul Hunter. But there had been more kissing, and easy-going talk about the gardens, and films they liked, and books they'd read. And, for now, she planned to keep it that way. She loved that one part of her life was simple, or something approaching it. For a moment, she wondered how she'd feel if it were the other way round — if he kept something like this from her. Was it being dishonest, not saying anything? Was it lying by omission? No, she decided, it was just choosing her own timing, that was all.

Her friends had just arrived, and Cal was chatting to James — saying something cheeky about Mae, Delilah guessed, by the steely look and playful slap she gave him.

James laughed again and Delilah's breath caught in her throat. Her eyes lingered on him, as he leaned on his spade. He was such a relaxed, warm presence to have around. And there was more. There was something very special between them, they both felt it. But it didn't have to unfold all at once.

Again, she told herself, *there will be time*.

Milly was there too, hanging back behind the others, more reserved and hesitant, and as she smiled shyly at something Bob said, Delilah was filled with a rush of love and appreciation for her. She'd been so brave, staying there with Tol's bleeding body in the woods.

Tol... He was back in hospital making a slow, carefully monitored recovery. Cal had been to see him and, as she'd hoped, he hadn't remembered anything beyond waking up in agony in the woods. Her mind strayed way back to what had happened between them at the party, before they'd fought: the pure animal attraction — feral, magnetic — like nothing she'd ever felt. Like nothing she'd known a girl *could* feel. Woman. Girl. Woman. She wasn't quite either. She was both, and somewhere in between, and that was okay. But how she'd felt about him then didn't matter now. She couldn't even think of being with him — not after all this. And anyway, there was James. She'd uncovered so much more of who she was since then, and she was standing at the threshold of a whole new world.

She gazed out of the window, watching her friends as they all looked up, following a bird of prey gliding across the endless blue sky above them. The memory of the Soul Hunter's vicious owl, housing his spirit, flashed in her mind. She wondered where he was now, *what* he was. Was he out there somewhere, floating through the real world, a wisp of consciousness looking for another home, a whisper on the breeze? Or perhaps he was holed up in the Dark Woods of Otherwood, waiting to gather strength, germinating like an evil seed. She didn't want to think about that now. There would be time to explore the possibilities. There would be time to discover more about her own magic, too.

When he came for her again, she'd be ready. And when she next went into the Dark Woods, she swore once again to herself that she'd be coming out with the rest of those poor trapped souls.

She remembered that Kae Tempest song, "The Beigeness", picked up her pen again and continued to write:

All life is forward, you see, Dad.

And it's all there waiting for you, if you're ready to receive it.

So much life... so much blue.

With these final words, she put down her pen and hurried out into the sunlight.

The End.
For now, anyway....

Kelly McKain is the UK-based author of over fifty children's and Young Adult books and has been published in more than twenty languages. You can visit her children's fiction website at www.kellymckain.co.uk and her intuitive guidance/energy healing platform at www.soulsparks.space. To find out more about the world of the Green Witch books and the magical Green Witch path, visit www.greenwitchbooks.com. As well as being an author, Kelly is a mystic, healer, Green Witch and yogi. She loves horses, wild dancing, nature walks, sitting round the fire with friends and discovering the magic all around us.

LODESTONE
BOOKS

YOUNG ADULT FICTION

Lodestone Books is a new imprint, which offers a broad spectrum of subjects in YA/NA literature. Compelling reading, the Teen/Young/New Adult reader is sure to find something edgy, enticing and innovative. From dystopian societies, through a whole range of fantasy, horror, science fiction and paranormal fiction, all the way to the other end of the sphere, historical drama, steam-punk adventure, and everything in between (including crime, coming of age and contemporary romance). Whatever your preference you will discover it here.

If you have enjoyed this book, why not tell other readers by posting a review on your preferred book site. Recent bestsellers from Lodestone Books are:

AlphaNumeric
Nicolas Forzy

When dyslexic teenager Stu accidentally transports himself into a world populated by living numbers and letters, his arrival triggers a prophecy that pulls two rival communities into war.
Paperback: 978-1-78279-506-3 ebook: 978-1-78279-505-6

Time Sphere
A timepathway book
M.C. Morison
When a teenage priestess in Ancient Egypt connects with a school-
boy on a visit to the British Museum, they each come under threat
as they search for Time's Key.
Paperback: 978-1-78279-330-4 ebook: 978-1-78279-329-8

Bird Without Wings
FAEBLES
Cally Pepper
Sixteen-year-old Scarlett has had more than her fair share of
problems, but nothing prepares her for the day she discovers she's
growing wings...
Paperback: 978-1-78099-902-9 ebook: 978-1-78099-901-2

Briar Blackwood's Grimmest of Fairytales
Timothy Roderick
After discovering she is the fabled Sleeping Beauty, a brooding
goth-girl races against time to undo her deadly fate.
Paperback: 978-1-78279-922-1 ebook: 978-1-78279-923-8

Escape from the Past
The Duke's Wrath
Annette Oppenlander
Trying out an experimental computer game, a fifteen-year-old boy
unwittingly time-travels to medieval Germany where he must not
only survive but figure out a way home.
Paperback: 978-1-84694-973-9 ebook: 978-1-78535-002-3

Holding On and Letting Go
K.A. Coleman

When her little brother died, Emerson's life came crashing down around her. Now she's back home and her friends want to help, but can Emerson fight to re-enter the world she abandoned?

Paperback: 978-1-78279-577-3 ebook: 978-1-78279-576-6

Midnight Meanders
Annika Jensen

As William journeys through his own mind, revelations are made, relationships are broken and restored, and a faith that once seemed extinct is renewed.

Paperback: 978-1-78279-412-7 ebook: 978-1-78279-411-0

Reggie & Me
The First Book in the Dani Moore Trilogy
Marie Yates

The first book in the Dani Moore Trilogy, *Reggie & Me* explores a teenager's search for normalcy in the aftermath of rape.

Paperback: 978-1-78279-723-4 ebook: 978-1-78279-722-7

Unconditional
Kelly Lawrence

She's in love with a boy from the wrong side of town...

Paperback: 978-1-78279-394-6 ebook: 978-1-78279-393-9

Readers of ebooks can buy or view any of these bestsellers by clicking on the live link in the title. Most titles are published in paperback and as an ebook. Paperbacks are available in traditional bookshops. Both print and ebook formats are available online.

Find more titles and sign up to our readers' newsletter at
http://www.johnhuntpublishing.com/children-and-young-adult
Follow us on Facebook at
https://www.facebook.com/JHPChildren
and Twitter at
https://twitter.com/JHPChildren